MOUTH SHUT HEAD DOWN

A NOVEL ABOUT COERCIVE CONTROL IN TRAFFICKING

by

Geraldine Donaher

PARISIANPHOENIX.COM
angel@parisianphoenix.com
parisianphoenixpublishing.substack.com
@parisianphoenixpublishing
/parisan-phoenix-publishing
/parisianphoenixpublishing
@parisianphoenix
/parisianphoenix.bsky.social
parisian phoenix
PUBLISHING

To Tammy
A friend of Allee's from the very beginning

My silences had not protected me.
Your silence will not protect you.
AUDRE LORDE

Chapter 1

The door announces his arrival. It's always the door announcing his arrival, signaling me to become less. I shrink as he becomes more.

He's Tony. Doesn't deserve a title. Doesn't even care I stopped calling him "Dad."

It seems wrong, the way he gets to shout-stomp while Mom and I whisper-tiptoe. At seventeen years old, I should know how to fix the more and less in this family. Maybe I'm supposed to become so less I disappear. That might work. I could haunt him, freak him out by moving stuff around the room so he disappears and never returns.

Well, I have the disappear part down to a science. When the air about him becomes disturbed, prickly even, I freeze, assess the situation, and either pretend I'm invisible or make myself invisible. Pretending sometimes doesn't end well for me. Making myself invisible always works. He's not very good at hide and seek. Too much effort.

I never stay away too long. I always come back for Mom.

Even though I'm in the bathroom, that front door hitting the wall in the cramped entrance echoes in my ear. Kind of hard to go all invisible when you're in the bathroom taking care of business.

He slurs his words and calls out for my mom. "Barb, where the hell are ya?"

He's messed up. I do what I need to do the best I can, then pull up my pants. I know better than to flush. He'll know I'm in here.

I creep to the window and lift it enough so I can shimmy out and down into the alley. Sometimes he passes out on the couch, and all I have to do is wait in the bathroom until I hear him snore.

No such luck tonight, my stomach knots as he bangs on the bathroom door. I usually unlock it before I leave through the window.

That's how I kept his coming-in and my going-out a secret. No time for that now. He'll know how I get away and take the lock off the door, like he did to my bedroom. The bathroom will no longer be an easy escape.

God, I hate him.

"Girl, you in there? Where's your mother?" He bangs on the door again. "Unlock d'fuckin' door." It comes out a whispered threat.

He lowers his voice before a rampage. I need to leave.

Now.

I twist as I slide through the window, hang onto the sill, and then drop onto the frozen plot of dirt below. I run to a parked car two houses down the alley and crouch between the front wheel and concrete wall. I hear the bathroom door smash open. Tony bellows from the window. "Allee, get your sorry ass back here! Hear me, girl?"

I hug my knees and roll my head until I am a tight ball, becoming one with the car. I am a shadow.

"Stay out there all night!" He screams louder. "Hear me? Don't come back!"

He must walk away from the window because his booming voice becomes a slurred mumble-shout of my mom's name followed by more slamming.

I used to hide behind the couch and suck my index finger whenever he shouted or started throwing things. But when I was ten years old, furiously sucking, he dragged me out by my hair and shouted up in my face, "Stop being such a baby."

My mom rushed over and pushed him away.

It was the first time I ever saw her push back. He's big and hairy, towers over her. She told me to run. He forgot about me and went for her. I may have been only ten, but I was fast and ran all the way to my best friend Tanaya's house.

Her mom was walking out the front door as I took the concrete steps two at a time up to the porch.

"Hi Auntie T!" I yelled but didn't wait for a response.

I ran under her arm and up the worn carpeted steps to Tanaya's room. Tanaya was sitting on the bedroom floor, the brush with pink nail polish inches from her left thumb.

"Yo, Allee, look what my mom just got me! Sit down, I'll give you a mani-pedi."

She looked so normal sitting there. I wanted normal and obediently sat. Even back then, I knew not to talk about what went on in my house. Tanaya's dad-less, which seems to make a difference.

My first manicure at ten and I never sucked my finger again, behind the couch or anywhere else. I stopped being a baby. Instead, I hide behind parked cars in dark alleys and think about the more and less of things.

The alley's quiet tonight, cold with a light mist. The brick homes' backdoor lights are kept on all night to keep intruders from sneaking up back steps and into kitchens. The lights shine on the freezing drops, and the alley glitters. For a second, I forget that my seventeen-year-old life is cold and lonely. The world around me sparkles.

But then a crash from old Mr. Petruso's drops me back into reality. Lord knows what he's been doing in that house. Lots of weird noises, odd pieces of wood and metal stacked out by the curb for trash pick-up. Sometimes it spreads out and ends up in front of our duplex. We all wonder, but nobody asks. Not even the trash collectors.

Sometimes I stay for hours in the alley shadows, but the cold stings my fingertips tonight, and Tony's quieted down. It's safe for me to go.

God, I wish I had stuffed a coat somewhere out here.

I jam my hands into my front jean pockets and walk toward 5th Street worrying about my mom. I haven't seen her since breakfast. I like to warn her when Tony's a mess. He goes ballistic when she gets home later than him.

About a year ago, she helped me get a job at her friend's pizza shop so we can work on getting phones.

"Those prepaid phones are a good idea," she said. "We'll be able to keep in touch instead of worrying about each other."

Her getting me that job? Best thing ever. I don't have to become less at Pop's Pizza Shop. Or Tanaya's. I'll sleep at her house tonight. Her mom will help me find my mom.

It'll be much easier once we get those phones.

Chapter 2

Tanaya's mom opens the door wearing a worn Penn State sweatshirt and tight pants with big yellow and red flowers.

"Seriously, Auntie T? Please tell me you're wearing yoga pants as pajama bottoms and that's it."

God, why do people pour thick legs into spandex?

Tanaya's mom is usually for the more practical things in life. Her auburn hair has just enough gray streaks to look as if she pays for highlights, but she doesn't use her money for such things. She swears she'll grow old gracefully.

She's lucky. It's working for her.

Well, except for the yoga pants.

"Allee! Now don't get all judgy about my pants. They're comfy and that's that." She holds the door wide, like an embrace I don't have to return. "It's freezing out! Come on in, Tanaya's upstairs, getting ready for bed."

"Thanks, Auntie T. I was wondering if I could stay here for the night and if you know where my mom is."

Ms. Craig's a friend of my mom's from high school but told me to call her Auntie T. Whenever I show up on her doorstep, she never bothers with questions like why on a cold December night I'm not wearing a coat.

That's why I keep showing up. Adults who ask questions are trouble. Auntie T is the opposite of trouble.

"Not sure about Barb. I'll make a few phone calls and see what I can find out. When was the last time you saw her?"

"This morning, before school. I didn't work tonight, so I hung out in the library for a few hours then went home. I was alone 'til about thirty minutes ago. Tony came in."

I look down as I say his name. Can't trust my face won't give away that he's such a prick.

Honestly, it's embarrassing.

Auntie T pauses, and I get jumpy that she's about to break our unspoken rule and ask a question. But she doesn't.

"Head on up, fresh towel in the hall closet. There are clean pajamas in the bottom drawer. Borrow an outfit from Tanaya for school tomorrow." She gives me a reassuring smile. "Try not to worry about your mom. She worked today? Knowing her, she's out helping someone who walked into the store looking to get warm."

I nod then leave it to her and run up the steps. I can't wait to get a warm shower. Tanaya's putting on lipstick when I walk into the bedroom. I barely recognize her. I've always been jealous of her long lashes and eyes so dark it's impossible to differentiate between pupil and iris. Tonight she's wearing lash extensions. When she blinks, it's like her eyes are waving to me. She grins.

"Hey girl! What brings you by so late?"

Like every other time I show up here, I lie. Some things are better left hidden behind something that could have been.

"Mom and Tony aren't around. Gets kind of creepy at home by myself. Your mom's calling around to see if she can find my mom."

Tanaya likes to hold her springy curls away from her face with a colorful, extra-wide cloth headband. But not tonight. She's teased the curls forward. They surround her face like a wiry dark picture frame. Her lips, coated in a shiny blood-red color, are the focal point of the overall picture.

I stand next to her and look in the mirror. I only come to her shoulder, and she's not even wearing shoes. My dirty blonde hair frizzed from the cold mist, and my practically non-existent lashes offer nothing. Tanaya's just four months older than me, but the freckles scattered across my nose and my bone-thin torso make me look like a kid next to Tanaya's flawless golden skin tones and sexy curves.

"What are you doing? You look about twenty-five years old!"

I turn from the mirror and plop onto the extra twin bed with the silky comforter that hugs me to sleep whenever I nestle down into it.

"Shhh!" Tanaya gently closes the door just as I hear her mom talking to someone on the phone, asking if they've seen Barb.

"Why so secretive, Tanaya? And more importantly, why are you dressed like that?"

Her sequined camisole catches the light and brightens her face, like a model in a photo shoot. She sits next to me on the bed and pulls something out of her back pocket.

I don't take my eyes off her face and ask, "Girl, what are you up to?"

She holds it up.

"What the……?! Where'd you get an iPhone?"

I take it. The crisp lines and smooth black finish have a weight that feels comfortable in my hand.

"Did Auntie T get you this?" I can't imagine her switching Tanaya's refurbished Moto 5G for an iPhone. I dust off the front with my shirt sleeve. Not because it's dirty. It just feels right to caress it like that.

"Where'd you get it?"

Tanaya snatches it out of my hands and slides it into her back pocket as she gets up.

"My new boyfriend got it for me."

She glances sideways with a sly grin, then looks in the mirror to add another layer of blush.

This is news. We tell each other everything.

Well, I thought she told *me* everything.

"Where'd you meet him and when did you hook up?" Nothing makes sense. "And what the hell did you have to do to get him to give you an iPhone?!"

I want to be excited for her, but something's not right.

"It's not that expensive. He said he gets a deal through work and put me on his plan." She shrugs. "God, Allee, what are you? My mom?"

This shuts me up, and I lower my eyes, pretending to pick at a spot on the comforter. But just for a minute. I jump up.

"What's his name? Where'd you meet him? When can I meet him?"

Tanaya looks in the mirror and plays with one of her ringlets. "I met him a couple of weeks ago. At a party over on Snake Road. You didn't want to go so I went with Dorie and Carissa. There were some older guys there. They were nice, and I hooked up with Stretch. We hit it off, and I've been seeing him since."

The make-up, her clothes…

"What are you doing? Sneakin' out to see him in the middle of the night? And who has a name like 'Stretch'?"

She gives a smug smile that means, *You couldn't possibly understand what I am about.*

A panicky feeling cuts through my core, like our friendship is in need of life support. I have to do something before it dies.

She's trading me for Dorie and Carissa. And a guy called Stretch. Seriously?

I swallow the panic and play it cool.

"God, Tanaya, how old is he?"

The phone vibrates, and she reaches for it.

"Look, I gotta go. That's him. Don't worry you'll get to meet him. Don't tell my mom. I owe you."

She slips on a silvery jacket and picks up ankle boots that were sitting on the floor. She doesn't bother to put them on, though. Auntie T would definitely hear those clunky heels. Tanaya prowls into the night as I look out the bedroom window at a black car idling in the alley. She rounds the corner, boots secure on her feet, and bounces into the front seat. If I hadn't just seen her leave the house in that metallic jacket, I would have never known it was her.

The uneasy feeling expands in my gut.

This can't be good.

And...

There's no way that jacket's gonna keep you warm.

Unaware, Auntie T continues talking on the phone in the kitchen. I can't make out the words, but she's asking a lot of questions.

Chapter 3

"Allee, Allee, wake up, honey. It's me. Auntie T. I need you to wake up."

The soft voice has an edge to it, a dread like it doesn't want to disturb my sleep, but something important is happening. Not like I'm late for school or anything like that. She would've screamed from the bottom of the steps. Like a hundred times before.

This is different.

"What's going on?" I sit up and do a quick look to Tanaya's side of the room.

What if she didn't make it back to bed yet?

But she's there. A ringlet mess of black hair cascading all over her pillow. I look outside. The morning sun hasn't burst warm colors onto the dark sky. It's early.

"What time is it?"

Auntie T's eyes are red and wet.

"What is it? What's the matter?"

She whispers, "Let's go downstairs so we don't wake Tanaya, okay?"

I slip out of bed, and she puts an arm around me.

This is weird.

In the hallway, she clicks the bedroom door closed and whispers, "They found your mom, Allee. Let's go downstairs to talk."

She looks shaken, like she can't stand on her own. Is that why she put her arm around me? I'm scared to move. My feet keep me from walking down the hall.

"Tell me now. What's going on?"

She sighs, and it sounds like her insides just fizzled and died.

"Please, Allee, come down with me."

There's nothing to do but follow. My feet fall in behind her, and I think about becoming less.

Two police officers, a man and a woman, stand in the living room. They look up as we walk down. The guy's old, at least 45, and gives a weak, "G'Morning." He looks quickly away and takes a step back, like he wants to be here even less than me. The female officer, who seems way too young to be in a police uniform, says, "Hi Allee. Allee Gray? I'm Officer Smith. We need to talk to you about your mom. Will you sit with us?"

"Where is she? She's hurt?"

My eyes dart back and forth between the two officers then rest on Auntie T's sad, swollen eyes. Auntie T takes my hand and tries to pull me to the couch.

"She's gone, Allee. There's been an accident."

My feet plant themselves and I shout, "What d'you mean an accident? Gone? What happened? Tell me!"

Auntie T shuts down, cries. I made her cry, and I don't even care.

I snap at the girl-officer, get up in her face. "Where is she?"

Instead of backing away from me, she stands her ground and softens her voice.

"Allee, we found your mom, deceased, in the kitchen of your home. We took her away so we can figure out what happened and give you all the information that led up to her death."

She puts her hand on my arm, and I fight the need to run to my house, to check for myself. This is all wrong. They must not know who my mom is. How could these cops know what she looks like? My mom is probably safe, sleeping on the couch in our living room. She likes to sleep on the couch in the living room when Tony isn't passed out on it. But I look at Auntie T, her face red and flooded.

"How?" escapes my mouth.

I let Auntie T touch me this time, let her take my arm and lead me to the couch. She sits close, our thighs touching. A second ago, I hated her and what she was saying. Now, I want to put my head on her lap and not think or talk or listen.

I stare at the area rug under the coffee table. My brain tries to find a pattern among the rough material, "jute," I think Auntie T called it, a mismatch of rectangles and squares. An occasional trapezoid. I'm aware that these are stupid thoughts. That I shouldn't be finding shapes on a rug at a time like this.

Auntie T tries to bring me back to the things I don't want to think about.

"Allee, look at me. We need your help. Okay?"

I raise my eyes and answer, "Yeah, sure."

But I can't look at her so I focus back on the rug. Something's building inside me, just under my skin, and wants to get out. It's bubbling like an angry pot of water on the stove. I imagine turning down the heat. Sometimes that works with my feelings. Like when the pot of water settles with a turn of the knob.

But it's not working today. So I imagine slicing my skin. One cut and the bubbling anger can flow free. Be outside of me.

And then, I just know. I look at Auntie T.

"Tony did this."

It isn't a question.

She nods.

I should have stayed home. I could have saved her. Instead, I ran away because I was too weak to stand up to Tony.

I'm a coward.

Chapter 4

He shot her. No one knows where he got the gun, and he's not talking.

I can't look at him for too long during the preliminary hearing. It's been two weeks, and I still feel a mixture of a sick-to-my-stomach and a wild-hatred-in-my-veins feeling that's hard to control. It makes my knee bounce even though the top half of my body sits mannequin-still. Auntie T places her hand on my leg. The warmth sends a calm through me, and my knee settles.

I didn't have to be here if I didn't want to. But I need to see him because part of my brain doesn't believe that anything bad has happened to Mom. I keep thinking I'll see her again.

Auntie T said I wouldn't have to talk, and she would sit with me. I'm at my best when I only have to look and listen to what's going on around me. Not having to say anything is why I came.

Tony looks small now. And old. I look away from time to time to give myself a break. There's a handful of people scattered around the benches, more like pews — but this is definitely not a church. No stained glass windows or ceiling art like we studied in art history sophomore year. But the judge does seem like he's sitting up behind an altar. Two women look over at me and Auntie T, then quickly turn away. If you ask me, they seem a little too interested in our story. The priest-judge and lawyers keep referring to my dad as *Mr. Gray*. I keep thinking about changing my last name.

A coroner-lady calls the autopsy "preliminary" but is pretty certain how Mom died. She talks about Mom's bruises, the new ones. And the bullet's entry and exit wounds.

"There's a bruise across her right cheek and a pool of blood behind her right eye. She was either punched or hit with a fist-sized hard object."

With my peripheral vision, I see Auntie T put her head down at this. But I don't take my eyes off the coroner. I wonder what she thinks about my mom and me because I'm picking up on some kind of judgment, that she's better than us. Like, because of her nice suit and perfect blond bob haircut, she'd never allow herself to be found dead on a dirty kitchen floor.

I want her to stop talking, but she keeps going.

"There's an abrasion on the other side of her face and a large wound on the back of her head. Her blood was found on the kitchen counter ... "

The judge asks about old bruises. They talk about things that were normal to Mom and me, things we kept secret from the world because it was none of their business. I listen as if they're talking about someone else's hellish life. Those two nosy women keep looking over, and I can't stand it anymore. I stare right back at them, glaring as if I can bore right through their eyeballs into their brains.

They turn away. But I don't.

The blond bob steps away from the microphone, and breathing's a little easier for me. A cop settles behind the microphone. He talks about "Mr. Gray" passed out next to Mom's body. And how the serial number had been scratched off the gun. I look at Tony again. His head is down. I want to go shake him. Scream at him. Let him know how much I hate him.

He looked like this every morning after a crazy tirade of beer bottle throwing, name-calling, and hair-pulling. I wear my hair short ever since I got smart enough to know that braids just ask for trouble. Tony'd sit all sad and ashamed on the couch. I'd listen from my bedroom and wonder about the two sides of Tony Gray.

"You know I try, Barb. I just can't stop. I get so mad."

On and on he would go, until Mom told him not to worry, as long as he was trying. I'd walk out of my room, and they'd be hugging. He'd cry and tell me he was sorry.

Him crying, her hugging, and me thinking, *What the f...?!*

I asked Mom about it once. She paused, slid her lips to one side of her face.

"That's what family does, Allee. Forgive."

I still don't know what to make of all that. I look around the courtroom and wonder who will hug him now. Will they tell him not to worry and let him walk free? Am I going to have to do the hugging?

A disgusted feeling washes over me, and an actual, "Fuck!" breathes out of my lips.

Mom wouldn't like me saying that. Auntie T squeezes my hand, and the disgust floats away. I look away from Tony and turn to her. She gives me a gentle smile, and I squeeze her hand back.

They take him away in handcuffs, and I'm glad I won't have to hug him. He doesn't turn around to look at me. Thank god. I hate the persecuted look that always went with his apology.

A woman I don't know, a "Cara" something or other, wants to see us in a room down the hall. She's explaining how the police gave her all my information and that as a seventeen-year-old, I'm a minor. Auntie T cuts her off.

"She's staying with me."

Cara nods, and sets up a time to come to the house and check it out. Then, she asks if I want to stay with Auntie T.

That boiling feeling in my veins is just under my skin, on my forearm. I dig my thumb nail into the soft skin to feel calmer.

I answer, "Yeah, I'd like to stay with Auntie T."

I look at my Auntie T, sitting just next to me, and the tears run down my face.

"Thank you."

She nods, tears in her eyes, and takes my hand.

"We got this."

- - - - -

God, I hope I'm not a baby. It's been three weeks since I saw them take Tony away, three weeks of me hiding in this bed under the silky comforter, thinking about my mom and watching Tanaya sneak out a couple times a week. Usually, she slips out right after Auntie T leaves to clean office buildings in the city.

Since I came to live with them, Auntie T picked up the cleaning job because her waitressing job isn't enough to feed the three of us. Yeah. I'm a baby hiding under a blanky, missing my mom, and Auntie T is the babysitter.

I like to stay in bed and think about Mom. Sometimes images of Tony being awful burst into the memories, like he's haunting me.

Wasn't it supposed to be the other way around? I was supposed to haunt him so he would leave me and Mom alone.

I hate how he treated her. Tony shouldn't have treated anyone like that, especially my mom. How could she take it? Over and over again?

I choke on a sob.

What the hell? I should have been there to help her. Help her? Who am I kidding?

I couldn't even go and identify her body. Auntie T did it for me. The blood stirs. It rushes in my veins and wants to get out. It pulses in my ears. I need to release it before it pushes me further and further away from …

I don't know where it's pushing me. But a cut, even a little one, stops all those thoughts, releases the pressure. Can't be that bad if it gives me a sense of calm. I'm not hurting anybody.

Cara, my I-don't-have-time-to-actually-talk-to-you case worker, told Auntie T I should see a shrink. I refuse to let anyone inside my brain. Cutting seems okay to me because it works. No reason for me to tell anyone about it. Adults wouldn't understand, and then they'd call me crazy. Which is an excellent reason not to see a shrink.

Auntie T said we can compromise.

"You don't have to go see a therapist if you get yourself into school by the first of February. It's been almost a month, Allee. You need to get out of bed and back into the real world."

I have three days to get my shit together.

I turn to face the wall and allow myself a few peaceful moments with memories of my mom from over a year ago:

The More-Bang-4-Your-Buck dollar store is less than a mile from school and around the corner from the library. I opened the front door, reindeer bells clamored on the glass, and I guessed what was inside the large cardboard box next to the check-out counters, "Christmas stockings."

Just the week before, the leftover gourds and pumpkins from Thanksgiving were taken out. The orange, gold, and red tones around the store were all gone, too. Everything was now red, green, blue, and white. And plastic poinsettias. Lots of poinsettias.

I peeked into the large carton and saw that once again, I was right. It was filled with palm-sized red felt stockings.

"Hi, Allee!" Arban called from the third register as he finished ringing up a customer's cleaning supplies, "Your mom's dusting vases."

"Thanks, Arban!"

I walked down aisle eight, and saw my mom on a stepladder, reaching upward with a feather duster. Each vase needed to be dusted inside and out once a week.

"God, Mom, how do you not go crazy working here, dusting those things?"

Her dark hair had a salt-and-pepper thing going on. It was short, like mine, but spikey so it looked kind-of badass. She smiled.

"It gets me away from the cash register so I can hear myself think." She backed down the stepladder. "And look how clear they are now!"

I thought it pathetic that she even cared because the vases would cloud over again by tomorrow morning. The ceiling fans were coated in thick black grime, circulating gross particles around the store. What did I learn in biology? Dust is filled with gross microscopic bugs, mites or something. Disgusting.

She hugged me.

"And it's a job."

I hated her dead-end job, the minimum wage, the menial tasks they made her do. Yet, there she was smiling like she owned the place.

"Sure, whatever. Listen, I'm going to hang out at the library for a while. Any ideas for dinner?"

She pulled money from her front jean pocket.

"Here's a ten. Head over to the new pizza place, Pop's, on Third Street. Pick up a cheesesteak or slice of pizza for yourself. Don't worry about your dad or me. I'll get something for us."

She climbed back up the step ladder.

"Listen, Allee, I've been thinking maybe you could get a job…"

"What?! No way I'm working here!"

She laughed, a full belly laugh, the kind that is so embarrassing, heads turn and people stare.

"This is the last place I want for you. But a high school classmate of mine, Danny, stopped in yesterday. He's the new owner of Pop's Pizza. He's looking for help. I told him I think it would be good for you to have some money of your own. He said he'd make sure you keep up with your homework, and he'd even let you eat dinner there for free once you start working. Nothing fancy, but it would be something. What d'you think?"

"A job? Like a real job?"

The possibilities! The extra cash and a place to hang out instead of just the house, Tanaya's, and the library.

"I *need* you to get a job," she leaned down and whispered, "but Allee, let's keep this between you and me. I mean… your dad doesn't need to know about it."

She waited until a lady walked past us and disappeared up aisle seven. Then she lowered her voice even more, "I know I taught you never to lie but Lord knows Tony drinks right through my paycheck. He doesn't need to know. It'll be your own money. I may need help with bills every once in a while, and you can help me."

She stood up and dusted the top shelf of vases.

"We'll open a bank account for you at First Federal tomorrow after school. Pop's is perfect for you! I trust Danny. You'll have a place to eat dinner. You'll be safe when you're not at home, and you'll have some money for school activities." She rested the feathers in her other hand and looked down at me. "Maybe we can get phones. Those pre-paid phones are a good idea. We can keep in touch instead of worrying about each other."

I started the job at Pop's a week later, but Tony had gotten worse, drinking more and more. I had to help with the bills all the time. Even after a year of my working at Pop's, there was still never enough money for phones.

But we sure did try. Mom tried so hard.

I roll into a tight ball under the comforter and try to control the ache that's bubbling just below the surface of my skin.

I'll get a shower soon. Cutting will settle it down.

Chapter 5

Three days later and I'm in a place that I've managed to stay away from for three years—the guidance counselor's office.

"And how is it over at the Craigs', with Tanaya?"

Ms. Davis stops shuffling around the papers on her desk and sits back to give me all her god-damn attention. It feels like everyone in the world keeps looking at me these days. Paying attention to me in a way that no one bothered before.

"I was relieved to hear that Tina Craig offered to take you in. When I first called her about your schoolwork, she talked about how close you and her daughter, Tanaya, have been through the years."

Whether I want to or not, I have to report here every Monday morning before school. Auntie T said a failure to show up guarantees a visit with the shrink. Maybe this first time will be the hardest, but then it'll get easier.

Whatever.

All I know is that thanks to Tony, my life is screwed up even at school. What I want doesn't matter anymore. Adults tend to leave me alone if I do what they say, so I agreed to what Auntie T wanted, but I hate it. I feel like I'm on pause.

I pull the sleeve down, over my right hand and shrug. "It's fine. My mom and Auntie T, I mean Ms. Craig, were friends for years. Tanaya and I grew up together."

I must not be very convincing because Ms. Davis sits an awfully long time looking at me. Then, she sighs and gets an idea, pulls a paper from a manila folder.

The print at the top is upside down from where I sit, but I can easily read it:

The most important thing is to enjoy your life
—to be happy—
it's all that matters
~ STEVE JOBS

Frigging Steve Jobs. What does he know?

She glances at her notes, then looks up at me.

"A Dan from Pop's Pizza called. He asked if you wanted to go back to work. He says he has a paycheck for you."

Dan.

An involuntary pull flutters in my stomach. I sit forward in my chair.

"Dan called?"

Ms. Davis notices my attitude adjustment and suppresses a smile. I hate the scrutiny and shut back down, silently cursing myself for showing emotion. I slouch a bit and stare at the scuffed woodwork on the baseboard behind Ms. Davis's chair.

"Yes, twice in fact. Do you want me to call him and let him know you'll start up again? It will get you out of the Craig house for a few hours, few days a week. You may start to feel like you're back in control of some of your life. Ms. Craig and your caseworker think it will be good for you, too."

Back in control. What the hell does that mean?

I don't answer. Ms. Davis sighs and sits back in her own chair. It creaks, but I don't look up.

"It's up to you, Allee. Want to try? He said it's been over a month since you worked there. You can talk to Dan yourself about your schedule. I'll try and reach him today."

I don't look at Ms. Davis's face. I don't want her to see how disjointed I feel inside, like my pieces aren't touching. Or they're put together all wrong. Like a jigsaw puzzle that someone shoved together without caring what the final picture looks like.

Instead of meeting her eyes, I look at her kinky brown hair, parted off to the side so it tumbles around her face in an uneven way. The mother-of-pearl button at the top of her green cardigan catches my eye, and then I notice the rest of the sweater. Unlike me, Ms. Davis pushed the sleeves up to her elbows as if she's ready to get to work—like I'm some big project.

Jesus Christ, can my life get any worse?

But I nod. Maybe it will help so I can feel like me again. I have

18

no idea what the final puzzle is supposed to look like because there's no box showing me where the pieces go. I know nothing will ever be normal, but I wish I could find a puzzle piece to rest on. Maybe Pop's Pizza is one of the puzzle pieces I can stand on while I figure out where all the other pieces go.

I pull my sleeve further down, over the knuckles of my left hand.

"Yeah. I'll stop by Pop's on my way back to the Craigs' after school today."

"Okay. I'll call him and let him know to expect you this afternoon." Ms. Davis writes on a paper before looking up. "Is there anything else I can help you with, Allee? I'm here to help with anything. Cara, Ms. Craig and I are all here to help. All you have to do is ask."

Sounds easy, except I don't know what to ask for. This pause is everything. My feet, my words, my thoughts, my eyes, my ears seem stuck in thick mud like those mud-loving zombie frogs we learned about in Biology. Gross. Effective for preservation? Maybe. But definitely not helpful if trying to ask for help to get out of the mud.

I want to ask her where Tony is to make sure jail is making his life miserable. But I keep my thoughts and feelings just under the mound of mud so it doesn't crack. Cracks are bad for mud. It'll break into thousands of pieces and add to the confusing puzzle inside me. I won't be able to control anything if the caked-on dirt that I've packed around me falls away. I'll be exposed, which even zombie frogs figured out, is bad for preservation. When my thoughts and feelings bubble up inside I add more mud, pat it down, keep calm. If they find the knife under my mattress and figure out that at night I think about stabbing Tony, they'll take me to some god-forsaken foster home. Or worse, a padded cell.

Maybe they'd send me to juvie. Do they lock kids up for just thinking about killing someone?

Instead of asking about Tony, I ask about my stuff.

"Can I get a couple of things I left at the house? I need them."

"Are you missing something particular?"

Am I missing something particular?

It takes everything in me not to say, "Yeah, my mom. I'm missing my mom."

Instead, I shrug.

"I want to look around. See if there is anything I can take. I mean keep."

Tears well up in my eyes. I pinch the inside of my wrist to stop them.

Mom's voice floats around inside my head, saying, "Stay quiet. People only know what you tell them. Stay quiet and everything will be okay."

Ms. Davis sits back in her chair. "I'll have to check with your caseworker. Let me make a few phone calls. Maybe I can drive you over there after school and then take you to Pop's Pizza. I'd like to meet Dan anyway."

The start of the first period bell clangs. Ms. Davis stands and ushers me to the door. Thank god it's the end of our session.

How many of these am I going to have to do?

"You have an eighth period today, right? Meet me here afterward. I'll work on getting the okay to take you by the house and then we'll head over to Pop's."

I nod and slip out. The last thing I want is her coming to the pizza shop. But what else can I do? I force my legs to walk. I keep my head down, stay close to the lockers, and cringe as everyone rushes past me. The air they disturb and their voices swoosh around my ears. They're probably talking about me. I would be talking about me, too, about the girl whose dad killed her mom.

Shit.

I want the floor to swallow me, whole. But trying to survive the last few months of high school has to be better than a shrink. I inch forward, down the corridor.

Tanaya runs up behind me, and my skin crawls as she slides her hand around my waist. I can't stand it when people touch me. One too many surprise smacks from Tony has left the surface of my skin on constant alert. I imagine piling more mud around me and resist the urge to push her away. This is a different kind of protection, though—Tanaya on one side and the lockers on the other. Between them, I'm hidden from all the stares. I concentrate on that thought, and not her hand on my hip.

Oblivious to all the thoughts and feelings I'm trying to keep under control, she laughs.

"What did Ditsy Davis have to say? You just get done meeting with her? Is she going to leave you alone now or is she destined to cramp your style forever?"

I manage a weak smile and change the subject.

"Well, look who it is! Miss Sneak-Out-Of-The-House-And-Have -Your Friend-Cover-For-You."

Weeks of her slipping out at night to be with Stretch is just asking for trouble. If not from Stretch himself, then from Auntie T once she finds out what Tanaya's been doing and I've been lying. Tanaya gives me a friendly push.

"Ah, c'mon, don't be mad. Y'know I'd cover for you."

I know she would but that isn't the problem. She's spending a lot of nights with a guy I've never met. I'm used to seeing guys around Tanaya, falling all over her. Not taking her away in the middle of the night.

"He's trouble, Tanaya. He never shows his face, just sits in the car shrouded by darkness and waits for you."

Like a creepy vampire. A shiver runs down my spine.

"I wish you'd tell me more about him so I could tell you why I don't like him."

"That's harsh. How y'know he's trouble?"

Tanaya's phone, the one he gave her, vibrates and she reaches to get it. I put my hand on her wrist.

"I don't like him, Tanaya."

She shakes my hand away. "You don't have to like him. That's my job." She turns to read the text and then smiles. "Come party with us down at Snake Road. Spend some time with him and his friends. We'll hang out." She slides the phone back in her pocket. "It'll be good for you to do something fun."

I don't want to go to the parties. Even Logan, the fryer at Pop's Pizza warned me about Snake Road gatherings. He graduated a few years ago and seems to have a pretty good handle on what and who to stay away from in this neighborhood. When I first started working, Tanaya stopped in for a bite to eat and was telling me about the Snake Road hang-out in a hidden plot, just off Adams Avenue. Logan was wheeling the bucket into the janitor closet, shaking his head as I asked her more and more questions. It's hard to believe that conversation was a year ago.

When he walked out of the closet he called over to us, "Nuttin' good ever comes out of Snake parties."

That's all I needed to hear. Had enough of my own troubles. I never bothered with Snake Road.

But I don't like hanging out at the Craigs' without Tanaya. Last Friday night, Tanaya went out with Dorie and Carissa. Auntie T kept checking on me, asking if there was anything I needed and bringing me glasses of water. By the end of the night, there were four full glasses of water on the dresser.

That, and having to lie when Auntie T asks about Tanaya's new friends and why I'm not with them makes me cringe.

So, I tell Tanaya, "Maybe I could head over with you one night, for a little bit and then leave."

We stop just outside my Algebra classroom, and she gives me a quick hug.

"It'll be a blast! Gotta run. See you in Lit!"

As Tanaya runs down the hall, I slip into Mr. Devlin's room for the designated fifty-five minutes of integer hell. I've tried to catch up on all the missed work, but I'm lost. I've missed three weeks of school and now nothing makes sense. Mr. D asks for homework, and I quickly write my name on the top of a piece of blank paper, number 1-20 down the margin. I pass it up the row with everyone else's and hope it buys me time to catch up. He usually shoves our homework into a folder to look at later.

But it's not my lucky day. He flips through the homework right then and there, stops and looks up at me.

"We're going to have to set up study-homework partners."

And then, as if life isn't bad enough, he singles me out.

"Allee, what free period do you have?"

I look around. "Me?"

"Yes, you. What free period?"

"Third period study hall."

Everyone turns and stares, pity floating out of their eyeballs, and I slide down, down, down in my seat.

"You need to catch up, Allee, or you'll be taking this course all over again in the summer."

Shit. I shouldn't have handed anything in. He wouldn't have noticed until he had to record homework grades. So stupid!

I put my hands in my lap, under my sweater, and pull at the skin on the inside of my left wrist. He looks out at the class.

"Does anyone have third period study hall to help Allee catch up?"

No one moves. I don't blame them. Who the hell wants to give up their free period to work with me? Mr. Devlin's been teaching here at least 20 years. He knows someone other than me has third period open. So he just stares out at everyone, waiting. I hear the sigh first, then see Dorie's hand.

"Great! Thanks, Dorie. I'll be sure to give you an extra point or two this quarter. Just work on the chapter she missed." And then he looks back at me and says, "She's a fast learner."

Gee. Thanks.

Dorie never bothered with me before. Now she'll hate me for taking up her time. There's got to be some reason she raised her hand, and I'm not thinking a sense of duty is her motivation. But what? I can't even...

Chapter 6

One more period, American Lit, and I'll be heading to the pizza shop. The first time I'm looking forward to something in what seems like forever.

Unlike most of the other seniors, I never miss eighth period. Mr. Jenkins is a great teacher. He shares the authors' lives along with the stories they wrote. It was fascinating learning about Alcott, James, Faulkner, and Fitzgerald. I missed most of Fitzgerald, but Mr. J said he'd give me a B if I read *The Great Gatsby* and hand in a one-page summary. It's a short book. I'm almost finished the assignment and ready to start with the next writer.

Conversations stop as everyone strolls in after me. It's not because I'm finally back in school, and they all feel sorry for me, thank god. It's all about Mr. Jenkins. Everyone has a sense of weird reverence for him. He never addresses us before class, always just starts by writing on the board. We're so tired of listening to adults drone on and on, there's genuine appreciation for how Mr. Jenkins hardly opens his mouth. We enter and sit, reading the board as he scribbles THE GLASS MENAGERIE and TENNESSEE WILLIAMS. Under that, DYSFUNCTIONAL FAMILY, and he draws a big circle around it.

Without saying a word, he has our attention. I'm hungry for information on the Tennessee guy. Jenkins turns, nods his head, then back to the board to write NOVEL. Then crosses it out. He scribbles faster, SHORT STORY and crosses that out.

He turns to us, and everyone waits. This class may not be the smartest at Emberton High, but we care enough to show up for eighth period. That means something, and he knows it. The less he says, the more attentive we become. He turns his back to us, underlines FAMILY and adds A PLAY ABOUT to the left of it.

With a *snap,* he caps the marker, puts it down, and waits. Timing is everything, and it takes just a second for the conversation to start.

"Yo, Mr. J, what's that 'dys' word?" Ty calls out. There's no pretending to know stuff with Ty. His questions reveal an innocence most of the others laugh at. I think he's pretty brave to just speak up and ask. Mr. Jenkins believes in freedom of expression, no one has to raise a hand in his room.

"Jump into the conversation when you feel like it."

Ty has taken it to heart.

We've been conditioned, though. Generally, we're guarded, don't voice questions or thoughts. But, Jenkins is patient, holding his opinions, and lets us talk through our thoughts without interrupting. There aren't too many teachers at Emberton like him.

He doesn't answer Ty. Kim usually fills Mr. J's gaps.

She calls out, "Dysfunctional. It's dysfunctional, and it means the family is messed up bad. Like, broken."

Mr. Jenkins still doesn't say anything. He looks around the room and waits. He's awesome, a showman. I barely make comments in class, preferring instead to watch how he works the room, keeping everyone on topic. Sheer genius, really, and if he didn't have such a god-awful dandruff problem, I would've crushed on him. There's something legit about the way he treats us with regard, respect when most adults don't bother.

I find it attractive. That's all.

But when the white flakes fall on his dark shirts, I'm all, *yeah, no thanks.*

The least he could do is buy white shirts.

No one has anything to add out loud, but we're all thinking the same thing: A story about a messed-up family. Big deal. Show us one that's not.

Mr. Jenkins turns back to the board, circles PLAY, and finally speaks, "It's a play about family. And the play is comprised of just four people."

He writes:

MOTHER – AMANDA WINFIELD

SON – TOM WINFIELD

OLDER SISTER – LAURA WINFIELD

TOM'S FRIEND – JIM O'CONNOR
"That's it." *Snap*.

I can't help but notice there's no dad in this dysfunctional story. I sit back in my chair and cross my arms.

As if reading my mind, he continues, "Now, you may be wondering, 'Where's Dad?' Well, he's referred to in the play but never actually shows up. There's even a picture of him hanging in a place of honor."

He walks over to the bookcase under the line of windows and picks up a pile of paperbacks.

"You have your homework. Read the play and we'll discuss the importance, or lack of importance, of each family member."

He passes out worn paperbacks with TENNESSEE WILLIAMS in caps at the top of the cover and THE GLASS MENAGERIE in the middle. Half the cover is ripped off my copy, but I don't care—it's a goldmine. Notes are penciled all around the margins on almost every page.

I sit up, grab the pen out of my back pocket, and write ALLEE inside the torn cover. *Easy A—Thank you whoever used this book before me.*

Tanaya looks over. "You have notes on every page! Here, swap books with me."

There's no way I'm giving up this book. "We'll study together, I promise, but I'm holding onto the book."

Where I do the minimal amount of schoolwork in English class to get a passing grade, Tanaya studies and does extra credit to pass. We've been friends since first grade, and it's how we fit together. I help her understand all the things we have to read for school, and she helps me with everything else: the social stuff, the ability to fit in with the crowd, talk with boys, put on make-up, and wear the right clothes. Tanaya's got that down to perfection.

Or, so I thought before Stretch slithered into her life. Now, I don't know who or what Tanaya is trying to be. But whatever she's playing at, Tanaya is looking good.

She gathers her thick curly black hair and slides it over her left shoulder so when she relaxes in the chair, she doesn't lean on it.

"Thanks, Allee. I can always count on you."

Mr. J slides the chair out from behind his desk and sits. "Start reading it now so there's no excuse tomorrow when we begin discussions." Everyone groans and he raises his voice. "And yes, you'll want to bring it every day so we can reference your comments. One point off your grade every day you don't bring the book into class. In other words, don't lose it, keep it close. Make it your best friend."

I love how books often reveal that for every person with a better life than mine, there's another with a shittier one. Reading about other people's problems puts me in good company and I often think how I'd fix the characters' lives. And what about the Tennessee Williams guy? Why would Mr. Jenkins want us to spend time talking about his play?

I push my chair back, open to the first page, and rest my chin on the top of my wrists.

"Talk to me, Tennessee. What could you possibly want to tell me?"

- - - - -

It's the first time we've been assigned a play and I find the format kind of choppy at first. But, I like the flow of the conversations. I'm on Scene Three when the end-of-the-day buzzer sounds. Tom Winfield has just crouched towards his mother and is on a rant about visiting opium dens and becoming a hired assassin. I want to keep reading but instead, I get my things together to meet up with Ms. Davis.

Tanaya walks out of the classroom with me. "Thank god that's over! Ever read anything so boring?" She rolls her dark eyes, then stares at me. "Am I right or am I right?!"

I dog-ear page twenty-five and shrug. "Yeah, boring."

Some things are better off not admitting. Tanaya would think I'm crazy if I tell her I can feel Tennessee Williams reaching through time and space to hold my hand and pull me into his play. I can't wait to go to the library to Google questions about the book. Tom's mom talked about a Mr. Lawrence and his filthy writing. That would be interesting to research. And what kind of music is glass menagerie music? I want to be able to hear it in my mind whenever I think about the story.

But it will have to wait. I smile when I think about Pop's Pizza, Logan and Dan.

Dan called and wants me back.

The awkward mishaps this first day back to school should make me want to crawl back under the comforter in our shared bedroom. But instead, I'm genuinely happy about going to Pop's.

"Listen, I'm heading to the pizza shop. Will you tell your mom I'll be getting in late?"

Her phone vibrates.

"Yeah, sure." She looks at the phone and walks slowly down the hall. She doesn't bother to say good-bye.

"Okay, see you later," I call after her as I head toward Ms. Davis's office.

Tanaya doesn't look up. Or back. I don't think much of it. Except, just my luck, she has two phones and I don't have any. Don't really want one anyway. Not without Mom.

Chapter 7

I walk into Ms. Davis's office as she's putting papers into a leather bag. I plop into the chair, and she gives half a smile.

"Allee, I couldn't get the okay to go back into your house, but we can head over to Pop's Pizza. Dan's there waiting for us."

I nod. "There's not much stuff at the house anyway but I'd like a few things. Can you keep trying?"

"Sure." She lets out a sigh. "But your mom was renting, and the owner already cleaned out the house a couple of weeks ago. I'm trying to find where he put everything." She pauses to check the buttons on her sweater, then looks up at me. "It seems he threw most of it out."

I nod again because I do understand. My mom could take great care of dusting the dollar store vases, but never cleaned the house. We used to, together. Mom and I would dust, put things away, sing on the way to the laundromat. A faint smile twitches in the corner of my lips as I remember our march to 5th Street, pillow cases stuffed with dirty clothes.

But it all stopped about five years ago. Tony started drinking more and more, and it was too depressing to clean up the house. Once we did, he'd come in and trash the place. We tried to stay on top of every-thing, but then, we just stopped caring.

I still kept up with the laundry. Even Tony's. I loved getting the stink of stale alcohol out of his clothes. Saturday mornings, I'd pillow-case everything and head to the laundromat just before it opened at nine. I'd get my choice of the best machines as long as I was the first one there.

It was a mantra, Mom's thought process:

"No reason to smell, Allee. We'll keep ourselves presentable. Okay?"

She'd be at work, and I'd do laundry. There's something reassuring about the thump-thump and swish-swish of the machines. The smell of warm cotton and Bounce sheets mixed with steady rhythms lulled me to sleep in the plastic yellow chair next to the window. Such a peaceful environment. And safe. I felt safe there.

Tony never showed up at the laundromat.

My job and the bank account were the last two things my mom did for me and the only things I need. They're all that matter. Seems right that everything else in the house is gone.

"Hey, what's that on your arm?"

Ms. Davis's concern pulls me back, out of my memory.

Crap!

I'm holding *The Glass Menagerie* and a notebook across my chest with my left arm. The sleeve of my hoodie bunched up to show part of the paper towel I taped around my newest cut.

I'm not ready to talk about that just yet. Can't even wrap my head around why I do it, so I don't think about it much. Kind of refuse to admit it happens.

It started three days after I moved into the Craigs'. Auntie T popped into the bedroom and asked me to empty the dishwasher. Tanaya was out with Dorie and Carissa, and I think Auntie T was starting to think I'd never get out of bed. I was thinking the same thing.

But when she locked the front door behind her on her way to work that night, I realized the least I could do was empty the dishwasher. The quicker I emptied the dishwasher, the quicker I could climb back under the comforter.

I roll-slid out of bed. The walk down the steps reminded me about the two cops telling me about Mom. The jute rug, still under the coffee table, made my blood boil.

Still does, whenever I walk past it.

I absent-mindedly emptied the dishwasher until I lifted the silver-ware out of the baskets. I put them in the right sections of the utensil drawer, except for the small paring knife.

It glistened in my hand, and I understood something as clear as if it was scribbled on Mr. J's board: with one slit, the emotions boiling just below the surface of my skin would have a way to escape.

Admittedly, I often thought about cutting, just never did.

And now, it's just normal. Cutting gets me out from under the comforter because the only way to do it, without leaving a bloody mess, is in the shower. So, when I'm expected to do stuff, like show up at school for Monday morning sessions, I get out of bed, get my intense feelings under control, and get squeaky clean with whatever new bodywash Tanaya is experimenting with.

That's actually three good reasons to cut.

I give myself a few seconds to answer Ms. Davis by sliding the books into my backpack. Then I pull the sleeves over my knuckles and swing the backpack onto my shoulder.

"Oh, nothing. I put a white thermal under my hoodie because I couldn't get warm this morning."

Ms. Davis tilts her head and tries to look into my eyes. I focus on the mother-of-pearl button at the top of her cardigan. For whatever reason, she decides not to say anything about my lame excuse. She collects a few things off her desk.

"Okay. Well, let's go. We can talk about why you're cold in the car. Do you think you have a fever?"

"Oh, no!" I assure her. "I'm good."

The last thing I need is to go to the doctor's. I'm going to have to be more careful around Ms. Davis.

She parks in front of Pop's Pizza. She doesn't know we're supposed to walk in the back, through the alley. Dan explained on my first day to use the back door, like family walking into the house. But Ms. Davis doesn't need to know that. She's not part of the family.

I open the front door, and the bells jingle. A soreness in my gut, like a bruise, spreads out as I walk through that door. A quote from Maya Angelou that I memorized in fifth grade pops into my mind:

The ache for home lives in all of us.

I never understood that line. Until today.

It's the same ache I get when I think of Mom. You'd think they'd be different, the missing-her feeling and this glad-I'm-here-at-the-pizza-shop feeling. I guess that's why it lives in all of us. Those who have and those who don't share the same aches. Loss and love seem to feel the same.

That's weird.

And confusing.

Logan turns from the oven and gives a nod—no smile though, just a concerned look that seems to read every secret I have hidden away. I look down and make sure the sleeves of my hoodie cover my arms.

Dan walks around the counter and shakes Ms. Davis's hand.

"Thank you for bringing Allee."

And then he does something no one's bothered to do over the past few weeks—he takes me into his arms. My first reaction is to push him away, but his arms seem to shelter me from everything, so I allow myself to disappear into his embrace. I don't know why it doesn't hurt, like when everyone else gets too close.

I haven't cried since the morning after the arraignment, when I was in bed remembering Mom on the stepstool dusting vases. In Dan's arms, I feel myself coming undone. My eyes grow hot and wet. It's hard to breathe, and a lump grows in my throat. After a couple of seconds, I need to breathe, so I push him away.

If I hurt Dan's feelings, he doesn't show it. He guides Ms. Davis into the booth closest to the door. I don't want to be part of their conversation and so I walk over to Logan. He saw me push Dan. I know it 'cause he doesn't bother with a hug, high five, or any words of comfort. He busies himself by flattening dough on the counter and then spinning it up in the air.

"Coming back soon? Kind of hard with only the two of us in here. We sure could use your help."

I'm surprised. "Dan didn't hire anyone to take my place?"

"Nah, not your nights. Just waiting for you to come back."

He pours red sauce on the dough and sprinkles cheese in four circles, like a bullseye. It's Pop's Pizza's special style.

"Separates us from everyone else," Dan explained when I first asked about the design.

The phone rings, and without thinking, I go to answer it. I stop with my hand on the receiver.

"Oh, I forgot, should I answer it?"

Logan smiles. "Well, everyone else is busy. And he hasn't bothered to put the online ordering option on the website. Go ahead."

I tuck the receiver between my shoulder and ear, grab the purple sparkly coil that keeps the pen from walking away, and slide the tablet closer to the phone.

"Pop's Pizza. What can I get for you?"

And with that, I forget all about how much I hate Tony, how much

I miss my mom, and how Tanaya sneaks out of our bedroom to do god knows what. And how, in order for me to deal with all those things, I have a small knife nestled between my mattress and box spring. A knife that releases big emotions bursting inside me.

After about twenty minutes, Ms. Davis gets up to leave.

Dan yells over to me, "It's up to you. Want to work tonight? You can work now, until closing, if you want."

I walk around the counter. "Not tonight, Dan. I'm pretty tired and trying to catch up on missed homework."

"Okay. How about tomorrow? I'll expect you after school."

"Sure."

I pick up my bookbag, and *The Glass Menagerie* peeks out of the front pouch. I think about the characters in that play. My mom set up this pizza job. My mom would want me working, keeping busy. Doing something.

I look at Dan.

"Y'know, I, um, changed my mind. I can get homework done between taking orders tonight."

Dan smiles. "Sure, like before, homework comes first."

He seems relieved, but Ms. Davis's about to pop a blood vessel.

"How will you get back to the Craigs'? Will you have to walk home? It may be too soon for you to be wandering around the streets at night by yourself. Today's the first day you've been back to school. After working tonight, you'll be exhausted."

The heat rises, boiling below the surface of my skin. The mud is cracking. I steady my voice but it comes out all snappy.

"I always walked before. The Craigs' live even closer than I did, a couple of blocks. I'll be fine."

Ms. Davis hesitates. "I don't know, Allee."

She looks at Dan for back-up. As if the two are trying to be my parents. I resent their hovering and seethe.

"I'm not a baby! Even my mom knew I could fuckin' walk home by myself!"

Ms. Davis looks as if someone slapped her. Dan takes a step closer, doesn't take his eyes off me. His brow furrows, and his voice cuts through the tension that filled the small shop.

"There's no cursing in here, Allee. I can't risk you talking to customers like that. If you work here, you have to be respectful. Never a reason to curse."

I want to hate him. Throw Dan onto the pile of hate, sit him on top of the whole shit load, and flip him off. I glance over at Logan, sure that he's on my side.

But Logan lowers his eyes, turns to the fryer.

I'm utterly alone in my messed-up life. The pizza shop slips away from my grasp, sliding away on an angry mudslide. Ms. Davis can allow it to slip into oblivion, this sanctuary that my own mom secured for me.

I want to run and hide. Crouch down and disappear.

But then I realize... Mom didn't allow cursing, either. What is wrong with me?

I will myself to do what needs to be done to keep this job. I turn to Dan, soften my voice.

"Yeah. Sure. Forgot myself there."

And then back to the woman with all the power. I keep my voice even, controlled.

"Sorry about that Ms. Davis. Don't know what got into me. Really. Won't happen again."

Dan doesn't say anything, and Ms. Davis busies herself by looking in her purse.

"No problem, Allee. You've been through a lot."

Finally, she takes keys out of the zippered pocket and looks up. Her face is red, which makes me feel crap about myself. She coughs.

"Okay then. If you're set, I'll call Ms. Craig so she knows you're working tonight. Hopefully you can get a good night's sleep and start fresh in the morning."

Dan walks Ms. Davis out to her car, and it's obvious they're talking about me. Dan is nodding his head as Ms. Davis keeps talking, swishing her hands this way and that. Pulling her purse strap back onto her shoulders when her hand movements make it slide down. I want to know what they're saying.

At the same time, I don't want to know. I'm afraid they know too much about me. Care too much for me.

It won't be good if they figure out about the cutting—that I'm messed up in the head.

Two kids walk into the shop, so I step back behind the counter, and the phone rings. Thank god. Taking care of customers and answering phone calls quiet the thoughts crowding my mind.

"Pop's Pizza. What can I get for you?"

Chapter 8

It's everything I want in a job. Five days a week, I get a warm pizza slice or two, and Dan lets me have a Coke to wash it down. Since I came back, after my mom… Well, he's been making me eat a salad, too. The first time was with the stern directive, "No more pizza and Coke for you unless you eat a salad."

Seriously.

I go into the walk-in and bring out an already prepared salad on a Styrofoam plate. Logan chuckles as I toss it onto the counter. Which ticks me off.

"You think it's funny? I think it's sexist. You don't have to eat a salad every night."

"No, Dan just tells me to eat my pizza faster and get back to work. Tonight, he added some shitty comment about the new designs in my hair line."

He turns his head sideways, so he can see his reflection in the microwave door. It's a zigzag that makes him clean cut, but with an edge. I love his brown skin and black hair. And his eyes are as dark as his hair, like they've been colored with the same beautiful crayon. I wonder how long it'll take for the hair to grow in and if he already has another design planned. He turns quickly, and our eyes meet. He grins, lifts his chin upward, and points to his hair with an inquisitive look.

I smile. "I like it. It's sick."

He laughs, and I look down at my salad as a blush warms my face. He grabs another dough ball from the walk-in and starts kneading it at the end of the counter.

"Dan cares, Allee. No strings attached. Swear. He cares. You can trust him."

I fork a tomato and nod, but *no strings attached* seems a little too good. I give a non-committal, "Hmmm," and finish the salad. Keeping my eyes and ears open before jumping right into paranoia, or trust, is always the better plan. It would be rude not to eat the salad anyway.

I swallow a mouthful of tomato and say, "Well, he's got to upgrade the food ordering system. I can't believe he didn't do that while I was away. What do we have to do to convince him to get it online? The website looks pretty good. Who does it for him?"

Logan sprinkles the cheese bullseye on the pizza sauce.

"He does it all. Now would be a great time to bring up online orders. It was hard when you weren't here. He'll be more open to simplifying things now that he had to answer phones." He chuckles. "Dan would get so mad the way people would take forever to order, asking everyone in their house, or wherever they were, while he stood there waiting. We probably lost a few customers because he would just hang up on them."

"No joke?"

"Nope. Go ahead and say something to him. Can't hurt. He won't listen to me."

The bells over the front door chime, and three guys, twenty-some-things, walk in. I don't recognize any of them from the neighborhood or school. I drop the empty salad plate into the trash can and slide the pad over to take their order.

The first guy says, "I'll have the cheesesteak wit' fried onions, side of fries."

He's about 23 or 24, maybe an Emberton graduate. Maybe a drop-out. And tall. If he raised his arms over his head, he could proba-bly touch the ceiling. Well, not the ceiling. Definitely the ceiling fans. Where Logan's hair is a high top fade, this guy's long, black straight hair is pulled into a high ponytail. His sideburns outline sharp cheek-bones. His hair is better conditioned than my own, and his pale skin has a small jagged scar above his right almond-shaped eye.

I write down his order as he turns to the shortest guy, "Yo, Mouse, what're ya' gettin?"

The guy he's talking to is thinner and younger, maybe eighteen or nineteen, not quite twenty. Acne has left scars on his cheeks, and his greasy hair is parted down the middle. It's almost shoulder length. If he wears his hair longer to hide his big ears, it doesn't help. It parts like a curtain on either side of protruding ears. I don't stare, but I smile at the appropriate nickname.

Sliding his elbow toward me, he leans over the counter and whispers, "Sumpin' funny?"

I look down. "Nope. What can I get ya?"

He straightens, throws his shoulders back, and tilts his chin up to give the impression he's looking down at me.

"Two slices, plain."

At that moment, I'm sure of one thing—I hate this guy.

The third guy is looking in the refrigerator for a drink. Tall guy smacks the glass, and my insides jump.

"C'mon Frank, we ain't got all night."

I look back at Logan, make sure he's picking up on all this. He raises his eyebrows as if to ask if I'm okay. I nod and turn back to the customers.

Frank looks over at me and gives a wink with a reassuring smile. My insides calm a bit, but twitch again as the fridge door bangs closed. I drop behind the counter to pretend I'm looking for something on the bottom shelf. Loud noises, surprising movements make me duck. I take a few deep breaths, remember that Tony isn't here. Tony's in jail. I cringe, waiting for objects to fly at me.

There's nothing.

I whisper, "You're okay, Allee. You're at the pizza shop."

The 'Frank' guy puts his drink on the counter.

"Jesus Christ, Stretch! Take it easy! What the hell's got into you tonight?"

Stretch. He must be Tanaya's boyfriend.

A shadow falls around me as Frank leans over the counter.

"You drop somethin' down there? Whadda y'doin'?"

I stand slowly and give a side glance toward the guy he called "Stretch." He's pissed and snaps back at Frank.

"We got stuff to do. Unless you don't want to. Mouse and I can handle it fine without you."

Frank slides his Coke toward me.

"I'll have a pizza steak, no onions." And then he turns back to Stretch, "You know I'm in. Calm the hell down. Party's never in full swing until after 10:30."

I write down his order, and before taking it back to Logan, ask, "Anything else?"

He smiles at me. "Nah, that's it. Thanks."

This Frank doesn't seem to fit with the other two.

Is it because of the way he says, "Thanks," or the direct eye contact, or the soft smile? Why is he hanging with these losers? And his eyes, are they really so blue?

I tear their order off the pad and don't look back up to check his eye color.

"You know a person by the friends they keep," Mom always cautioned.

The guys with him? Definitely assholes.

I clip the order on the line for Logan and then head back to the counter. Stretch walks toward me, so I grab my Algebra book from the shelf under the counter, and sink to the floor, leafing through the pages on the ground.

He doesn't take the hint and leans over the counter, talks to the top of my head. "You go to Emberton?"

He pronounces it *em-ber-ton*, enunciating the second syllable and the t sound. That means he's not from here. Locals mesh the sounds together, it's *em-br-don*.

I don't bother to look up. "Yep."

I take out a piece of graph paper, lay it on the floor, and write my name at the top.

But that doesn't work either. He keeps talking.

"Shame you have to work. There's a big party down by Snake Road. Pretty much everyone will be there."

And then he pauses. I can sense him looking at the top of my head.

"Why don't you stand up so I can get a good look at you? Sweet thing like you shouldn't be hiding behind counters."

I freeze and wonder what Tanaya would think about all of this.

Logan's busy at the fryer and doesn't hear him. I'm safe behind the counter, and Logan is close. I shouldn't be frozen. It's silly. And the floor is gross—no matter how many times Logan mops it.

Why can't I stand up and talk to this guy?

I challenge myself to do what he asks and slowly stand, sliding the textbook and paper onto the counter.

But I keep my head down. I feel his eyes at the top of me, moving down onto my breasts and stomach. He leans a bit over the counter to look down at the rest of me.

Gross.

I mumble, "Need somethin'?"

And hold my breath.

"I don't know yet. Still thinking 'bout it."

He chuckles softly, and when he turns away, I release my breath. My knees are shaky. When he's on the other side of the shop, I whisper, "Yep. Asshole."

Then, I busy myself with the first math problem. Logan walks up behind me.

"Y'alright? Anyone rassin' you?" And then in a whisper, "I'll spit in his food."

"No, just jerks. You better not spit. We'll have the Board of Health in here, you'll get fired, and then Dan'll kill you."

Logan puts his shoulders back and lifts his chin toward them.

"Better watch themselves. Never saw them before. D'you?"

"Nope. But I think that tall guy is Tanaya's boyfriend. He invited me to a big party down on Snake Road. Supposedly, everyone but me will be there."

Logan shrugs and walks back to the fryer.

"Y'know what I think about that."

I write down the next math problem and answer, "Nothing good ever comes from Snake parties."

He chuckles. "Got that right."

Dan comes out of the office.

"Everything okay out here? I'm picking up on some sarcasm."

He shoots us a now-get-back-to-work-and-appreciate-that-you've-got-a-job look.

"All's good, Dan. Makin' sure no one's 'rassin' Allee."

Dan looks out toward the foyer, where the three guys are busy on their phones, looking totally innocent.

"Paying customers are paying customers."

He grabs his car keys out of his pocket and slides his tweed cap onto his bald head.

"With a smile, please. With a smile. I'll be back in about an hour. Walmart run for more paper products. If I could figure out a way to ration out toilet paper, I would."

The screen door bounces twice behind him as he leaves by the alley door.

Fifteen minutes and two phone orders later, Logan shouts, "Orders up!" a little louder than usual.

The three guys look over, and Logan stares them down. I enjoy the not-so-subtle messages boys often exchange. Girls have their own way to get a message across with "the look": sucked in cheeks, lips turned down, raised eyebrows, and neck shifted to one side, shoulders back.

I see it used, but haven't mastered it myself.

Boys are different. They're all about how loud, strong, and tall they are. I think Tony's stuck in that teenage intimidation time warp. Most seem to grow out of that stage. Look how normal Dan seems. And the teachers at school. It's just young guys—and Tony. When he was his loudest, I'd sit in the locked bathroom wondering why I couldn't stand up to him. I'd wait until he passed out.

Those last few moments of my mom's life…What was she thinking when he emptied all his rage on her?

She had nowhere to go.

These thoughts fill my mind at odd hours of the day. I can't control them and the guilt creeps in—over and over again. If only I had stayed at home that night, Mom would still be alive. Instead, I ran and hid. I pinch the inside of my wrist while Stretch pulls out his wallet.

He asks, "What time you get off work?"

Logan walks over and stands behind me, watching everything and ready to step in if I can't handle Stretch by myself. I lower my eyes and see the wad of bills in his wallet. Twenties, fifties.

Hundreds.

So many bills, the wallet barely shuts.

He hands me a fifty. My fingers shake as I count out his change, and my nerves cause the register door to slam closed a lot harder than I want. I stand there and don't answer, wishing him to disappear.

"I can come back and get you."

He leaves another fifty on the counter.

For a tip?

I shrug.

"Nah, thanks anyway."

I slide the bill back toward him.

"Oh, come on. You can buy yourself something pretty with that."

I don't seem to be able to take my fingers off the fifty.

Finally, he walks away, and I stuff the bill into the small front pocket of my jeans. My nerves have me all jittery, so I go to Dan's office to read more of *The Glass Menagerie*.

Logan pokes his head in after about twenty minutes, "You good?

Dan's not back yet, but the last order was just picked up. I'm gonna start cleanin' out the fryers."

I walk out to help close the shop.

"What the hell? That tall guy is Tanaya's boyfriend. I don't get it. There's something off with that guy. And did you see the cash in his wallet? Fifties and hundreds in there! Who walks around with cash? It has to be fake. Or, he's dealing something."

"Not to throw shade on your friend, but maybe that's what she likes about him. The cash flow."

I think about the fifty in my pocket.

Maybe.

He wipes the two baskets down with paper towels, then drops them in a solution of vinegar and scalding hot water. I grab the push broom and start sweeping the restaurant area.

"He gave her an iPhone. Maybe you're right. I sure don't get it."

Well, if I'm honest… *kind of* don't get it. But kind of *do* get it.

Logan starts at the top of all the appliances and systematically wipes the chrome.

"They've been going out for a while now, though, huh? 'Couple months? Notice anythin' that seems off? You know, trouble Tanaya may be gettin' herself into?"

I don't tell him about her sneaking out. None of his business.

"I just don't like him. And she jumps whenever he calls or texts. It's like her life is his now."

He shakes his head. "Doesn't sound right. But maybe she likes that. She's probably in love with the guy."

He's got a point. Could be more than all the things he buys for her. Maybe she likes the way he looks at her, makes her feel.

Ick. Cannot imagine that.

Thank god I live in the opposite direction of Snake Road. Wouldn't want to run into the three of them on a dark street.

Chapter 9

A week later and I have to run all the way to eighth period to talk to Mr. Jenkins before everyone walks in and he starts his scribbling. Two sophomores, maybe freshmen, walk out the door as I slide into the room.

"Yo, Mr. J! Can I ask you something?"

"Sure, Allee, what's up?"

"What happens if I can't find my copy of *The Glass Menagerie*? I've been looking all week. It's gone."

He looks somber, as if I told him I lost a puppy.

"It's five points off your final grade."

"What??!! They're falling apart, every single book! Can't I just get another? For Christ's sake, five points? That's stupid."

"Now hold on there, Allee. They're all the same edition. We use the same ones to reference pages and for direct quotes on quizzes and tests. It's hard to replace the exact editions. It's not like the one we use is still in print." His eyes soften. "What have you been doing since it disappeared? I graded the last quiz. You did very well. Is Tanaya sharing hers?"

I wish. Would have made my life much easier.

Between my extra hours at work and her hanging out with Stretch, we hardly see each other.

"No, um, I've been real busy at work, so I hit the library after school. They don't have a copy of the play, but I read what I can online. Sometimes there's no computer available. It's frustrating, Mr. J. Can't even imagine why someone would've taken the damn thing in the first place."

Except, of course, that notes are written all over the pages.

"Alright, calm down." He walks over to the shelf. "Here's another copy, it's in sad shape, but at least you can read it whenever you can, instead of sitting in the library."

No cover and it starts in the middle of Act Two.

Whatever.

I slide it into my backpack. Kids are coming into the room as I walk away from Mr. J, he calls to me, "Listen, Allee, I know you're going through a lot. I'll wait to take the points off. That will give you a few months to find it, before I have to lower the grade. Okay? Does that help?"

I roll my eyes, sarcasm falling off my tongue. "Gee, thanks."

If Mr. J registered my attitude, he doesn't show it. He looks in his top drawer and takes out a black marker, preparing himself for literary combat.

Why is life so unfair? I wasn't even the one who misplaced it. Someone steals something, and I have to deal with the consequences? I kept it in the same spot, the small section in the front of my backpack.

I watch as everyone files in and takes their seats. Someone's messing with me, and I wonder who.

And why?

Mr. Jenkins writes LAURA WINGFIELD on the board. And then in classic Jenkins style he underlines it, draws five lines around it, and waits for the stragglers to shuffle into the room.

He nods to Jacquin, who is always last, and closes the door.

"Let's get started, shall we?" He pops off the cap, "Tell me, in one or two words, about Laura Wingfield. I only want simple descriptions."

Tanaya yells out, "Daughter."

"Okay—we can start with basics. I'll add 'sister' to that because it's understood."

Jacquin shouts, "Crazy Bitch."

Everyone laughs except for me and Mr. Jenkins. I feel for the girl—even though she's weak and a little messed up. Ever since my mom died, I have a nervousness like Laura. It used to be just at my house when Tony was lurking about. But now it's all the time. People are draining. Some days after school, if I don't need the computers at the library, I go to the Craigs' and shut out the world.

Three thirty in the afternoon? Doesn't matter. I crawl under my lavender comforter to escape all the people at school and to mentally prepare for the customers at work. People are getting harder to be around. What they say and how they look at me sticks to my insides, and I can't stop thinking about them.

I wonder what that feeling is called. Does it have a name? Whatever it is, it's growing. It isn't only images of Tony killing my mom or for my mom leaving me all alone. Or everything that happened before it all ended. It's the way kids whisper and look at me in the lunchroom. The way some people come in for pizza and start giggling.

I'm sure it's about me— what I'm wearing or what I said.

I never actually sleep those afternoons, but curl into a ball under the comforter and feel the blood coursing through my body, traveling around, and bumping into the sticky things inside me.

And then I do what I need to do in the shower to make it all stop – cut.

And don't think about it too much. Until the next time I need it.

Sometimes I wonder if I should tell someone about these feelings inside me.

But watching everyone laugh at Laura as a "crazy bitch" proves that I shouldn't open my mouth about it. Some things are better kept a secret.

I can hear Mom whispering in my mind, "Things tend to blow over Allee, if we leave them alone."

Things will get better. I just have to wait it out.

Mr. Jenkins is tired of waiting for everyone to stop laughing.

"That's enough. Quiet down." The room settles and he continues. "'Crazy Bitch' is not sensitive. How about 'mental illness'?"

Without waiting for a response, he writes MENTAL ILLNESS on another line.

Sharique stands up. She always stands to talk which, for whatever reason, I find super annoying.

When all eyes are on Sharique, she says, "I don't think she's crazy or mental or anything. I think she's just shy. Why does she have to be messed up in the head? I wouldn't like to limp. People would stare and think bad things about me, like, 'What the hell's wrong with you that you can't walk right?'"

A few of the other girls agree. Walking around in public with a limp would be social suicide. Therefore, a great reason to stay in the house.

They're talking over each other, and the boys join the conversation. They definitely wouldn't want to be with someone who has a limp, unless she was really hot.

"Like Tanaya," Jacquin shouts. "I'd definitely take you out on a date, Tanaya, even if you had a limp."

Tanaya wiggles then sits straighter in her chair, sucks her cheeks in, and winks at him. The rest of the boys whistle and howl.

This makes Mr. Jenkins shake his head. He shouts over all of them, "Settle, everyone settle down."

The room quiets and Tanaya crosses her right leg over her left knee. She starts swinging it so it kicks out from under her desk. She's wearing new boots. The black leather looks real, hugging her leg all the way up to her knee. The toe and heel are pointed, a silver buckle crosses over the ankle. Never saw them before today. They do not look comfortable.

But, they are bangin'.

When Mr. J continues, it's in his normal, I'm-in-full-control-of-this-situation voice. "Something is keeping Laura from bettering her life. We can say she is living with a form of mental illness, even if it's only a slight one. She's unable to get to school, unable to hold down a job, unable to socialize with people. She spends all her time with glass figurines. Once her mom dies and Tom leaves, she will have no way to care for herself."

He hesitates and looks over at me. I freeze, don't move a muscle, but am totally aware that all eyes are on me.

I want to mouth off at all of them, "Don't you dare think my life is like frigging Laura's!"

But I stay quiet, shrug, and slip further down in my chair.

Keep quiet. Don't let anyone know what you're thinking.

The hate rushes to my center, pulses in my heart.

Why can't Jenkins buy goddamn Head-n-Shoulders and get a handle on the dandruff problem?

And then like an angry river after a storm, the resentment rises: Laura has a mom. And Laura's mom cares. Only a crazy bitch wouldn't appreciate a mom who sets her up for classes and tries to get her a job. Laura hides behind stupid glass animals. She even lies to her mom and spends her days wandering around neighborhoods like a stupid mutt. Laura is weak.

I'm not like Laura.

I force all this deep inside, push it down, and give Mr. Jenkins a cold, dead stare. What does he know anyway? Probably had a great childhood and feels like he can fix all his students' problems.

Asshole.

But I don't say it. Control. To lose control would mean being sent away.

Mr. Jenkins goes on to talk about anxiety disorders, and as I listen I'm even more determined not to turn out like Laura ... even more determined to get back to work, to keep busy, to be normal.

Tanaya swings her leg as everyone talks about Laura's mental illness, and Mr. Jenkins scribbles on the board. I tune them out and just copy what's on the board into my notebook. As I write, I fixate on the tip of the fine-point pen as it scratches lines onto the paper.

Chapter 10

Auntie T greets me over the hum of the 11:00 news. "Hey, Allee! Tired after such a full day?"

"I'm more than tired. My legs ache from standing, and I feel like a grease pit. Everybody wanted cheesesteaks tonight. I stopped counting after thirty."

Grease explodes throughout the kitchen with cheesesteaks. Because pizzas slide into the ovens, they're much cleaner. But there were only ten pizza orders the whole night. Dan was mad at all the grime and had us scrub everything. My fingers are pruned, and on top of the greasiness, I smell like vinegar and bleach.

But with Logan, it was fun. And busy. And perfect. It may have only been my imagination, but I swear he stood closer to me whenever we talked and brushed gently up against me when he walked past to get to the back line. Maybe it's only wishful thinking. Not sure, yet. But one thing's for certain, I'm looking forward to working again to be near Logan.

I walk to the bottom step. "I'm going to shower and hop into bed."

But I stop for just a second to watch her from the small entryway. It's weird, someone sitting in a chair carrying on a conversation and then turning back to watch the news. Whenever Tony was home and I'd walk in, he'd ignore me. If I talked to him while he watched television he'd bark, "Can't you see I'm watching TV?"

With Tony, I was either invisible or the target. I never knew what to expect.

I stand there waiting for something, or someone, to burst in and suck me back into the chaotic world of Tony.

But there's only Auntie T. She must sense I'm still standing here because she turns to me and says, "Well, welcome back. I'm sure a shower will feel refreshing."

I walk up the first step, but then notice she's still in her Applebee's uniform, black-tie shoes resting off to the side of the couch.

I clear my throat and ask, "How was your day?"

She looks at me and chuckles, "Well, you should know! You're in the food industry. I was so tired when I came in, I couldn't even walk up those steps! My feet are killing me. A couple of birthday parties, too. Please don't ever ask me to sing 'Happy Birthday.' Ever!"

It's this exchange that I love. The food, the roof, the bed, the peace and quiet are great. But in my old life, I still had Kraft Macaroni and Cheese, a roof (a leaky ceiling when Mrs. Estes left the water running in the bathtub, but still, there was something over my head), a mattress on the floor, and days and days when it was quiet because Tony was on a drinking binge. But I never had the conversations that are normal in this house.

I ask, "Do you have to go and clean office buildings tonight?"

"Thank god, not tonight. Tomorrow I will, though. I'll jump in the shower after you and get a good night's sleep for tomorrow's long day.."

"Okay. I'll let you know when I'm done. Tanaya up there already?"

"She came in about an hour ago and said she was exhausted. I expect she's sleeping."

There's a good chance Tanaya already slipped out and is with Stretch. But I answer, "Okay. I'll be extra quiet."

I start to walk up the steps and slide my hands into my coat pockets. With such a busy night at work, I scored with tips. My fingers wrap around the cash, and I walk back down to Auntie T.

"I want to give you something, you know, to help."

I hold out the wad of cash.

Auntie T looks at it, then shakes her head.

"No, Sweetie, you keep that. You work hard, and we're doing fine here."

"I used to give money to help my mom. We helped each other, you know. Like partners."

She doesn't say anything, just looks into my eyes and makes a "hm" sound.

"You know, for bills," I say. "Food and electric bill. Stuff like that."

She takes it from me.

"Okay, Allee. I actually appreciate that. How 'bout we do this. Whenever you have some extra cash, I'll use it to help with the food bill. I'm not going to ask you for it. Okay? I didn't take you into my home to have you paying for your keep. But I appreciate the gesture, so when you have extra, you can hand it over." She puts it in her apron pocket and smiles. "You're like your momma, you know? She was a very generous person."

I head upstairs with a flutter spiraling around my heart until I open the bedroom door. Tanaya's not in the room.

I walk over to the window and hope to see her hopping in or out of Stretch's car. I slide the window open and hang out a bit, watching up and down the alley. The late February air lost January's sting. It's brisk, but with a hint of better weather to come.

But, no Tanaya.

"Tanaya, what the hell are you doing?"

I lower the window and head into the bathroom. I turn on the water and drop my clothes. Carefully, I unwrap the paper towel taped around my arm. Three thin lines run down this forearm, crisscrossed with older scars. The slit from yesterday is a pretty shade of red, almost pink now. It's sore to touch but starting to heal. I look closer at it, amazed at how skin knows how to heal.

I think about the sharp tip on the fine-point pen I used in Mr. J's class. I want to retrieve the knife from under my mattress, a simple cut in the shower. No one would know.

But I'm exhausted. The steady rhythm of the shower calls to me, and I step in. Besides, I want to go quickly, so Auntie T can shower and get to sleep.

I close my eyes as the water massages my head and shoulders. I had to shower quickly in my house, or Tony would bang on the door to take a piss. But the Craigs' have another small bathroom on the first floor. There's no yelling or banging to use the toilet.

Whoever thought to install the very first guest bathroom was brilliant. Even knowing that Auntie T needs to shower, there's no urgency. She won't bang on the door and yell at me to go faster. She treats me like a person. Like my mom did. I have every right to a nice shower, like everyone else.

When I'm done, I dry off, carefully patting my forearms, then put on a soft cotton long-sleeve pajama top. I noticed a few weeks ago that newer cuts heal quicker if I don't wrap them tightly while I sleep.

I take care so they don't get infected. A trip to the doctor is something I don't need.

I almost yell down the steps to Auntie T that I'm finished in the shower. But that wouldn't keep up the lie that Tanaya's asleep in bed. I feel guilty, but go to the middle of the steps, and lean over the banister.

"All ready for you, Auntie T."

She has dozed off so I call out a little louder.

"Shower's ready for you!"

She opens her eyes, taking a moment to remember where she is, and smiles.

"Thanks, Allee. See you in the morning."

I crawl under my comforter and look over at Tanaya's empty bed. Everything would be much better if Tanaya was sleeping safe and sound in her own bed.

"Come on, Allee. It's late. You slept in."

Someone is rubbing my shoulder. Instinctively, my eyes widen, and my skin prickles into action. I shove my arms under the comforter and sit up. "Get off me!"

Auntie T backs away from my bed.

"Easy, Allee. Just trying to get you up. You're late for school. Tanaya left half an hour ago."

It's not Tony trying to mess with me, or Ms. Davis trying to take a look at my arm. It's the lady who welcomed me into her home, staring at me, eyes wide with fear. I scared Auntie T.

What the hell is wrong with me?

She takes a step toward me.

"Do you feel okay, Allee? Maybe working is too much for you. You usually hear me when I call up to you."

"No, no, I'm fine. I was having a bad dream." I pull the pajama sleeves down to my wrists, toss the comforter off, and swing my feet out of bed. "I'm sorry I snapped at you. Must have been that nightmare. Thanks for waking me. I'll have to hurry."

I start looking through drawers for something to wear and Auntie T walks out the door.

"I'll get you a bite to eat, okay?"

God, why is she still nice when I'm a pain in the ass?

"Yeah. That would be great. Thanks, and, um, sorry for not knowing it was you waking me up."

"Sure. No problem."

Which makes me feel even more crap about myself.

It's how my mom reacted to my younger, brattier self. No lecture, no reprimand, no threat. She always expected me to be kind, polite, and respectful— because that's how she treated me.

And then it hits me...

She's dead. My mom is dead.

I run past Auntie T and into the bathroom.

Close the door, always close the door. Lock the door, always lock the door.

It's a conscious decision.

Auntie T always lets me close and lock the door.

My eyes burn and I feel as pathetic as I look, dry-heaving into the toilet. I stifle a cry, but can't stop the flow of tears. They make small ripples in the toilet water.

"Allee, you okay? Are you sick?"

Auntie T calls through the door.

I steady my voice.

"Yeah. I just threw up. Maybe I shouldn't go to school today."

I flush the toilet even though nothing's in it. Well, except for salty tears.

"Good idea. I'll call Ms. Davis. She'll probably call you later. I'll tell her you're going back to sleep so she doesn't bother you for a few hours. Is that what you want?"

"Yeah, that sounds good. Thanks, Auntie T. I'll get a shower then get back to bed."

"Don't forget I picked up that other shift tonight. I'll be back for a quick dinner and check on you, but then I'll have to head out for the night shift. Then, out to clean offices. Try and sleep. I'll text Tanaya, let her know you're sick."

I manage a weak, "Thanks," close the toilet lid, and sit.

"I'm heading to the grocery store now. I'll pick you up soup and crackers. Think you can stomach anything else?"

I don't feel like eating, but say, "That's perfect. Thanks."

"You know, Allee, since I've picked up a few extra shifts, I think we should get you a phone."

I slump forward, put my head in my hands, just let the silent tears do their thing. Can't stop them anyway.

She keeps talking through the door.

"It'll be a lot easier for all three of us. Keeping in contact even with just a text. What do you think? It's not much more to put you on my family plan."

I can't. Don't want one. The phone was supposed to keep me connected with Mom. But the dead don't text.

I take a deep breath, to steady my voice.

"I really don't want one, Auntie T. That's nice of you and all, but I just, well, phones were what Mom and I were trying for. Now that she's not here, it's too..." Sometimes, if you tell adults you need time to think about something, they leave you alone, so I add, "How about we talk about it in a few weeks?"

"Yeah, sure. I'll leave you be. I'll stop by and put the soup on the kitchen table before I head back out to work."

A few minutes later the front door shuts and locks behind her.

How could I feel so safe and comfortable at the pizza shop last night and so shitty this morning? I try to remember the peaceful "busy" of last night, and the feel of Logan so close to me, but other images crowd out the pizza shop. I pull my knees up and wrap my arms around my legs, rocking on the toilet.

How many times did I sit like this in my own home, waiting for my mom's knock on the door, her whisper, "Allee, you in there? You okay? I'm here. Let me in."

I'd unlock the door, and she'd hug me. Everything would be okay—for a little while anyway.

But there's no Mom anymore.

The one person who knew all my secrets is gone. The thought burns, searing into my stomach and my brain. Back and forth I rock, trying to soothe myself. The only other person who knows all about me is Tony. And he's locked up. I want us all together again, the familiar, the home, no matter how bad it was.

Tony and my mom were my only family.

How crazy is that? Wanting Tony if it means I get Mom back?

That can't be right..

I remember all the pain, still feel it in my bones. But he was sad, so he drank. It's not like he wanted to hurt us. He didn't know any better. He always apologized.

On and on, my mind tells me he's not such a bad guy.

And I kind of believe it.

Until I remember Mom, in the ground, under the headstone Auntie T bought and is still paying for because there's no one else to bury her.

How can I want Tony now? He killed her.

The holes in the walls, the name-calling, the stink, the clatter of cans, the pulled pony tails. Was it better than not having anything? Anyone?

The thoughts, feelings, images run rampant in my mind, and my blood surges. I have to stop it, control it. I turn on the shower and walk into the bedroom. I take the knife from under the mattress, the roll of paper towels from downstairs, and a change of clothes from the dresser.

It's all so methodical. It works. It silences everything. Slows everything down.

Steam fills the bathroom, and I ache for the release.

It's genius, of course, cutting in the shower. No evidence, no need to hide anything. Totally exposed and vulnerable.

I don't have to figure out anyone else. I can just concentrate on me.

Chapter 11

Tanaya flicks the light on. "Yo, Allee, wake up! Y'alright?"

And before she pulls my comforter, I secure the sleeves over my wrists, grab the cuffs, and roll into a fetal position. She flings the comforter onto the floor.

"God, Tanaya, it's freezing! What d'you want?"

"Checking on you. Davis called me into her office today. You better get your butt out of bed. Back to school for you so people stop paying attention to me, asking me shit. I can't stand them in my business!"

I roll out of bed and grab some socks off the floor. No matter they don't match and are dirty. The room is freezing.

"What she want?"

"You know—the normal adult-all-up-in-your-face shit."

"Specifics, Tanaya, did she ask about anything?"

I sit back on the bed and pull the comforter up off the floor and wrap it around me. It grounds me. I feel secure.

Tanaya looks in the mirror and adds some clips to her hair. "Yeah, she wanted to know if you were sick last night. Since I didn't see you last night, I told her I thought I heard you puking in the bathroom, but couldn't be sure."

Not far from the truth. I can work with that lie.

"Where d'you go every night, Tanaya? I'm starting to worry. You're sleeping out more than here. What if your mom walks in one night and checks to see if you're in bed? And how are you not exhausted? Your energy is not normal!"

"Don't you worry about me. I take very good care of myself. Besides, good ol' T never checks. Too busy with her jobs and tired. As long as I keep my grades above 70 and don't get in trouble at school, she'll never know. Or care."

"What's wrong with you?! The only reason she works her ass off with double shifts and that cleaning job is for you—and now me. She cares, a lot."

Tanaya stops fixing her hair and rolls her eyes.

"For god's sake, lower your voice. Whatever. She's a mom. That's what they do. Her jobs are like yours, ridiculously low-paying. She wouldn't have to work all those hours if she found a half-decent job like the ones Stretch sets up for me." She adds a glass rose barrette to her hair. "And besides, Stretch cares for me. Makes sure I have what I want, protects me from jerks and," she turns and smiles at me, "it's great sex."

I slide to the edge of the bed. "Oh my god, Tanaya! What have you been doing?! And what's with all the make-up and now straightened hair? And new clothes?!"

"Jealous?" She giggles and walks over to the closet.

It's such a mess, she struggles with the sliding door until it bangs into the wall. She wrestles a large, black garbage bag from the back and rummages through it, pulling out black boots, red leggings, and a black low-cut silk blouse. Gold beads are sewn around the low neck-line. She's been stashing all the new clothes on her side of the closet.

What else is she hiding from me?

"Where did you get all that?"

The sick feeling grows in my gut.

Tanaya laughs. "Now don't you worry that little head of yours. Ms. Davis reminded me today that you've been through so much. I wouldn't want you to concern yourself with me."

She shoves the outfit into her pink and green floral backpack, sits next to me and gives me a hug.

"I'm heating up the dinner Mom brought home. And the soup she said you didn't eat today. Are you hungry now? Or are you too sick? I can bring some chicken up to you, sicky."

"Knock it off. The mom-act doesn't quite fit you."

I shove Tanaya off the bed, and she laughs as she falls. Her laugh makes me a little sad. I miss the fun way we used to tease each other. I grab the pillow from behind me and give it a hug.

"I miss you, Tanaya."

She gives me a crooked smile and a slight nod.

"I'm right here. Not going anywhere." She walks over to the door. "Dinner'll be ready in about ten minutes. Come on down and eat with me and T. You know how much she loves you, right?"

And then she heads back down to the kitchen.

That's the thing about Tanaya. She's so sure of whatever she's doing and convinces everyone that it's the right thing. I think of all the scenarios Tanaya could have gotten herself into, and none of them are good. The iPhone and bags of new clothes at the bottom of the closet are just the start. She also has new earrings, and the other day showed up at school with another piercing hanging out from a short Hollister tee: a belly button ring.

Maybe I'm paranoid.

But sex with Stretch?

Ugh.

I don't want to think about what Stretch might have her doing....

Tanaya has passing grades, and Auntie T is proud of her. Whatever she's doing can't be too bad if she's keeping her grades up. Grades seem to be what most adults care about anyway.

But still, her changing so much in such a short amount of time can't be good. Can it?

At dinner, I notice black circles under Auntie T's eyes, and she's very quiet. I hadn't eaten since 5:30 the night before, and the smell of chicken makes my mouth water. We never have enough for seconds, and I've noticed the last few weeks that Auntie T eats less and offers part of what's on her plate to us. I make a mental note to give her more of my tips.

Tonight, I'm starving and only feel a little guilty eating everything on my plate, all the soup, and the rest of her dinner.

Tanaya doesn't bother to make conversation. In fact, Tanaya doesn't even look up.

She wolfs down her food, stands and announces, "Well, that was a great dinner, and I'd like to stay and chat, but I gotta run — math test tomorrow."

So much for hanging out with me and Auntie T. She walks over and puts her plate in the sink.

"Carissa's picking me up in about five minutes to study at the library. It closes at 10 tonight. You working 'til after midnight, Mom?"

"Yeah, I'll leave here in about an hour. Make sure you get a good night's sleep, Tanaya. Don't want you getting sick like Allee."

"Will do, Mom. Allee, you okay cleanin' up the rest so I can get out of here? Some of us need to study for the grades we get."

Playing the I'm-not-as-smart-as-you card is just an act so she can go out. I hate that she's lying to Auntie T, but I nod.

"Yeah, sure."

"Thanks, Allee!" She grabs the bag with the new boots and clothes. "I'm going to wait out back. See you!"

She bangs the door closed and is gone. Again.

The whole charade is flawless. There's no reason Auntie T wouldn't think Tanaya is going to the library and would be in bed by 10:30. Or would suspect that Stretch is probably picking her up, not Carissa.

"I'll clean up Auntie T. Why don't you take a nap before heading back out to work? I had a whole day to rest."

She smiles. "Thanks, Allee. I'd appreciate a cat nap. Can you make sure I'm awake in 25 minutes so I can get ready to go back out?"

"Yeah, sure. I'm going to get some studying done. I'll watch the clock."

She gets up but hesitates in the doorway.

"Allee, everything's okay, right? I'm not missing anything, am I? You're doing okay, and Tanaya isn't doing anything she shouldn't, right?" She pauses. "Nothing's going on that I should be aware of?"

I stare at a piece of gristle on her plate.

Keep quiet. Don't say anything. This is not for you to tell. Tanaya is a big girl and can take care of herself. Tanaya is your friend.

I'm too nervous to say anything and clumsily drop a fork. Leaning to pick it up gives me a hot second to think carefully of what to say.

I stand and casually ask, "What do you mean?"

"I'm so busy working. I feel like I'm missing something."

I can't look at her, so I stack all the utensils on top of our plates and walk over to the sink. I put the water on to rinse them.

"I think everything's okay. Ms. Davis says the best thing parents can do with teens is eat dinner with them—and you do that with us most nights."

She chuckles. "She thinks it's that easy, huh?" With a sense of urgency that makes me think there's some truth to a mother's intuition, she adds, "You'll let me know, though, right? If anything is going on that I should be aware of?"

Betrayal sickens my gut, rises in my throat. I choke the truth down, turn off the water, and make Auntie T a promise.

"I'll keep my eyes open and let you know."

It was half-hearted but good enough that she walks into the living room and lies down on the couch. I finish with the dishes and tip-toe upstairs to work on a rough draft for Mr. J's assignment: Laura Wingfield's role within the family compared to your own.

I guess the Craigs are my new dysfunctional family. Shouldn't be too hard to write about my roles: secret keeper and liar—the foundation of family.

The fine-point pen isn't in my backpack, so I look under the bed. Nothing. I crawl over and look under Tanaya's. There's the copy of *The Glass Menagerie* with my name on the inside of the ripped cover.

Son of a bitch! *You lying, cheating, stealing bitch!*

No wonder she's getting 80s in this class.

Sitting back on my heels, I stare at the torn cover and wonder what to do. Her lies are getting out of control. I toss the book back under her bed. I don't need it anyway. With a 92 on my last quiz, the book is a crutch. I think just fine on my own. I will have to hand it in, though, and explain where it was to Mr. J. I guess I can just lie to him. God, lying is the new norm.

But do I let Tanaya know that I know? Or play dumb and watch how this whole shit-show unfolds?

I plop on Tanaya's bed to think about my next move. A small tin of Altoids rattles under her pillow. Absentmindedly, I pop the lid and pour some mints into my hand. But they're not Altoids, they're pills, in rainbow colors.

Most of them have *M* on one side and *30* on the other. There's a few blue pills, stamped with a dolphin.

What the hell, Tanaya? You are out of control!

I don't know her anymore. She's a stranger getting into serious shit. I put the pills back into the tin, slide it under the pillow, and jump back onto my own bed.

So what? None of my business. I have enough troubles of my own.

But I do care. In fact, I'm scared. Tanaya can get really hurt if she's not careful.

And there's Auntie T. This will kill her.

My stomach aches, pulling in two. I can't concentrate on the essay. I'm pissed... and sad.

Always, pissed and sad.

After fifteen minutes of writing and rewriting the first sentence,

I toss the paper to the floor and go to wake Auntie T. I watch her sleeping for a second before disturbing her. She's so peaceful, content.

I decide to keep my mouth shut about what Tanaya is doing. Maybe she has a perfectly good reason for everything. I'll go to the next Snake Road party and check things out before I say anything.

It's better to be sure. Maybe the Altoid tin isn't Tanaya's. Maybe she doesn't know my book is under her bed. Everything could just be a misunderstanding.

But something's tugging on my insides. I try to ignore it, but it feels like a warning of some kind, like something bad is about to happen.

Chapter 12

Well, I learned something new about myself. A day to hide under the comforter is fine. Two days? Totally can't do it.

School is actually turning out to be the distraction I need from all my thoughts and feelings.

Who would've thought?!

Ms. Davis has a peach-colored cardigan on today. The top button is diamond-y. Catchy and easy to look at.

She starts right in with the questions, "So you're okay? You feel better? No need for a doctor visit?"

"God, no! I puked twice. That's it! Is this why you took me out of study hall?" I pull the sweatshirt sleeves over my fingers and fold my arms. "I'm fine, really. In fact, I need to meet with Dorie so I don't fail out of school. Can I go?"

Ms. Davis writes a few notes and then closes the manila folder that's open in front of her.

"Yeah, sure. You working tonight? I'm wondering if you should take a few days off? Want me to call Dan? Tell him you can't come in?"

"No!" I shout and sit forward in my chair.

Immediately, Ms. Davis's right eyebrow raises about an inch. It's my reminder to calm the hell down. I fall back into the chair and start an inner dialogue: *Counselors hate hysterics. Counselors can call your caseworker, and they'll send you away because of hysterics. Hysterics will keep you from your job, which gives you freedom.*

Out loud I say, "It's just, when I go to work, I feel good. I like being there. Please let me go. It's all I've got left that's mine. Please."

Ms. Davis's eyebrow lowers. I'll have to remember that it works to tell her how positive the work experience is for my mental well-being.

Truth. I can't sit at the dinner table with Tanaya and Auntie T every single night. So depressing, watching Auntie T worry as Tanaya flounces in and out of the house. I hate lying. Hopefully, after work tonight, I can check out what's going on at Snake Road and get a better idea how to fix everything.

"Really. I'm fine," my voice is controlled, reassuring.

I'm surprised at how confident I sound.

I add, "If I feel sick before the end of the day, I'll let you know. Then you can call Dan."

She nods. "Okay, sounds good. Come see me anyway before you leave. I want to know for sure you're feeling better. I think it's been a while since you've been to a doctor. Do you remember when?"

OMG! What a pain! There's no way I'm gonna let her take me to the doctor.

But I force a smile and stand.

"Nah. Mom and me weren't big on doctors. But, I'll check with you on my way out this afternoon."

God, the babysitting has to stop.

But I'm not dumb. Babysitting will only stop if I cooperate long enough to show how responsible and mature I am. Two more months til my eighteenth birthday. Three more months 'til graduation.

I got this.

I run to study hall. Dorie's sitting in the back of the room and gives a nod to the seat next to her. "I didn't think you'd show."

I pull out my math text and roll my eyes. "Ms. Davis. Need I say more?"

This makes Dorie smile. "No. I get it. Your life is pretty screwed up on so many levels, isn't it?"

If she's trying to be mean, I don't feel it. In fact, it shows an understanding I don't get from most people.

"Yeah." I nod. "My life's pretty rough right now."

I feel a tingling on my forearms and look down at my left arm. Nothing to see, the sweatshirt covers the slits that release all the shit in my life. Dorie looks at it, too.

"You good?'

"Yeah," I look at her and smile. "So, let's make sure I graduate out of this place."

She smiles. "That's the plan."

- - - - -

It's hard sitting next to Tanaya in English Lit. I decide not to accuse her of taking my copy of *The Glass Menagerie*. I want to give her a shot at honesty. Maybe it slid out of my backpack, and I kicked it under her bed without realizing.

"Tanaya, did you see my copy of *The Glass Menagerie*? You know, the one with all the notes. I lost it at the end of last week."

She doodles a daisy on the cover of her notebook.

"Nope. Haven't seen it. Bummer. That book would be a great help on all these quizzes."

"Mind if I take a look through your stuff in the bedroom? You know, under the bed and through the closet? I may have shoved it somewhere, not thinking. Or it fell out of my bag and slid somewhere."

She stops doodling and looks over at me.

"Yeah, sure. You working after school? I'll give the room a quick look, too. I'm sure we'll find it."

And then she goes back to doodling a fat caterpillar wrapping itself around the daisy stem.

The lies, the excuses, the planning. I'm losing her. I want to shake her and scream, "What are you becoming? Stop it! It's me, Allee!"

Instead, I mumble, "'Kay, thanks."

The class quiets as Mr. Jenkins scribbles SYMBOLISM on the board, circles it, and then draws five lines.

Tanaya's hand shoots up… *Oh for God's sake. You're going to lie to me in one minute then raise your hand to answer in class? I want to throw my pen at her.*

We don't even have to raise our hands.

Mr. Jenkins nods. "Go ahead, Tanaya."

"The collection of glass animals."

He writes GLASS MENAGERIE on one of the lines and then UNICORN under that. "Keep going, what other symbols can you name?"

Tanaya's only too happy to list them. "The fire escape, flowers, and alcohol."

They roll right off her tongue, memorized from a short list penciled in a margin. I'm certain of it now. She's a book thief.

Jenkins can't write fast enough, and the more she talks the more I want to pull her braid.

Pull her braid.

I shake my head to get rid of that thought, but it grows, the image from years ago ... *Tony in the kitchen mad that I finished the Cheerios. Came up from behind. I didn't know he saw the empty box in the trash. I didn't know he was hungry. Somehow, I was supposed to know things like that. He up and yanked my braid so that my head snapped back, spoonful of Cheerios flying across the kitchen.*

I can still feel the yank and the snap in my neck.

And then the slap for making a mess with the Cheerios.

I look over at Tanaya and don't feel like pulling her braid anymore.

"Good," Mr. J says. "How about one more. Anyone else?"

The room is silent. I can only think of one more and call out. "The record player, music?"

He nods and writes MUSIC/MOVIES.

"Excellent. We could add more, but let's keep it to these."

He turns to the class. "Alright. Let's go. Can anyone explain to me the symbolism of one of these objects?"

Everyone shouts different ideas as Mr. J writes as fast as he can. The ideas hang off the lines like tree branches. I want to be part of the discussion but can't be bothered. Neither can Tanaya. She sits and draws stupid little flowers and bugs all over her notebook. I can't stand not knowing and lean closer.

"Wow, Tanaya, pretty cool you know all this stuff! Stretch tutoring you when you're with him, or did you pick up on all those symbols yourself?"

She tilts her head. "Jealous, Allee, that I know more than you for once?"

I shrug. "You told me you thought it was all boring. That's all."

Mr. Jenkins calls over, "Allee, Tanaya, want to share with the class instead of holding your own private discussion?"

"Just giving Allee some ideas. Helping her out."

Tanaya looks at her newest daisy, colors in a petal.

Mr. Jenkins says, "Well, we like it better when you share with the room." He looks at me. "Allee, anything you want to share?"

I sit back in my chair and shake my head. "I'm good."

He won't let it go. "We'd like you to add something about symbolism."

The board's full. I try to think of something amazing to add so he'll get off my back...but it's all been pretty much said. I'm losing ground, better to bail out.

"Nah, looks like you got everything."

I slide my elbow across the desk and lean my head on my hand.

"How about you, Tanaya?"

She sits up. "Yeah, one more."

God, I hate you right now.

Oblivious to my agitation or maybe enjoying it, she continues, "Amanda hates drinking, hates that her husband drank, and hates that Tom drinks. I think they're all related somehow."

He writes AMANDA'S AMORAL WORLD, coming off the ALCOHOL line.

I whisper, "Do you even know what that means?"

Mr. Jenkins turns around. "Nice Job, Tanaya."

Tanaya whispers back, "Maybe I'm smarter than you think."

"Really? Where do you think sex and drugs would go on that board, Tanaya? Hmm? Think it belongs anywhere up there?"

She turns, her hate boring into me. "Don't be talking about things you know nothing about, little girl. Hear me?"

"What did you just say to me?"

I heard her. Just can't believe it.

No—won't believe it.

She turns from me.

I whisper, "Tanaya, you playing with me? What's going on?"

She looks at her drawings, starts doodling again.

Mr. Jenkins glances at us but doesn't say anything. He puts the marker in the top drawer and slides it closed. "Okay, so next week, before we move on to our next American writer, the poet Maya Angelou. I want your final essay on *The Glass Menagerie,* three to five paragraphs."

People groan, and he quiets them, "Hey, hear me out, this isn't hard. Tanaya did most of the work for you."

Tanaya sits up in her chair.

"Put the definition of symbolism at the beginning of your essay. Then, explain one of these." He points to the board. "Or, create your own idea about symbolism. As long as it includes something or some-one from the play."

He taps the board with his finger. "Take notes now. It'll be an easy grade for you. Use examples from your life to convince me you can relate to the symbolism Tennessee Williams was writing about way back in the 1940s. Use the topic of symbolism however you see fit. But convince me you understand."

I open to the next empty page in my notebook as he continues. "Start it now. Today, I'm collecting last week's assignment about your individual family role as compared to Laura's or Tom's. Bring that assignment to me as you leave. You can finish it during this time if you didn't get a chance at home."

I write FIRE ESCAPE at the top margin of my notebook. A fire escape at my own house would have been a nice change from dropping out of the bathroom window. While the class whispers about the assignment, I'm drawn back to the bathroom of my old house. Trapped in a bathroom without a fire escape... but I made a way out.

Don't need a fire escape when you live on the bottom floor. Just crawl out the window, creep around the alley.

Escape looks different to everyone, but it means the same thing. Even for Tanaya, the way she escapes at night. I can't figure it out, though. She seems to be escaping to something worse. Is that possible?

I guess, for whatever reason, it's not worse to her.

Can it actually be better than a safe, warm house with me and her mom?

I don't get it.

Chapter 13

After work that night, I slip through the bushes and notice a few faces from school. I give a slight nod when they look at me, and I follow some over to the keg. A sleeve of red Solo cups is tossed off to the side, and a few handles are shoved into the keg's tub of ice.

Ice? Seriously? It's freezing out here.

Not wanting to draw any attention, I grab a cup, half fill it, and then step back to a large oak. I raise the cup to drink, but Tony has forever ruined alcohol for me. It's like the smell of Tony is poured into my cup.

Screw you, Tony.

I dump it into the brush behind me.

Partially hidden by the oak, I have a great view of the party. Only kids lining up for a refill can see me. I continue nodding, holding up my empty cup whenever anyone looks my way. But not many do. No one bothers with me. They never really did. And even less now that Tony killed Mom.

I touch the tree trunk, becoming one with it, like a shadow. I have become so less—I watch, listen, and think like the tree. It has stood over these parties for generations. It has secrets to tell. I close my eyes, put my ear to the bark and listen. I can be the shadow of a car's tire, a tree, anything. I see, hear, and think. But I don't have to do anything.

That is survival.

I feel Tanaya. She's close. I open my eyes and there she is, a few yards from where I stand.

She's getting comfortable on a makeshift bench—a piece of ply-wood atop two milk crates. I walk a few more feet, away from the keg and tree, closer to her. There's more brush behind her, just off to the side, and a small clearing in the middle of the thorny bushes. It's big enough to stand in, but just barely. The thorny bush embraces me like a hood and cape, a horror alternative to Little Red Riding Hood. No one driving along Snake Road can see me and only people leaving the party would see me from the footpath. The path is kept single-file thin to obscure the gatherings from cars, cops, grown-ups, and other party crashers. If spotted, I can pretend I'm leaving, too.

Because I'm behind Tanaya, we both see everything going on. Stretch stands with a group of younger girls on the other side of the lot. They're too far away to hear, but they're easily visible. Snake Road parties have always been a rite of passage for juniors and seniors. These girls, though? They can't be more than fifteen. Even from this distance, I can see the twinkle in Stretch's eye and the charming way he smiles at them. These girls are new and exciting to him.

They will do things for him.

Dorie walks over and calls to Tanaya. "Why so glum? Trying Goth these days? Black lace and leather suit you."

I don't want her to see me and take a step back into the bush, hoping it's not poison ivy creeping up my neck. I'd rather thorns.

Dorie plops next to Tanaya, and the plywood bends under the extra weight. Dorie is now facing away from me, too. I inch a little closer, away from the vine and thorns so I can hear them better. She's wider and taller than Tanaya. Her blonde hair forever braided tightly, falls to the top of her pants. There's talk she's a lesbian. No one bothers to ask or say it to her face. Dorie is secure in her space, never faltering. Like a blonde Amazonian, no one messes with her. Dorie just is. Doesn't give a shit about anything.

She's drunk and talking loud enough for me to hear. "Black lace is very becoming, but your thighs must be freezing! And you look pathetically depressed over here. Can I be of help? Need a friend?"

She puts a sloppy arm around Tanaya, and the girls rest their heads together. Tanaya is not drunk, in fact, she seems mellow. I can barely make out what she's saying, so I step to the smaller tree just behind them. Something about doubting Stretch. She turns toward Dorie, and I can hear her better.

"Is love supposed to feel like a game? If it is, I don't understand the rules. The love-hate feelings make no sense. I don't like this game."

Tanaya looks in Stretch's direction, and Dorie follows her gaze. So do I. Sadness blankets the scene, and I want to join them on the plank, to add my two cents. Love isn't supposed to be a game. True love doesn't have room for hate. Trying to mix them together makes for a nasty ending, like my mom and Tony. Instead, true love seems to exist in relationships that Auntie T and Dan offer. And like the one I share with Tanaya. Well, the Tanaya I knew before Stretch crept into her life.

And what about Logan? How would he fit into a relationship? Logan doesn't seem like the kind of guy that would play games with his friends or girlfriends. I wonder if he has a girlfriend. I wonder if he could ever like someone like me.

Probably not.

Dorie raises her voice as she defends Stretch.

"He doesn't care for them the way he feels for you, Tanaya. My god, look how he buys you gifts and spends so much time with you! Those boots, shit! Only mean one thing: 'This is *my* girl! Don't even think about it!'"

She laughs and pulls Tanaya in for a side hug. I can't tell if Tanaya agrees or disagrees with the bullshit Dorie's dishing out because she doesn't say anything, and I can't see her face. I know Dorie's wrong. Love doesn't need to buy expensive things to prove itself. I know my mom loved me. And we didn't have things. Maybe there's two types of love: a good-for-you love and a bad-for-you love.

Dorie reassures Tanaya by nodding over toward Stretch and his small entourage and then yells, "Bitches, all ov'em! Don't let'em get you down, beautiful."

Tanaya nods but asks, "He loves me, right?"

The three of us watch the small group as Stretch traces a line down a blonde's cheek with the back of his index finger. He pulls the top of her jacket tighter around her neck, like he's concerned about how cold she is. He meets Tanaya's gaze with a wink and blows her a two-finger kiss. Then he looks back at the blonde. They laugh, bend their heads toward each other. The blonde lowers her eyes then smiles at him.

The other girls stay to the side, laughing and whispering. They know not to get too close. This is the blonde's territory, she and Stretch have something going on, and they are to keep their distance.

Dorie sighs. "He's a tough one to keep all to yourself, Tanaya. But you knew that from the beginning, right?"

Tanaya's quiet, but then asks, "Why does he need all their attention?"

She keeps talking, but I can't hear and there's no way I can get closer without being seen.

Dorie laughs, which pisses me off because it's obvious Tanaya is upset. What does Tanaya see in that girl? Why has Tanaya traded my friendship for hers? Is it because she comes to these parties? I look around. Except for me, everybody does look like they're having a good time.

I don't get it.

Then Dorie's loud voice booms into the night, "C'mon, Tanaya, you're not jealous of a few girls? They're babies. What do they have? They want what you got, that's all this is. And you already got it."

Tanaya rests her head on Dorie's shoulder. There's laughter over by Stretch. Tanaya sits up, resolved by some shit Dorie said.

"Yeah, he's worth it," Tanaya says. "He takes good care of me."

"Atta girl!" Dorie's voice is sing-song-y positive. "He's a good guy, Tanaya. That's why everyone loves to be around him."

You have got to be joking me!

This is all wrong. I want to step in, push Dorie off the bench and talk sense into Tanaya. But maybe I'm just jealous because Tanaya's opening up to someone else. Something's been happening to Tanaya, and I know she won't listen to me. Sneaking out at night, stealing my copy of *The Glass Menagerie*, hiding pills—I don't want to make things worse, lose my friendship with her. Alarm bells go off inside me.

Where would I live?

Mom was always saying things like, "It's better to be quiet in a place that you know than in the unknown."

That's why we never reached out to shelters. She said she heard crazy shit went on in them. But I think Mom got some things mixed up. Crazy shit was actually going on in our home. It's only after living at Auntie T's that I started thinking about things like good-for-you love and bad-for-you love.

But, who am I to tell Tanaya what to do? I've never even had a boyfriend. She's the one who navigates the guy thing.

Dorie rummages through her backpack and pulls out two Wawa shorties.

"Here, I picked up a few hoagies to share. Turkey good enough for you?"

Tanaya takes one. "Yeah, you're an angel. I'm starving. Thanks."

Dorie stands. "There's the smile I've been waiting for! I'm going to walk around, say hi to everyone. I'll be back before you finish that."

Tanaya unwraps the small hoagie, folds the Wawa paper in half and places it like a napkin on her lap. I'm getting cold standing here, and I feel stupid hiding in shadows instead of hanging with my friend. She's the one who told me to come to the parties. I take a few steps to sit with her, but Mouse appears out of nowhere with two full Solo cups.

Crap!

I slip back into the bush. Like me, he must have been waiting for Dorie to leave, lurking somewhere close.

He asks, "This seat taken?"

Tanaya shakes her head, takes a bite, and nods toward the bench next to her.

Mouse offers her one of the Solo cups, then places it in between them on the plywood. He takes a sip out of the other one.

"Want half of my sandwich?" She tears the Shortie in half and hands the piece to him.

"Well, thank ye, beautiful wench!"

"What?! Mouse, that's not a compliment."

"Yeah, probably not, but I couldn't think of anything else off the top of my head."

"How about, m'lady?"

He puts his hand on her thigh. "Yeah, way better. I'll remember for the next time."

Tanaya turns to say something but doesn't get the chance, because Stretch descends on them, pulls her off the plywood. What's left of the shortie rolls off her lap and the Solo cup falls, beer spills onto her new boots

"God, Stretch, what the hell?"

She struggles to stand, and because of her outburst, everyone around us turns to watch. Stretch seems oblivious to them all.

"Whatcha' doing, Mouse?" Stretch stands over Mouse, contempt distorts his face.

Mouse doesn't say a word. He stares at the ground, waiting.

"I'm talking to you, Dickhead!" Stretch thunders.

Mouse holds up his half of the Shortie. "Sharing a sandwich, Stretch. Getting something to eat." He takes a bite.

The woods are quiet except for a car winding down Snake Road. Everybody watches, silently moving closer to the action. A few phones go up, on record. We're all still, watching Tanaya, Stretch, and Mouse. Tanaya reaches to Stretch and pulls gently on his arm.

"Hey, want to get out of here? Now that I've got beer all over me, I sure could use a shower."

Stretch doesn't acknowledge her, doesn't bother to take his eyes off Mouse.

Tanaya steps in front of him. "Come on, Baby. Let's get out of here. I've been watching you all night, wondering when we can go back to your place and be together. Just you and me."

She slides her finger inside the top of his jeans, around his belly and hips. He tears his stare away from Mouse and roughly puts his arm around her, pulling her into his chest. I want to grab Tanaya by the arm and get her out of there. Instead, my feet do what they've learned to do: stay perfectly still until everything blows over. Everyone must know this maneuver, because no one moves.

Tanaya smiles and says, "That's my boy. Let's go."

Then the crowd separates as she and Stretch walk toward the path.

I crouch and push back into the bushes. Tanaya leads the way and doesn't notice me. But Stretch stops for a second, looks down at me with a slight smile, and licks his top lip. My skin crawls as he chuckles and then follows Tanaya.

I let her go. It's what she wants. She wouldn't like it if I tried to stop her.

Only after they disappear onto Snake Road does the crowd relax. Everyone must be thinking about what just happened, worrying about Tanaya. But when I look around, I see that I'm wrong. Dead wrong. They're in small groups, laughing and chatting. They've moved on, couldn't care less what happened.

Dorie is drinking and laughing with a group by the keg. Nobody cares about Tanaya. Stuff like this must happen all the time. This is so messed up. She's got really shitty friends.

But I didn't help her either. I let her walk away. I'm just like them.

Chapter 14

I hear Auntie T shuffle up the steps around 1:30 in the morning. Soon after, her steady snores vibrate down the hall and keep me company while I wait for Tanaya. I build conversations in my head to convince Tanaya that she needs to drop Stretch's sorry ass. My reasons sway like an annoying pendulum. I can yell at her like a banshee foreshadowing her doom if she keeps up with this lifestyle or plead with her like a mom trying to get a toddler to eat carrots instead of candy because carrots are healthy and candy will rot your teeth.

It's almost three when the bedroom door finally creeps open. Tanaya slips quietly out of her clothes and into bed. She's crying and it softens my need to scream or plead. I want her to know I'm her friend. Even if only a shitty one.

I get out of my bed, slide under her covers, and put my arm around her.

"What's the matter? Y'hurt?"

She melts into me and sobs. There's nothing to say. I stroke her hair.

The sobs slow, and she falls asleep, safe in my arms. She's warm, and I like her close to me. We fit together, two pieces in the puzzle that is me.

I can't sleep. Or move. The streetlight at the end of the alley catches the scars on my forearm. Tanaya's hair covers most of them. Here we are—entangled. There's a small black rose tattooed on her collarbone. I never saw it before and wonder when she got it done. Of course, she never told me about any of her new piercings either; why would she tell me about a tattoo? It's small, no bigger than my thumb. Rose stems are usually straight, this one curls. It's probably one of those matching friendship tattoos some of the girls are getting.

I roll my eyes and imagine her and Dorie getting matching tattoos on a day I was busy at Pop's Pizza.

Whatever. She came home to me, not Dorie.

As long as we have each other, I know we'll be okay. With that thought, I drift off to sleep. It's dark and quiet, and Tanaya is safe.

- - - - -

When Tanaya wakes, it's abrupt with a push off my side. I secure my sleeves between palm and fingers as she mumbles into my sleepy awareness.

"Um, I've gotta go."

She crawls over me, but I grab her arm.

"Tanaya, you don't have to go anywhere. It's Saturday. Stay here. Let's hang out like we used to."

She shakes her head and pulls away. "Things aren't always that simple. I'm different from you. I want...." She stands next to the bed and looks around the bedroom. "More. I need more. My life's not here."

"What are you talking about?"

She walks away, starts rummaging through trash bags in the closet. I've lost her to what Stretch can give her. He turned her life away from safe and sound. She is willing to trade it for the rush of anything else. The excitement of a chaotic world. Tanaya is being sucked into the world that trapped my own mom year after year of Tony's abuse. Abuse that started sporadically and was sprinkled with just enough love crumbs to keep us guessing, wondering ... hungry.

"What does he do to you, Tanaya? Does he hurt you?"

She stands, shiny black pants and a pink top folded over her arm. "Like your dad, Allee? No. Not even close."

I can only describe those words as a stab, a quick jolt that momentarily stops my breathing. It doesn't register in my mind that she has left the bedroom until I hear her turn on the shower. The sound of water pushing through pipes behind the wall next to the bed reminds me to force air into my lungs.

She knew. All along she knew but never said anything to me.

Not knowing what else to do, I go down to the kitchen, toast waffles, and with a glass of milk, bring them up to her. She's back in the closet looking for something. Probably shoes.

The vulnerable girl from last night is gone. The thought of losing her to the chaos scares the shit out of me, but I sit on the floor and lean against her bed.

"I brought you something to eat. Sure you're okay?"

Tanaya stops looking in the bags and sighs.

"Yep."

She seems resolved, calmer, and sits on the floor next to me. I don't think she even knows how much her words about Tony hurting me stung. She nibbles around the edge of the waffle.

"Guys can be jerks, right?"

"Couldn't agree more." I hand her the glass of milk. "What's Stretch up to?"

"He thinks I'm fuckin' amazing."

"What's not to like? And you're a hundred times better than him, y'know?"

Tanaya shrugs again, like she doesn't believe me. "He buys me a lot of gifts and makes me feel beautiful. He spoils me." Her tone has definitely changed from last night. "I have things you could never afford."

Christ, do you think I'm jealous of what you have?

But, I keep my mouth closed because at least she's talking. Even if it is to just keep knocking me down.

The clothes "she can afford" from last night are at the foot of her bed. They're scattered with a week's worth of dirty socks and underwear. No better, no worse.

I'm afraid to ask the question, "In exchange for what?" because I know the answer but don't want to hear it. That little question and I'll be thrown right into Tanaya's fast, chaotic world of sex and drugs.

For a split second, I wonder if Ms. Davis is ever afraid to ask questions. Probably not. Can't be afraid to ask questions unless you already know the horrible answer. There's something about Ms. Davis that's all rainbows and unicorns. Naïve is a dangerous place to be because it feels safe to trust, to believe that people won't hurt you on purpose. That all people are good.

But all people are not good. Some hide behind charm, concern, generosity. Love.

Tanaya can't see the truth behind her relationship with Stretch. Or doesn't want to see.

So I don't ask. My mom tried to shield me from that world, but eventually it killed her. That world is the opposite of safe and sound. I don't want to have anything to do with it.

I remember something my mom told me and slide closer to Tanaya, our arms touching.

"Tanaya, if something makes you feel uncomfortable or makes you cry, then it's not right."

And then, because my own mom couldn't see it in her own life and I should've pointed it out, I add, "You need to drop him if he doesn't make you feel like the wonderful person you are."

She shrugs.

Sure is a lot of shrugging going on these days.

There's a slight sigh, and she says, "He spends a lot on me because he thinks I'm wonderful. He broke it all down last night. How much I cost him. What I'm worth."

That feeling in the pit of my stomach, the one I first had when I saw her run down the steps and out to his car, slices into my gut. I feel the blood drain from my face.

I grab her shoulder, turn her toward me, and yell, "Oh my god, Tanaya. You're not his property! Is he telling you that you are?"

She swats my arm away and puts the plate of half-eaten waffles on the floor. "Shut up, Allee! The last thing I need is Mom to walk in here and get all up in my shit."

She then grabs her pillow and hugs it close to her chest like a shield. She rocks, back and forth, as she sits there.

I kneel in front of her, my hands on her knees, and whisper, "Give it all back to him. Tell him you don't want it, Tanaya. Guys like that suck! He's a parasite, and you don't need him. I'll go with you!"

She looks up, her eyes pleading for something...help? But she changes her mind and looks away.

"Who said I don't want it? Why would I give it back?! For life here in this shitty bedroom? A boring life here with you and my mom? Forget it. I want more." She cocks her head and smiles. "Maybe you should think about your life, Allee. Is this all you want?"

This comes out too scripted. Like someone else asked her the same question.

Stretch?

Her cell phone vibrates under the clothes, and I slide over to pick it up. There's a text, but Tanaya snatches it before I can read it or see the number.

She seethes, "Don't touch my stuff!"

I hate that damn phone.

She turns away to read it and then slides it into her backpack.

"Listen, um, I'm gone for the weekend. Tell my mom I'm with Dorie, 'kay?"

She disappears back into the bathroom, and I pick up the plate and glass of milk and take them downstairs, toss the cold waffles into the trash.

When Tanaya comes into the kitchen, she's wearing silver wedges instead of the beer-ed boots from last night. The gross stale beer smell's going to be all over the bedroom. I'll have to wipe the boots clean today so Auntie T can't smell it when she walks down the hallway to get a shower. I lean on the counter.

"Where are you going? You must be exhausted. How are you even functioning?"

"I still have some stuff to get straight with Stretch. He stopped at Dunkin and is waiting outside."

"Before you go, answer me one thing."

She rolls her eyes. "What, Allee?"

"What's with the rose tattoo? When we were little you hated roses. Well, the thorns on them anyway."

Her hand rests on her collarbone, as if she just remembered the tattoo.

"Yeah, well, I guess I learned to ignore the thorns and love the flower."

She opens the door, turns before heading out.

"I'll see you later."

"Yeah, sure."

I watch from the window as she gets into his car. After they pull away, I head upstairs to get a little more sleep. Or, at least to hide, safe under my comforter.

On my bed is the missing copy of *The Glass Menagerie.*

Chapter 15

STRETCH: IN THE MIND OF A SEX TRAFFICKER

I know how to get a girl. It's pretty easy. They actually come to me now, wanting more. I show them how to get more. No big deal.

The blonde next to me? I smile and she smiles right back. That pretty smile means she's willing to please. I convince her what that means, show her how the more she pleases the more she gets.

It's always about more.

It's funny, how angry Tanaya got seeing this new one in the front seat with me. I love it when Tanaya gets angry. The fire in her eyes. Adorable. I'll smooth things over with her later. She's been asking for a Tiffany bracelet. Pricey, but she's bringing in tons of cash. I know a guy down on Fifth Street. He said he'd set me up.

She'll like that.

But now I have to concentrate on this new girl.

I look at her and ask, "Chloe? Right?"

She nods. Sometimes I forget their names but this one has a clean fresh look like a Chloe.

"So, you're eighteen?"

I know this girl is not eighteen, but they all have fake IDs. I ask so I can tell the cops,

"She told me she was legal! She had an ID. I checked!"

She's probably fifteen. A little too young for me. But some guys like that.

She giggles nervously.

"Yeah, eighteen. I uh, failed a couple of years in school. School sucks. I think I'll just drop out." She giggles again. "It's not doing much for me and I'm bored out of my mind." Another giggle. "I'm thinking of beauty school but I'll have to find the money to pay for that."

Giggle. Giggle.

"My mom says she won't pay for it unless I stay in school."

Giggle. Giggle.

Jesus Christ, I need her to shut up.

"Babe, you don't have to convince me. I'm not the cops. You tell me you're eighteen, I don't question it."

Giggle. Giggle.

Yeah, that has to go.

"You always giggle? Makes you seem about twelve. Ya'gotta stop that shit."

She shuts up. Doesn't giggle.

See? It's easy. They do what I want.

A quick look of uncertainty clouds her face, though, so I play the game.

"I didn't hurt your feelings, did I? I didn't mean to."

I take her hand to reassure her, and she relaxes back in the seat. Smiles at me again.

But no giggle.

It's Tanaya that's my calling card. The girls love the way she dresses, walks, talks—shows off herself with confidence. Once I start talking about Tanaya they listen, want to be like her.

I look over at Chloe, petite and clean, fresh. Now that she's not giggling I can see her potential. She's like a daisy, blooming open from a tight bud. Maybe we can have a small party tonight just the three of us. I'll give Tanaya the bracelet. The rest of the night will unfold as I want. It always does.

So simple, really.

Chapter 16

Before leaving for school, I shove *The Glass Menagerie* Tanaya had hidden from me—*stole from me*—into my bookbag. I don't want it anymore. Once I turn it in, I won't have to worry about those five points off my grade. I look at her bed. Tanaya never slept in it last night.

What do I care?

I walk down the steps, checking my symbolism essay for errors:

> Symbolism in literature: The use of an object, word, character, color, or action that stands for or suggests something else. The fire escape in *The Glass Menagerie* symbolizes something different for each of the Wingfield children. It has an important place in the play for Tom because it's his exit to the wide unknown world. For Laura, it's a way into the small safe apartment.
>
> Tom uses the fire escape to run away from family. Not escaping is to accept suffocation. 'Leaving' means his sister will have to fend for herself. She won't be able to, of course, but he leaves anyway.
>
> Suffocation is not a pleasant experience.

I stop reading to wonder about the similarities between Tony and Tom. If Tom had stayed, would he have developed a heavier drinking problem, start smacking his sister and mom around? Is Tennessee Williams saying it's better that Tom left? Or, did he write about it because he wanted to show how guys take off? Both Tom and his dad left. What the hell? The guys leave and the girls are stuck trying to live where they landed?

As far as I'm concerned, Tom and Tony? Assholes. Both of them. And cowardly.

There has to be another alternative. I stand by the front door and finish proofreading:

> Laura sees the fire escape as a way into a safe world; the small apartment and her glass animals. She doesn't want anything to do with the outside world because she is afraid. She needs to stay far away from freedom because freedom is scary for Laura. Possibilities are stifling when you struggle with self-doubt and anxiety.

"Well, that's not me." I fold the essay and slide it into my notebook. "I'm not weak. Or scared. I'd jump off that fire escape."

But what about Amanda, the mom? And my mom?

I shut and lock the front door behind me and think about their connection. Is there one? Amanda tried to do everything right for Laura, but Mr. J told us Amanda was a tyrant, a busybody, a terribly flawed character.

I think she was just trying to help. I think she knew she'd die sooner or later and Tom would be gone. Amanda was trying to keep her children safe. By controlling them, though. I guess that's never good.

What does that little crab in *The Little Mermaid* say? "Kids gotta be free to live their own lives." Or, something like that.

But at least Amanda stayed with them and tried to help. Isn't that something?

I walk the half mile to school and wonder what will become of Laura when her mother and brother aren't there anymore. One of two things. She'll starve and be found dead in the apartment once her body starts to rot. Or, she'll realize no one's giving hand-outs and she'll climb down the fire escape to get a frigging job. For god's sake, the dollar store is always hiring.

- - - - -

Tanaya isn't in Lit class. I look around. All the regulars are here. Dorie is sitting on the other side of the room checking something on her phone. No one's wondering about Tanaya. Everything seems so normal.

Even Auntie T assumes everything is fine because I pretty much let her think everything is. But something's definitely wrong. Even though it's annoying, I like it better when Tanaya is breezing in and out of my day.

She never disappeared for 48 hours.

I've got some worry going on. Other than the tears on Friday night, Tanaya did seem fine. But an empty bed for two nights in a row isn't good. I look over to where she usually sits next to me. An empty desk.

That isn't "fine."

Mr. Jenkins divides the class into groups depending on what symbolism example we picked.

"Read your essay to the group and see if anyone has anything to share. All insights are welcome. Don't be shy. I'm walking around because I want to hear what you have to offer. Speak up. Let people know what you're thinking."

The fire escape kids are told to work in the front corner of the room, near the windows. We drag chairs and form a lopsided circle. I plant my chair next to the windows so I can see if a black car pulls up and Tanaya hops out.

I know it's stupid. No sane senior is going to come into school during eighth period. Still, I feel better looking out for her.

Dorie drags her chair over toward my group. She's a "fire escape" person, too. She takes a paper out of her backpack then slouches when Mr. Jenkins asks who wants to go first. When no one offers, he volunteers Jared.

"Who, me?"

Jared hasn't even got his paper out and gets all jittery, knocking his leather bookbag onto the floor. The girls laugh and the boys make some weird barking noises. Jared turns red.

Mr. J sits on his desk. "Unless you don't want to."

"No, no, I'll go. It's fine. I just..."

He takes the paper out and stands behind his chair to begin. I never really watch Jared. He's a goofy kid who likes to touch people a little too much. Not crazy or creepy. He'll just touch an unsuspecting arm before he says, "Hi!" Or stand so close that you know exactly what he just ate, or wrap his arm around someone's shoulder while he walks down the hallway. All of those things make me not want to look at him let alone be near him. That would just encourage him. Maybe not crazy or creepy, but definitely uncomfortable.

No thanks.

But as he reads from his paper, I get a chance to get a good look without him noticing me.

"Symbolism is something in a story that makes us think of something else. The fire escape is a selfish way for Tom to leave and it makes me think of an easy way out of a difficult situation. My dad did the same thing, but he didn't have a fire escape. He ran out the back door … "

The things I don't want to say about Tony, Jared is sharing about his dad. Jared doesn't care how weak he sounds, and somehow this makes him seem stronger. He doesn't care what other people think. I didn't want to put my dad in my essay, but he plows through his essay, talking smack about his dad.

I zone out, watching Jared move around, swaying side-to-side as he reads. His hand trembles a bit and the paper shakes, yet he can still read the words. Probably read it over and over to himself before braving this group. Memorized it. But he can't look up at us.

His dad sounds like a prick.

I make myself pay attention at the end.

" … It's not Laura's fault that she's got a messed-up leg and plays with little glass animals. So, I think the fire escape symbolizes a selfish and cowardly way out for Tom. Family does better when people stick around and help each other."

Mr. Jenkins walks behind me and hears Jared's last few sentences.

He asks, "Does anyone else have any thoughts on that?"

No one joins in.

But I'm thinking about Tony. Maybe when cowards stay, they turn into bullies.

Hmmmm.

And then I have another thought: *What if my mom and I were the cowards for not leaving?*

This thought makes me feel sick so I quickly turn my brain off. Can't let all this literature stuff dance around inside the mind. That's a sure way to crazy.

Our group is quiet because Mr. J is still standing here. Everyone must be thinking confusing stuff like me. Maybe it would be good to talk about it, but eavesdropping adults blow everything out of proportion and don't know when to stop talking.

As if reading my mind, Mr. Jenkins walks away.

Dorie waits until he's out of earshot. "Yeah, I was thinkin' the same thing. My dad works two jobs ever since my mom got a new boyfriend and moved away. Maybe it's different, though, because Tom is

Laura's brother. I guess Tennessee Williams thinks each family member should go for their own dream? It's not like Tom promised to stay with them, like in a marriage commitment. If married people can't stick it out together in a family, doesn't seem likely siblings should have to stick it out."

I roll my eyes. It's not that I don't agree with her. Marriage traps people into nasty shit. It's just, like me, Dorie doesn't have a brother or sister. What does she know about siblings "sticking it out?"

Lou stands and stares at Dorie, his voice slicing through the classroom. "What? You think it's okay to bail on the other family members?"

So much for not drawing attention.

I look at Mr. J. He's acting all fly-on-the-wall over in the corner, eyes on his phone. I know he hears, aware of everything in this room. Serious respect for his choice to ignore.

Lou continues, his voice a little lower, more controlled. "My mom and dad run a corner store and two of my older brothers help with all the heavy lifting and accounting. I can't imagine if they up and left. The store would go into ruin and my parents would have to sell. They'd have no way to support themselves."

He sits down, and everyone starts talking at once. It's a lively conversation and I look back over at Mr. Jenkins. He's smiling, like he knows he unleashed some sort of magic among a bunch of kids. Or, he's looking at some hilarious cat video on his phone.

I try to pay attention to the conversations in my lop-sided circle group. Mostly sad shit mixed with a few family descriptions that sound almost hopeful.

I don't fit into any of these family categories. My story is different. One parent is dead and one is sitting in jail. There is no one left to be sad about, or fight for, or be proud of. I am in a family of one. How the hell did I get plopped on this earth without a single cousin, aunt or uncle?

Auntie T had explained it to me after she met with that Cara lady. They had looked, made some phone calls, tried to find a family member somewhere.

No one.

I don't open my mouth, nothing to say to this group. Sob, sob, sob. Who cares?

Not even me.

Mr. Jenkins interrupts my thoughts. "Do you know where Tanaya is?"

I almost forget to lie and shake my head. But I catch myself quick enough and stammer, "Yeah, um, sick. Yeah, she's sick. I think with the stomach bug I had. She was gonna try and come for part of the day, but I guess she didn't make it."

"Did she give you her essay to hand in?"

The end-of-day bell rings, and I stand. "No, I didn't even ask her for it 'cause I thought she was gonna make it into school."

He nods and asks me to bring it in tomorrow if she's still sick.

"Sure thing, Mr. J!" I slip out with the crowd, but my bothersome thoughts won't leave me alone. I head back into the classroom. "Mr. Jenkins, what if Tom had stayed? Would it have been so horrible for him to stay with his family?"

He straightens the pile of essays we all just tossed onto his desk, then looks up at me.

"No one knows Allee, it's just a story, a play. But that's what makes it a great piece of literature. It gets people thinking and talking about things."

I nod and turn to leave. "But, no answers."

He calls after me, "No easy ones."

Chapter 17

Like every other Tuesday, third period, Dorie is waiting for me. Consistent Dorie.

Doesn't she ever just not show up?

At least we don't have to meet every other day anymore. That was god-awful. She's business-as-usual and asks, "How'd you do on that quiz yesterday?"

I plop my backpack on the table. "Made sense, if that's what you're asking me. Won't know for sure 'til Mr. D gives it back. At least I knew what he was asking this time."

She smiles. "Good. That's good. You're not lost with all the terminology. You do all right on the next quiz, Devlin said we can stop meeting."

Because she's taking the time to help me, I think I should say thank you or something. But, honestly, if it didn't upset Auntie T, I'd be okay with the failing grade. Probably won't get into college anyway. Don't even know if I want to go.

Every once in a while, Ms. Davis has me fill out some special forms because of my "situation." Seems like universities have funds set aside for kids like me. Sounds so lame. Like I'm some sort of an afterthought, a charity case. Most of the other seniors already have acceptance letters.

I mumble a thanks to Dorie and sit across the table from her. She doesn't hear me. I really don't care.

I'm here, aren't I?

There's no test or quiz until after next week, so that means we can just work on the homework. When I have questions, Dorie talks me through the answers.

Not a bad set up, really.

We find the homework page, then each number our own sheet of graph paper.

She doesn't look at me but asks, "So, you know where Tanaya is?"

My stomach does a flip thing, and I keep my head down so she doesn't see my cheeks color. I start tracing over my numbers 1- 20, add little periods next to each number.

She asks again. I feel her eyeballs glaring at me. "Where's Tanaya?"

"How should I know?"

I pull the textbook closer and write the problem next to number 1. She keeps staring at me. I pretend she's not.

"Come on, Allee. No one's seen her since Friday night. You telling me you didn't see her since then?"

"I didn't say that. You asked me if I knew where she was." I look up at her. "Saturday morning, she told me she was going to hang with you."

Her eyes get big, eyebrows raised. She looks like the surprise emoji, except she's not as cute.

"That doesn't make sense. I didn't see her all weekend. Friday night, I saw her leave Snake Road with Stretch. Haven't seen her since. What are you talking about?"

"Saturday morning, she told me to tell Auntie T she was going to be with Dorie all weekend. So that's what I told Auntie T."

She sits back in her chair. "So that's why the cops called the house. You told them she was with me."

"Well, what else was I supposed to say?"

She leans forward. "Fuck you, Allee! Why'd you say anything? Stirring up trouble."

"I told you. Tanaya told me that's what she was doing."

I'd like to say I'm confident, sure of my response, proud of myself for sticking to Tanaya's script. Honestly, I feel kind of sick. I look away from Dorie because she's staring at me like she wants to rip my face off.

I think she knows more about Tanaya and Stretch. Like me, she's hiding something and that must be why she's so angry. I'm done being afraid, so I stare back at her and tell her what I know.

"I was there Friday night. I saw Stretch get mad at Mouse and then leave with Tanaya. Why don't you tell me what's going on, Dorie? I heard you talking to her, telling her it's not a big deal that Stretch and that blonde were hanging on each other. Why didn't you tell her to drop his sorry ass? Tell her not to go out with him anymore?"

The male sub in the front of the room looks up from his phone. "Girls, quiet down. This is study hall."

Dorie whispers, "What? Why would I do that? You're a moron, Allee. That's between Tanaya and her boyfriend. I'm not getting in the middle of any love quarrel. You just don't do that." She chuckles. "But you wouldn't know about that, would you? Never dated anyone, have you?"

"Fuck you" is what I want to say, but push forward with, "Tanaya's your friend. Do you really think Stretch is right for her? Good for her?"

Dorie sighs like I really am a moron and can't believe she has to explain such basic things to me. "It's not up to me, or you, Allee. That's Tanaya's call. Who are we to say what's good or bad for her?"

That doesn't seem right, though. What if, like my mom, it's hard for someone to see that something is bad for them? Shouldn't we tell them? Shouldn't we try and help them see? Not saying something seems to cause bad things to happen.

Now, Mom's gone. And Tanaya's gone, too. Or, at the very least, she's run off with Stretch.

I keep my hands on my lap, under the table. The more I think about all this, the harder I pinch the inside of my left wrist. I look down and see red skin around the fresh thin crescent nail marks. Scabs and scars from cutting are still safely hidden under my sweatshirt sleeve. Quickly, I pull the sleeve past my knuckles to help me stop pinching.

Dorie stands.

"You know what? I can't do this today."

She packs up her backpack and walks out of the room. The male sub in the front of the room lets her leave. Doesn't even look up from his phone. Stopping a girl leaving study hall encourages extended conversations on menstruation. Better to assume they're going to do what needs to be done in the bathroom and let them walk out. Some days, just before a dance or big party, or if a couple just broke up, the entire study hall seems to take place in the girls' bathroom. On those days, it's always just me and the guys left in the classroom. Historically, tribal women did menstruate around the same time and no one's going to question a group of teenage girls.

I look out the window, at the city skyline, convinced that Tanaya's in big trouble. I don't have a cell phone, so her not getting in touch with me is no big deal. But Dorie has a phone. Dorie should know where she is. Dorie's been her best friend lately, not me.

If she could, Tanaya would've reached out to her best friend.

But, I do know one thing. Dorie's wearing a spaghetti-strap top today, and there's no black rose tattoo, or any other tattoo, on her collarbone. Tanaya didn't get it as a sign of friendship with her new BFF.

Maybe I got the whole friend thing wrong.

Chapter 18

The next morning, Wednesday, Auntie T tells me Ms. Davis wants to see me before school. It's not even a Monday, and here I am, walking into this lady's office.

Ms. Davis doesn't even wait for me to settle into my chair before starting with the questions. "So, have you heard from Tanaya? Anything to share that could help us find her?"

I give no reaction, don't even squirm a bit, stay perfectly still. Everybody keeps asking me about Tanaya. The cops, Auntie T, Dorie, Mr. J, customers at Pop's, and even random kids in the hallways. Even the third floor janitor asked me if I had any news about my friend.

That made me cry, and I ran off without answering him.

I think a lot about the night she fell asleep in my arms. I promised to keep her secrets, but every day she doesn't show up, the shittier I feel about the whole thing.

Yesterday, someone threw a wad of paper at me in Mr. J's class. It hit me in the face then landed on my desk. There were enough snickers that Mr. J stopped scribbling about Maya Angelou and turned around to face us. I brushed the wad off my desk and onto my lap so he couldn't see it.

He teacher-stared at us.

"Is there a problem I'm unaware of?"

No one moved or answered.

"Okay, then let's get back to note taking, shall we?"

I didn't read what was written on that paper until I was at work:

Comfy in Tanaya's house?

Assholes, I thought and threw the paper away.

But it did pile on some more guilt. Instead of just sleeping in her bedroom, I should be out looking for Tanaya, helping her. Not too sure how to go about that yet.

I wish I could tell Ms. Davis about it. All of it. I mean, here she is staring at me, waiting. But adults mess around with stuff too much, make things worse.

I force myself to look right into her eyes and say, "No, I already told you, the cops, and everybody else, I have no clue where she is."

I pull at my sweater sleeves, tuck the ends into my palms, and look away.

I feel a little bad lying to her. Yesterday at the end of the day, she ran off flyers with Tanaya's picture and the Missing Person phone number. She asked me to go with her and hang them on telephone poles down Fifth Street. We even delivered them to all the businesses. Some of the shop owners couldn't be bothered. When we told Dan, he got mad as hell at them and stormed out of the pizza shop with some flyers and tape. When he came back, he didn't say anything. I took the long way back to Auntie T's that night after work. Sure enough, Tanaya's face was hanging in every one of the shops that turned us down earlier.

Dan can be very convincing.

Ms. Davis leans forward, rests her elbows on the desk, and with an edgy tone I've never heard before, says, "Allee, it's been five days since anyone has seen Tanaya. She may need help. Is there anything you can remember? What about over the weekend? Was there anything out of the ordinary?"

I remember Tanaya's clothes, her iPhone lighting up with a text, her tear-streaked make-up, and her heaviness as she slept in my arms. Remembering her nestled under my arm makes me crack a little.

Something must register on my face because Ms. Davis whispers, "You remember something. Allee, anything you say might help. We don't know until you say it."

But saying something would break the promise.

I miss Tanaya. Like I miss Mom. What's the use of having a friend if she's not around?

And there's Auntie T. My god, she's not talking to me. Or looking at me. She'll kick me out of the house when she knows all the lies.

And Dan will fire me.

Logan will hate me, too, for not helping a friend.

Everybody at school knows I'm not on social media, so they'll throw more paper notes at my face to get up inside my head.

"Allee, spill it. Tell me what you're thinking."

Ms. Davis's words jolt me back into our space, this room, my chair. She's staring at me, expecting more. Who am I fooling? I'm just a coward afraid of losing Tanaya's friendship, the warmth of Auntie T, and her home. All at the price of Tanaya's safety.

What is wrong with me?

I remember the way Tanaya shook as she sobbed on Friday night.

I stare at the baseboard behind Ms. Davis's desk.

"Well, she was crying, not exactly vomiting. I told people she was sick because she wouldn't want people knowing she was sad. She trusted me to keep her secrets, so I did."

"Oh, Allee, we need to go tell the police."

I look up at her in horror. *Cops? What the f—?!*

Ms. Davis's eyeballs are pleading with me. "If I went with you, could you tell them everything you remember? Anything that could help them find her?"

I'll have to tell them everything: the clothes, the sneaking out, the pills, Stretch.

I probably shouldn't say anything.

I think, *Poor Auntie T.*

But I'm really thinking, *Poor me. I won't make it out on the streets.*

Maybe Auntie T will let me keep the comforter.

And Stretch will know I told. When he finds out I talked to the cops, he'll come looking for me. I'll have to leave Auntie T, even if she doesn't kick me out, so he doesn't mess with her.

I should leave right after I tell the cops everything. I'll grab the comforter and go.

I look up at Ms. Davis. "Okay, I'll go with you to the cops. Someone called her right before she left. She ran out Saturday morning. It was the last time I saw her."

- - - - -

The police station is a busy place filled with serious people walking way too fast down narrow hallways, in and out of small offices like mice scrambling around a maze. The interrogation rooms are scattered down a hall that juts off to the left, around the corner from the main desk. It took a while for Ms. Davis to contact Cara and Auntie T, to get permission to be my guardian during this visit with the police. Cara is still busy and Auntie T still…numb. But once everything got cleared up on paper, Ms. Davis and I are ushered into a room similar to the interrogation rooms on *Dateline*: windowless, round table, camera up in the corner, a few chairs. Nothing else.

There's a young plain-clothes cop working a tape recorder and a disheveled older guy getting ready to jot down notes on a yellow legal pad. He reminds me of that *Columbo* cop because his shirt is buttoned wrong, his collar all lopsided around his neck.

I want to ask, "Rough morning?" But I don't. I figure I'll keep my words to just answering his questions. Nothing more.

Takes about two hours—his questions and my answers: Tanaya always slipped out at night to be with Stretch; he bought her new clothes and jewelry; the phone was in his name; blue pills with a dolphin on them, and some rainbow colored pills, were stored in an Altoid tin; no, I never saw her use them; everyone met at Snake Road parties; Tanaya came home crying Friday night between two and three in the morning and left Saturday around eight a.m.; she left in Stretch's car; he was driving.

On and on, his questions and my answers.

And with each answer? I'm a traitor. But I can't deny that as the words come out, a load is lifting.

The sloppy older cop writes notes on pages and pages of yellow paper. Once I start answering a question, he never interrupts, just lets me talk as he scribbles. Basically, I'm retelling Tanaya's story. That camera up in the corner…Why does he have to write stuff when that thing is capturing everything?

Getting everything off my chest makes the bad feelings, like guilt and cowardness, go away, but other feelings settle into their place. I can't quite identify what they are while I'm talking, but by the end of the interview, I'm pretty sure they're exhaustion and anxiety mixed with a lot of self-doubt. My knee is bouncing under the table, like a super ball getting closer and closer to the ground, picking up speed, pounding on the cement in an alley.

I can feel Ms. Davis's eyes on me, but I don't look at her. I don't want to see what her disappointment actually looks like. I concentrate on getting my knee under control so she doesn't think I'm a complete mess.

Sloppy cop, I didn't catch his name and he's not wearing a nametag, finishes some notes and flips to another empty page. He looks at the other cop.

"Blue dolphin pills? Ecstasy, right?"

The younger cop nods and says, "Yeah. Can't be sure what else is in it unless we get one from her stash and test it."

Sloppy looks back at me. "I need names and then we're done here. Think of anyone that Tanaya would have been in contact with? Tell me if they're classmates, close friends, or just someone you noticed that seemed out of place."

He pauses, grabs the point of the pen with his other hand. "I'm particularly interested in the names of the Snake Road crowd. Understand?"

This question I don't like and I stare back at him.

He challenges me. "What, you don't want to find your friend?"

I slouch deeper into my seat. "I'm not a snitch."

"Didn't say you were, did I? But you're here and your friend's not. How much do you want to actually find her?"

That doesn't deserve an answer.

"Screw you," pops right out of my mouth.

Ms. Davis leans toward me with that edgy voice again. "Allee, get it together. Tell them what you can about those parties." And then she turns to the cop. "This is a very sensitive topic. If Allee gives names, you have to be incredibly careful not to let the kids know who gave you their names. Allee's safety has to be taken into account."

He taps the pen impatiently. "Of course. A list of names is how we start inquiries. We'll talk to all the seniors, maybe juniors, too, so no one will suspect they were on a list."

They both look at me and I roll my eyes.

"You'll have to talk to the freshmen and sophomores, too."

Chapter 19

Each time I give up a name, I realize running away and living on the streets is going to be my only option. People do it all the time; it can't be that bad. I don't deserve the roof over my head, the food, the bed, the conversations, the friendships, the job. The comforter.

Well, I deserve the comforter. It was a gift from Auntie T when I turned twelve.

I'll disappear so everyone can get on with their lives. That's the way to feel better. I won't have to look at Auntie T, Dan, Logan, Dorie, or anyone else. And they won't have to look at me. Maybe that's how everybody gets rid of that cracked feeling. Just disappear.

Sloppy Cop takes one more look at the list then interrupts all the thoughts running around in my mind. "She probably took off and is having fun with her boyfriend."

What?! How did he come up with that idea?

I mean, I want to run away, but Tanaya was loving her new clothes, jewelry, even Stretch.

"We'll put her name and picture out to surrounding districts. We've found hundreds of runaways over the past few years. I'm sure she'll turn up. In the meantime, contact us if you find out anything new. Okay?" He hands us business cards with district phone numbers. "The name and number on the bottom of that card can help you with more ideas on how to get information out to the public."

They're not even taking this seriously. Tanaya wouldn't have gone anywhere without Stretch.

Wait. Is Stretch still in the area?

I sit forward in my chair. "Bring Stretch's sorry ass in here and you'll get some answers. Why don't you start there? Look for him and I'm pretty sure you'll find Tanaya."

I swear, the younger cop rolled his eyes. At me.

Ms. Davis stands and pulls on my arm. "Thank you, officers, for all you're doing to help find her."

Once we're outside, I ask her, "Can you take me right to work?"

She puts her hand on my shoulder, and I struggle not to shove it off.

"Maybe you should go home and rest, Allee. That was a lot."

My brain is so wired, there's no way I can go home. Talking to the cops meant I set things in motion, people will know I opened my mouth. And Auntie T still isn't talking to me, or looking at me. She hasn't gone back to work yet, so it's just her ignoring me in the small rowhome.

God, I miss our conversations.

First things first, I've got to get Ms. Davis's hand off my shoulder. It's another weight. I put some space between us by walking towards her car. Once I'm over by the passenger side, I lie.

"Auntie T went into work for the first time today. No one is home and I don't want to be alone. I can't just sit around in the house, waiting. I need to work."

"Really? Because she was at home when I called earlier to ask about accompanying you to the police station. She said she was still having a hard time leaving the house."

She looks at me expecting some kind of an explanation.

I am so bad at the lying thing.

"Please. I just can't … She's so sad and I don't know what to do, say, to fix things."

Ms. Davis gets into the car but doesn't say anything. She nods and drives me to Pop's. I think the police station stuff was a little too much for both of us because she drops me off with a quick, "Everything will be okay, Allee."

And then drives off.

I think I'm starting to appreciate her a little more.

Pop's is packed. I run behind the counter and start taking orders and answering the phone. Dan slides a little to the right to give me room.

When the dinner rush is over and Dan is tucked in his office, Logan throws a pizza in the oven for us to share. He yells over to me. "Heard anything about Tanaya yet?"

I wasn't going to tell anyone about my visit with the cops, was just going to let people find out without me initiating anything. But the pizza shop is quiet, and while I still have a dread in my stomach about Auntie T kicking me out, there's no denying I am feeling calmer.

When I was in my old house, I used to walk the neighborhoods at night and feel the calm of everyone sleeping in their homes. Interior lights out, quiet and away from Tony's craziness, there was no inner boiling of my nerves and feelings trying to crack the surface of me. Walking down sleepy streets, aware that people were safe and warm made me feel protective of them—like a warrior princess, calm but ready for battle.

Back then, I didn't have to cut for calm.

Something tells me I should be figuring out the connection between all my calms – the late night walks, the cuts in the shower, answering the cop's questions, and Logan. Yeah, I get a nice calm whenever Logan is around. Or, whenever I'm thinking about him.

While Logan waits for the pizza, he wipes down the chrome at the top of the ovens. He's probably weirded out by me not answering him.

I take a deep breath, calmness expanding in my chest.

"I was at the police station today, telling the cops all I know about Tanaya."

There's a slight pause to his movements, but then he continues wiping.

"I thought you told them everything when they went and talked to Ms. Craig, at the house, Monday night."

"Yeah, about that. I was, what did they call it today…withholding information."

There's some food stuck on the oven door. He scrubs, doesn't answer, doesn't look at me. Normally, I would accept this from people, prefer it to their questions.

But, not from Logan.

Haven't figured that out yet, either. Why I want to be invisible to everybody but Logan. I pick up the tray of ketchup bottles I'm refilling and walk back to him, to finish them on the counter near him.

"Tanaya was sneaking out of the house most nights. Staying out until two or three in the morning."

He stops scrubbing and walks over to me. "Seriously? Where was she going?"

"Not sure where she was going, but she would jump into Stretch's car." I unscrew another ketchup bottle and wipe down the inside of the squirt top. "He was buying her a lot of things."

Logan does a sighing thing, and I look up at him. His face looks genuinely sad, like he figured the whole story out without asking any more questions. But I want to tell him everything. Sharing with Logan seems the right thing to do so I start talking and don't stop until he knows all that I know.

"Shit, Allee, sounds like Tanaya got herself mixed up in some crazy stuff!" He pulls the pizza out of the oven and hands me a Coke. "You alright? You must be exhausted."

I crack open the soda. "Nothing a little caffeine won't fix."

He slides a salad over and chuckles. "Don't forget your veggies. You look pretty lousy. Maybe tomatoes and lettuce will help."

"Gee, thanks!" I smack his arm and take a bite of the pizza just as Stretch, Mouse, and Frank barge through the door. I push my food off to the side and grab the pad and pen. My hands shake and I look over at Logan, to make sure he realizes who walked in. He knows, gives me a nod then walks into the office to get Dan.

My voice shakes, "Know what you want, guys? We just started cleaning the fryers, so no fried food. But, we can cook you up anything else."

I start doodling on the pad so I don't have to look up at them. Pressing pen to paper keeps my hand steady.

"Yeah, make it three cheesesteaks and three Mountain Dews." Stretch looks back at the other two. "That good for you, guys? Want onions?"

Frank wants onions this time, but not Mouse. I walk back to put the order up as Logan and Dan come out of the office. Logan must have explained everything to Dan because Dan doesn't take his eyes off the guys.

He walks up behind me and whispers, "You good, Allee?"

I give a slight nod and Dan slides into the first booth, so he can watch everyone. He opens up his laptop and starts tapping away on the keys. I'm pretty sure he's not really doing anything specific, like creating an on-line ordering option which we really need, but he looks impressive sitting there.

Stretch doesn't miss the exchange, stares at me, then gives a tight-lipped smile and slams his hand on the counter. I jump back, ready to bolt. Dan looks up and Logan comes around and stands behind me.

"You're Tanaya's friend, aren't you? She talks, or talked about you all the time! Told me how you said she should start working here instead of hanging with me."

Stretch shakes his head and laughs, as if that was the stupidest thing anyone could have suggested.

Then he squints at me. "I remember seeing you at Snake Road last weekend. Right?! That was you, hiding on the path that leads to the road." He finds this even funnier, laughs so hard it takes him a second to add, "Like a little kid in a closet, hiding from Daddy."

Immediately, I drop my head. Words are jumbled in my mind, and I can't think of anything to say. My feet are stuck to the floor.

"You know, Tanaya spoke about you more than any of her other friends. Makes me think you know where she is."

I stare at a small chip in the countertop. It's shaped like a ladybug. I imagine it lifting up and flying out of here.

Stretch raises his voice. "Are you listening to me? I think you know where she is."

Logan speaks up. "What about you?"

Stretch smirks. "What about me?"

"Do you know where she is?"

"Nah. Haven't seen her since Friday," he points to me, "when this girl was spying on us at Snake Road." He chuckles. "Besides. Tanaya's my top girl. I need her back."

Top girl? She loved him, and that's all he thinks of her?

Disgust and anger force me to look up at him. The words come out in a whisper, but they come out. "You're a fuckin' liar."

This makes him laugh again. "So, you're not just a babe, you can talk. And dirty, too."

The heat rises from my gut, pulsates around my body. "Yeah. And today I talked to the cops."

This makes him stop laughing. "The cops, huh?"

"Yeah, I saw her run out to your car on Saturday morning."

Frank and Mouse look nervous and come forward to hear better, but Stretch puts a hand up and they step back.

He lowers his voice. "You've been talking to the cops, have you? Well, I'm glad. Tanaya has some things that belong to me, and I'd like them back. Let me know if you hear from her. Tell her I want to talk to her."

He puts a hand in his jacket pocket. I gasp. Dan stands and comes over in one quick step.

Stretch looks around at all of us, like a caged animal. But then shakes his head. "Just a pen, people, just a pen. Calm the hell down."

No one moves, and he turns to write his number on the paper menu taped on the counter. "Here's my number, case you hear from her."

He leans over the counter until he's inches from my face. I lower my eyes and he whispers, "You will let me know, right? Someone who hurt her wouldn't be writing his phone number down for you to contact him, would he?"

It's like when Tony would get so calm and whisper, right before the rage. I can barely shake my head. I stare at the ladybug shape, and don't move.

Instead of lashing out at me like Tony's next move would have been, Stretch takes a loud, deep breath in, sniffing the air around me to bring me into his body. I stop breathing so he can't take anymore of me. Like with Tony, I can't walk away on my own.

He whispers into my ear, "Lilies."

Dan walks behind the counter and pulls on my arm, tells me to go, and take a break in the back office.

He then tells Stretch, "Okay, that's enough excitement for one night. Pay now, then do us all a favor and wait out front for your food so we can close the shop. I'll bring it out to you as soon as it's up."

Logan and Dan are whispering, but I stay in the safety of the office. They're worried about me, and I hate that. I don't want to think about their feelings. Can barely handle my own.

Exhaustion. So tired of everything and everyone.

A new *Fishing* magazine is on his desk. I leaf through it and start reading about lures and tackle boxes. But that single word, *lilies*, plays around and around in my mind, stuck in my head.

I throw the magazine back on the desk. Why doesn't Stretch know where she is? Is he lying?

The front bells clink on the glass door and Logan pops his head into the office. "Dan just walked the food out to them, want to get some air out back?"

"Yeah, change of scenery would be good."

The wind blowing down the alley cools the blood racing through my body. With Logan close, I feel more than just calm with him now ... what do I feel?

Solid. I feel like I'm standing on solid ground. But not stuck.

Solid ground, a thin slice of dark sky looming above, and rows of stores lining each side of the alley create a safe space to breathe and just be.

"So, wha'd'ya think, Allee?" He lights a cigarette and gives me a sideways glance. "Stretch is trouble, for sure. But d'you think he knows where she's at?"

That afternoon, in the police station, I pretty much said that Stretch had something to do with her disappearance. But now, I have my doubts. "I don't know, Logan. He's angry because she has something of his. If he knew where she was, wouldn't he take whatever it is from her himself?"

"Yeah, I was thinkin' the same thing. But what could she have of his?"

"Well, I've been in denial these past few months. You weren't exaggerating when you said she's in some crazy shit."

I remember how jumpy Tanaya got as soon as she got notifications on the phone, I add, "She was always on edge."

Tanaya's smile, the way her eyes twinkled when she heard a joke or shared something funny had been gone for quite some time. The spark wasn't there anymore.

I whisper, "Logan, what if she's *gone*? Like 'gone,' gone?"

Logan drops his cigarette, toeing it into the concrete. "Let's not think the worst. Just try and remember if there's anything else to tell the cops, anything that'll help them find her."

He walks over and gives me a hug. A solid, calm hug that makes me wonder if it's a normal friend-thing to do between a boy and a girl. I wonder if I'm supposed to do something more in his embrace.

Nah.

It feels just right being held. So I let him hold me.

Chapter 20

Next morning, Auntie T is sitting in the wing-backed chair watching the morning news. She doesn't bother to look up at me as I walk down the stairs. Still doesn't acknowledge I'm around. I'm starting to wonder if living like this is worse than living out on the streets. I decide to make breakfast to get some conversation going.

I look in the fridge, then yell into the living room.

"We're out of milk, Auntie T. I'll go down to Larry's Deli and get some. Anything else I should pick up?"

Past-dated bottles of mustard, ranch dressing, and ketchup are scattered on the top shelf. Their insides have oozed out, crusting over the tops and sides of each container. There's a shriveled pepper. It's leaking in the produce drawer. As I toss it into the trash, pepper juice drips all over the place.

Lovely.

Auntie T would've never let the fridge get this bare. Auntie T always made sure Tanaya and I had enough. She'd go without so we could eat. Now, it's my turn to take care of Auntie T. She seems to be disappearing somewhere deep inside herself. I need to help Auntie T before I lose her, too.

Hopefully, it's not too late. Auntie T isn't dumb. Last Monday, the day Tanaya didn't come to school, I came home from work as cops were leaving the house. Auntie T stared at me, like she knew I was hiding something.

She hates me.

I wipe the pepper juice off the floor and inside the refrigerator drawer, then walk into the living room. She sits motionless, looking at the television.

"I'm heading to Larry's. For some milk. I'll make you coffee."

I wait for a nod, a smile, something to show she can hear me.

But there's nothing.

I kneel in front of her.

"I'm going to get some milk. How about eggs and bacon? I'll make us a nice breakfast. Okay? I'll be right back."

She turns slowly, but doesn't look at me. A week of her not talking or looking at me is killing me. She takes a twenty from her pocket. I pat her hand, give a weak smile.

"No worries, I got this. I'll be right back."

It's three blocks to the corner store. The sun has melted the last of the March snow into a gray slush. I'm wearing my oldest pair of sneakers, with the small hole by the left big toe because I don't want to ruin work or school shoes. These soles are in good enough shape to handle slush.

In the past, whenever Tanaya complained about the little row-home, Auntie T would remind her, "Just five minutes by foot to get whatever we need."

The memory makes me think maybe Tanaya's somewhere close. Maybe I can find her and make it up to Auntie T.

I round the corner and am about to skip up the store's two steps when I see Mouse talking to Frank. They're just past the storefront, down by the curb. Mouse's ears are as noticeable from the back as the front. Frank is laughing about something and doesn't see me. I slip quickly into the store as a young couple walk up the steps behind me.

I can keep Mouse and Frank in my peripheral vision as long as I stay by the dairy case.

God, I hope they don't come in here.

I jump when the cashier yells over at me, "Hey, are you gonna buy anything? You're wasting energy keeping the door open! Look through the glass for what y'want, then open the door, get what y'want, shut the door, then bring it to me. God! Let's go already!"

Rude. This guy must've never gotten an attitude smack.

I grab some milk, and with a bang, the dairy case closes.

"Oh, yeah, sorry, I was daydreaming." I carry the milk to the counter. "Wait, I forgot the eggs and bacon!"

"Jesus Christ, what is the matter with you kids these days?" He leans on the counter, "C'mon, c'mon, girl. I've got stuff to do."

Heading back to the dairy section gives me the opportunity to get one more look out front. They're deep in conversation.

What the hell are they up to?

I pay for everything and slide past an older man as he swings the door open. Mouse and Frank are now arguing about something and don't notice me. I walk down the steps and duck into the alley that separates Larry's from the junkyard next door. I hide behind a pile of old tires.

Stretch's black Dodge rounds the corner and ends up on the curb a few inches from their feet. They're not even ten feet away from me, I push back into the concrete wall and crouch behind the tires.

Stretch's voice is that controlled rage that serial killers on TV usually have before they do something gross, like Dexter. Like Tony.

"You two do anything stupid to Yaya?"

Yaya? That must be Tanaya.

I hear him spit. "Well, did you? Spill it so I can fix it or kill you myself."

Frank answers first. "No, Stretch! What the hell? She's your girl. We don't touch what's yours." I can't see him, but his voice gets louder as he walks closer to the car. "What happened? Cops talk to you? Did you find out anything new?"

Mouse sounds closer, too. "Is that where you've been? Police station?" He seems disinterested, cocky even. "Christ, are they going to call us in, too? Damn pigs."

"Yeah, they're probably gonna drag you both in, so get your stories straight. They asked me when I last saw her, and I told them I gave her a ride Saturday morning, and then I dropped her off near the boulevard." His voice gets louder, angrier. "Because that was the last time I saw her! They said they found her phone on the ground, outside the house on Emberton Avenue."

I hear movement, then it sounds like someone bangs into the side of the car. "I asked you, Frank, to go pick her up because I was with Chloe. That's the last time anyone heard from her. The last place they got a ping on the cell tower. What the fuck did you do?"

Frank stammers. "Nothing, I swear! I had those two girls we met at the party the night before. They were still with me. We started partying again. I was trippin'. I wouldn't have been able to drive. I don't even remember you calling."

I don't move or breathe.

"Come here, you little shit."

For a split second, I think Stretch is talking to me. But then he adds, "Closer, Mouse." Anger seethes with each word. "So you can hear me."

There's a slap, then two more, each time the slaps get louder, harder. I don't sense any movement from Mouse. He must be standing there, taking it.

Stretch lets out a short laugh.

"The cops better find out what you did to her before I do. Don't like anyone else's shit on my back, my face, or anywhere near me. I swear it, Mouse, you little... Start disappearing now. Before I change my mind."

Mouse snarls. "Well, isn't this convenient. You two want me to take the fall."

Stretch isn't buying it. "Fuck you, Mouse. What did you do?"

Mouse stays calm. "Nothing. I don't know what you're talking about. I don't even have a set of wheels to have done anything."

Stretch calls to Frank. "Goddammit, Frank, were you too gone to remember anything? Notice anything different about your truck the next time you got in it?"

Frank hesitates. "I remember it still being in the back lot when I came 'round. I didn't notice anything different about it." He pauses. "Maybe Mouse took it. Honestly, Stretch, I don't even remember you telling me to get her."

Stretch is silent, no one talks. I think Stretch is hatching a plan because his hand hits the side of the car door, four quick taps. Then, one loud smack.

"So, the Emberton house is the last place we know for sure she was. And then, maybe, the truck. Can't imagine her leaving by any other way. I didn't get any notification of suspicious activities in the neighborhood. I listened to all her messages, read her texts. She was mad that I was late, but didn't say she was walking anywhere. And I know she wouldn't get into someone's car if she didn't know them. She's not stupid."

Then, Stretch lets out a sigh like he just resolved all the issues and accepted fate.

"Frank, don't let Mouse back in your apartment. Get rid of all his stuff. Everything. Throw it in a dumpster, but not around here."

Mouse yells. "You can't do that!"

Stretch ignores his outburst. "Extra careful, Frank. Torch your truck..."

Frank's response is frantic. "My truck, Stretch? My truck?!"

I hold my breath, expecting Stretch to freak. But he continues as if he doesn't hear them.

"Then, report it stolen. It's too flashy anyway. I told you to get something that'd stay under the radar. We can't get our hands dirty with Mouse's disappearance. Divide Mouse's stuff, all his shit, into small bags, different convenience store bags. Boost a car and head down around the Eastern Shore. Use the dumpsters behind the Royal Farms, diners, any little shops. If anyone asks, we don't know where the hell Mouse went. He just cleared all his shit and left."

Frank doesn't question him this time. "Got it, boss. It'll be done by the end of today."

Stretch continues with disgust, "Why are you still here, Mouse? You're done. Dead as far as I'm concerned. Start traveling, I don't care where you go."

Mouse is livid. "Think I'm dumb, Stretch? I disappear and the cops think I'm guilty. Takes the heat off you two, buys time. My only question, why me and not Frank? It's gotta be him. I don't even have fuckin' wheels."

He's so defiant, confident even. I believe him.

But Stretch spits, "Fuckin' moron! I see the way you look at Yaya. Let's just say I trust Frank and you haven't earned it. I question your loyalty. I better not see your face again."

And then Stretch takes off, screeching off the curb and onto Fifth Street. I peek over the tires, but he makes a U-turn and heads back towards us. I drop to the ground behind the pile of tires.

Crap, did he see me?

I lie perfectly still, my body pushed up against the wall, shielded by tires, and try not to think about all the dog piss that's been sprayed onto the concrete throughout the years.

When I can't hear the screech of tires anymore, I crawl to the edge of the tires and peek around the corner. Mouse is walking toward the Broad and Emberton station but then turns. I duck back just as he yells, "Well, lots of luck to you Frank! It's me today. You'll be next."

Frank doesn't answer. I hear him run across the street and the beep of his truck unlocking. Once his truck pulls out into traffic and roars down the street, I head quickly back to Auntie T. I replay everything they said in my mind so I don't forget anything.

Could Mouse have done something to Tanaya? He and Stretch are both skeevy. Could have been either one. Except, Mouse is so tiny. Tanaya wouldn't have been afraid of him.

And then there's Frank. Sometimes it's the one you least expect, the nice ones. Would he have let Mouse drive his new truck? Would he have noticed if something bad happened in it?

Probably not.

Maybe Frank was so strung out on meth, he hurt her and doesn't remember. Or, remembers but doesn't want anyone to know.

This new information complicates everything.

Ms. Davis always tells me to talk about stuff that's going on. Talking to people about my own stuff is too hard. But talking about Mouse, Frank, and Stretch? Trying to find Tanaya? This stuff I can talk about. I just hope the cops don't think this is proof that she ran away, and they don't look for her.

Chapter 21

Once I get home, I leave a message with the police answering service then look around for Auntie T. She isn't here and didn't leave a note. Her Applebee's black sneakers are gone, so she must be at work. I cook some eggs and bacon for myself and decide to use the day to get caught up on all my homework.

It's quiet and lonely. At 4 o'clock, I walk around the neighborhood. Tanaya's pictures all along Fifth Street stir up even more loneliness, and I start to talk to her. I don't care what people think as I walk and whisper. I can't help myself, and it makes me feel better. I tell Tanaya about Dorie and how she helped me with my math, how sad Jared seemed reading his symbolism essay, and how much I miss her. Then, I spend a lot of time promising her I'm going to take care of Auntie T. I even ask Tanaya for some ideas on how to get Auntie T talking to me again.

She doesn't have any good ideas about that.

It's dark by the time I get back to the house, and I fall asleep reading Maya Angelou's *Gather Together In My Name*. I wake up to Auntie T howling again. First time I heard it, I thought it was a cat in the alley. But then I realized it wasn't coming from outside the window. It was coming from down the hall, on the other side of her bedroom door.

Like all the other nights, I want to go in and do something, say something to help her feel better. But all I can think about are my lies and how I should have said something a long time ago.

I take the small knife from under my mattress and tiptoe into the bathroom. I turn the shower on but still hear her. Once I step under the shower, I can't hear her anymore. There's just me and water pulsating onto my head. The water quiets her cries and my thoughts.

The small thin blade draws small blood droplets. I like to match the crisscross patterns on each arm. It's oddly soothing, the slice through soft skin.

Or it was.

Since Tanaya disappeared, cutting just isn't the same anymore. Emotions release, but they don't lift up and away. There's no full calm. The anger, guilt, sadness hover close.

The scars are making me feel worse, too.

When I look at them, I hear Tony, laughing. "Knew you were a freak, Allee."

And Auntie T, shuffling around the house during the day, walking into a room to find something, forgetting what she wanted, and then walking into the next room to see if she can remember. Howling in the middle of the night. Her grief for Tanaya makes me realize my mom would have been beside herself with worry about my cutting. I think about not doing it anymore and then I think about doing it even more. It's so confusing.

Maybe just one more time and it'll work again. The calm will return.

The warm water massages my back, and I put the knife to my forearm. I like to see water drop onto the blade. It creates pretty domes shining on top of the smooth, flat surface. They slide down as I turn the blade and methodically slice, creating another line on the design that is me. The design I can see. The design that is my creation. The design that I control.

Fresh cuts never sting until water hits them. The pain reminds me I'm not numb, that I'm alive. I feel. And I will heal.

I sense my mom very close. I pull the shower curtain back expecting to find her leaning on the sink.

But there's no one. I close the curtain and try to ignore her presence. I felt her before—on a walk to work, sitting alone in the library doing homework, or when I cry myself to sleep. This is the first time in the shower, though, with a fresh cut.

I ignore her, but she doesn't go away.

"It makes me feel better, Mom," I whisper.

She doesn't believe me. I sense her asking, 'Does it, really?'

I look down at the knife and all the lines at different stages of healing cut into my skin.

"No, not really." A sob catches in my throat. "I mean, it does, at first, but then it doesn't."

I wait for my mom to say something else. To be disappointed in me. To yell at me.

I peek back out toward the sink, but there's still no one there. It's just me in the bathroom.

But Mom's memory breaks into my sadness as the one good memory. I force myself to think of her and let everything else fade away. I close my eyes and try to remember her smell, the salt and pepper spiked hair, and the smile when I walked into the More-Bang-4-Your-Buck.

Remembering her is comforting. I hear her voice, outside the bathroom door after Tony would fall asleep, "Allee, unlock the door, it's okay. Everything is going to be okay."

I want to stop the cutting, hurting myself, because of Mom.

I sit down in the tub while the water rains all around me. I drop the knife out of the tub, and it falls with a clang onto the tile floor.

- - - - -

I wake early the next day and run all the way to school. Ms. Davis usually arrives early in case someone needs her. Her door is ajar, so I don't bother knocking.

"I need to tell you something."

I plop on the edge of my usual seat, a big change from the slouch I save for adults.

Ms. Davis's busy filing paperwork, but puts it all aside to give me her full attention.

"Sure, what's up?"

I imagine my mom sitting in the chair next to me, telling me to be honest. I take a deep breath.

"You know how I always tell you I'm okay and don't want to talk to a shrink or anything like that?"

"Yeah, that's fine, when you're ready you'll go. You've been a model teen staying with the Craigs, coming to school, and working at Pop's. No one will make you go. But now that Tanaya is missing, do you think you need something more?"

I nod. "Yeah, I think that's a good idea."

She pulls a form out of my file.

"Whatever you need, Allee. I can call for you, set it all up with your case worker."

Ms. Davis gives me that I'm-here-for-you look, and I put my head down. I'm ashamed to tell her. I'm just one disappointment after another. Why do I care so much what this lady thinks of me?

"You know, Allee, no one expects you to shoulder all this by yourself. Life is not supposed to be something you do all alone. I've been here for you and will continue to be here for you."

I'm afraid if I don't tell someone now about the cutting, I'll chicken out and never be able to admit it to anyone. Then, I'll never stop.

One at a time, slowly, I push up my sleeves and show Ms. Davis the soft underside of my arms, just enough that the bottom of puffy pink and white scars peek out.

Ms. Davis sits back in her chair, eyes misty.

"Oh, Allee. I'm sorry you're in so much pain."

I look at her, not at the cardigan button, but at Ms. Davis. Her eyes hold mine with a look of compassion that makes me cry. As the tears fall, Ms. Davis walks around the desk and gathers me into her arms.

Chapter 22

Three days later and Ms. Davis is driving me to an appointment downtown. This lady knows how to get things done.

She tries to get me talking about the weather, the three-legged dog hobbling across the street, and the Maserati that just sped past us. I give one-word answers, and then Ms. Davis stops trying.

A young receptionist has a vine tattoo creeping out of her blouse. It seems to grow toward her ear and then disappears around the back of her neck. She points into the waiting room and asks us to take a seat. There are four chairs up along the wall and a torn couch by the door. Ms. Davis and I sit on two of the chairs because the worn checkered upholstery on that couch cries, "I've seen some bad stuff." Vine-tattoo-girl disappears for about two minutes, then comes back and asks me to follow her. I get up, and Ms. Davis stands, too.

The receptionist looks at Ms. Davis and says, "Just Allee."

I follow her, but I really want to turn, run past Ms. Davis, jump over the gross couch and head back outside. But that really would be crazy, so I just follow the vine.

She gives the second door on the left a quick knock, opens it wide, and ushers me in. I turn to say thank you, but she's already closing the door. A middle-aged woman comes from behind her desk with outstretched hand.

"Well, hello. I'm glad to meet you, Allee. I'm Dr. Winters."

I accept the outstretched hand and mumble. "Hi."

I'm distracted by the hand. Perfectly manicured nails don't seem to go with her stretchy pants and oversized sweatshirt.

Probably yoga pants. Seriously.

Dr. Winters walks around her desk and sits. She gestures to a chair, and I assume my normal slouch. There's a bookcase behind her. Not many books but some knick-knacks are scattered about. I like it. I can look at them instead of her.

"I've heard a lot about you," she says. "And I have a question before we begin."

I think she's going to jump right in and ask about the cutting. I suck the air in around me to get rid of the ache in my stomach and manage a weak, "Sure, what?"

On the shelf, just past her right ear, there's a 3-D puzzle of the Earth. I wonder how it stays together as a globe. The puzzle pieces have to be curved for it to sit like that. They have a shine to them. Are they plastic?

Interesting.

"Your name. On the phone, Ms. Davis pronounced your name as 'alley.' When I first read it, I assumed you pronounced it the French way because of the spelling."

I shrug. "It's pronounced like an alley."

Next to the 3-D puzzle of the Earth is a green and white plant, big leaves on top, smaller ones on the bottom. Seems to be growing upside down. I really don't know anything about plants, but this one gives the impression it's confused.

Perfect plant for this office.

Dr. Winters writes something in her notebook.

"Such a beautiful spelling, such a beautiful word. I've never seen it before as a name."

What is this lady getting at?

Adults play all sorts of games. I'm not in the mood to play.

She looks at me for a few seconds before starting again.

"This is an intake, a way to get to know each other. No pressure, nothing to be nervous about. I'm here to help you with whatever you want. And, we can take as long as you want. Okay?"

I nod, but think *This was a bad idea. I've gotta get out of here.*

There's an empty chair next to me. I look at it for just a second, imagine my mom sitting there. I pinch the inside of my wrist. It grounds me, makes me feel like I'm in a set place. I look up and Dr. Winters watches my hands, sees me pinching.

Shit.

I'll have to tread carefully with this lady. I rest my hands on top of each knee and take another deep breath.

Play it cool, Allee, play it cool.

"So, tell me, why are you here? How can I help you?"

Lots of images flash through my mind and I allow them to play out, no rhyme or reason to their order: the torn copy of *The Glass Menagerie*, the black and brown feather duster moving in and out of glass vases, sitting quietly on the toilet seat as beer cans crack open on the other side of the door, setting up my bank account with my mom, Tanaya walking next to me at school. I stop that last one. What was Tanaya talking about? She had been excited about a party down on Snake Road and wanted me to go with her. I wish I had gone with her more. Maybe I could have helped her instead of hiding behind that dumb tree and in the prickly brush. I close my eyes to bring the image of Tanaya into focus.

I should have known more about what was going on with you, Tanaya. I am so sorry.

Dr. Winters interrupts my thoughts.

"Allee, what are you thinking?"

I open my eyes. She's sitting forward, hands folded on top of the desk.

But I'm not ready to share, and I shake my head. "Oh, not one thing. Everything. No order."

I push the guilt down and think maybe cutting isn't such a bad thing. I start to scratch the back of my neck, but I don't want the scars to show on my arm, so I put my arm back down, put my hands in my lap. I don't know what to do with myself. Everything is awkward, forced, unnatural.

I look back at the empty chair, roll my eyes. This is all a mistake. Something pink catches my eye in the corner of the top bookshelf, the fuzzy hair of a troll doll. It grins down at me with wide eyes, expecting more, like it's saying, "C'mon, you got this. Just open your mouth."

Dumb doll.

Dr. Winters writes more stuff on some paper, then she clicks the pen and asks, "Allee, why don't you tell me about work? Ms. Davis mentioned you work in a pizza shop."

Work. This is something I can talk about.

"Yeah, I work after school and most weekends at Pop's Pizza. It's a great job. Doesn't pay too much, but Dan and Logan are great. And I get free dinner."

"Do you hang with them, outside of work?"

"God, no!"

I laugh at the thought of doing anything with Dan other than folding pizza boxes and filling inventory orders. But then there's Logan. Why hadn't Logan and I ever hung out? Probably because working so many hours together kills the possibility of doing anything else. I remember his hug and start to smile, but then wipe it off my face before this shrink notices it.

Dr. Winters nods slightly. I decide not to talk too much. I hate when they nod.

"How about other friends?" she asks. "Do you have a 'tribe' to rally around you?"

"A tribe? Whatever that means, probably not. Too busy studying and working. That's all I got time for."

She writes something else. I want to ask, *What did you just write there?* But lack of interest is always a better strategy.

She continues, "So the pizza shop sounds like a good place. How about school?"

Right away, I think of the wad of paper smacking me in the face and the words: *Comfy in Tanaya's House?*

I don't tell her about this.

"Good, school's good. Can't wait to be done. Little less than three months and I'll be free."

She smiles. I nod for absolutely no reason and think, *Why the hell am I nodding now?*

I stop nodding and look at her, actually at her, for the first time. Her eyes are green.

She smiles which makes me look away. Ugh, she sees me. It's easier when people don't see me. Invisible is safe.

The silence is awkward. *Painful* comes to mind. I realize I'm holding my breath, maybe that's causing pain. I release the air, and it seems to roar into the room.

Now I'm just disappointed in myself. I glare up at her for making me feel shit about myself.

But, she's looking at papers, ignoring my breathing noises.

I think she knows about the cutting but doesn't want me to know she knows... wants to give me some space to sit in my crazy thoughts. Most adults would have said something by now and I'd hide behind whatever they said. But not here. This lady knows her shit. She doesn't do anything to make me feel better about myself. She just lets me sit with myself. My thoughts, my feelings.

Hmmm. Not sure how I feel about her knowing more about me than I know about me.

I take in a deep breath. Fine. I can just sit here, too. We'll just sit in silence. I am invisible.

She looks up and smiles. I look away.

After what seems like forever, she breaks the silence.

"I'm here for you, Allee, no one else. Whatever you want, whenever you want."

This makes my eyes get misty.

Crap.

I pinch the insides of my wrist to make the tears stop before they flow out. I feel them building in the corners of my eyes. I don't care if she notices the pinching now because that's better than tears. Tony always got worse once tears showed up. My nails dig into skin and just like that, my eyes dry up. I am back in control.

Gently, she asks, "Is there anything on your mind?"

Seriously?

Why should I have to tell her if she already knows? I'm not stupid.

"Well, what do you already know about me?"

This makes her right eyebrow raise a bit. Which makes me smile. I like giving adults something to think about. They always think they've got everything figured out. They don't know shit. And they all do that eyebrow thing, but in different degrees.

Her eyebrow lowers.

"I know that what other people tell me is not necessarily the truth. So, I don't believe anything until I hear it directly from the person coming to see me."

Hmmm. Serious respect for that answer.

Then she gives me a grimace, or is it a grin? Whatever, it lets me know she gets it, this awkwardness. It's something she deals with all the time, and it doesn't bother her. I think this lady has a lot of secrets she holds for people, and somehow she doesn't let it tear her up inside.

I'd like to know how she manages that. The secrets inside me rip me to shreds.

Chapter 23

There's one desktop computer at the Craigs'.

Tanaya, Auntie T, and I had shared it for checking emails, Amazon orders, and school assignments. I always preferred the library computers, but used the house one whenever I needed to finish assignments early in the morning or had to check on messages from teachers. I don't bother with social media, and Tanaya never bothered with it on the house computer. She used her phones.

I have less access now because Auntie T sits for hours and hours at it. Sometimes I find her next to it with her head tucked into her elbow, sound asleep. One day, when she was at work, I did a quick check on the search history. It showed all the different ways she was spending her time.

Searches were as dark as "Top Ways Teen Girls are Killed," as sad as "Is Your Teen a Runaway?" and as normal as "Easy Chicken Recipes." The recipe searches were confusing because Auntie T hasn't cooked anything since Tanaya disappeared. I told Dan, and now he has me bringing sandwiches and salad home to her.

So, it's not only easier to use the library computers for everything I need, it's also not as depressing.

I usually stop at the library on my way to work. It's comforting: the people coming and going, the hush of conversations, the smell of books. It gives me a break from Tanaya's absence at school and Auntie T's sadness at home. And that my mom is dead. Throughout the years, no matter what was going on in my life, I've always had the library.

If the computers are busy, I sign-in to reserve the next one and start on other homework. I usually only have to wait about fifteen minutes until a computer is free.

One time, I lost track of time and was late for work. Dan was furious and made me cry.

When he saw my tears, he stopped yelling and kept repeating, "Allee, I'm so sorry. I was scared something happened to you. I'm sorry. I didn't mean to yell."

He pulled me in for a hug, which surprised me, and I didn't know what to do. I was used to Tony pushing me away when I cried, not pulling me in. And the tears were confusing, too. Why *was* I crying!?

And then I remembered Dan's hug when I first came to work after my mom died, when I stopped in with Ms. Davis. I lifted my head out of his embrace enough to mumble, "Okay, okay, Dan, let me go. Why you huggin' me?"

He held me at arm's length but didn't let go. "You scared me!"

"I scared you? That's why you were yelling at me and then hugging me?"

Dan pulled me back into the bear hug and sighed. "I don't want anything bad to happen to you, Allee. That's all."

The flood of emotions made it impossible for me to say anything. I wanted to push him away, but a part of me thought maybe he really needed the hug. Like, it was helping him somehow.

Awkward, yes. But I really needed this job, so I decided to just stay with the awkwardness. You know, if it helped him or whatever.

He finally let go and said, "We need to get you a phone, Allee. Then, you can text me if you're running late. Or, I can text you and remind you about work."

At the mention of "phone," I had wanted to throw up. Phones were supposed to be for me and my mom. A hug, yes. A phone, no.

"I don't want a phone. No phone for me."

And besides, phones are trouble. Look what it did to Tanaya — taking her away from me and attaching her to Stretch, minute by minute, day or night. Makes me hate them, all of them.

Like Auntie T, Dan dropped the subject. I vowed to never be late for work again.

Two days later, and here I am in the library again, but this time, keeping watch on the time ticking by in the upper right-hand corner of the monitor.

Fridays in a library are pretty empty. I have some time before heading to work and type in "allee."

The page fills with definitions, images and YouTube pronunciation choices. I learn that *allée* is the past participle of the French verb "to go."

Why haven't I ever searched this before?

My eyes scan the screen, and then I see it:

> al·lée
>
> /a lā/
>
> *noun*
>
> an alley in a formal garden or park, bordered by trees or bushes.

"I wonder if Mom knew," I whisper and click on *13 Stunning Allées* from the *Architectural Digest*.

Beautiful natural paths cut through tree and shrub borders. It reminds me of the buildings and concrete walls on either side of the city's alleys, but instead of gray sharp edges and chipped cinderblock, the rich colors invite the viewer to enter. The grasses in the pictures are lush, the flowers lining the borders, so vibrant. I click on the images and visit each website.

After a while, the clock in the right-hand corner catches my eye – 4:10.

"Crap, I'll be late!"

I grab my backpack and run all the way to Pop's Pizza.

Dan isn't waiting in front of the shop like the last time. Logan taps his wrist two times and then puts his finger up to his lips as I run in.

He walks closer to Dan's door and yells, "Hey Allee, when you're done filling those salt shakers, check on the ketchup bottles."

I smile and mouth *Thank you,* as I grab two shakers from the booths on my way toward the counter. The phone rings as I walk by, and I pick up the receiver to take the first order of the night, "Pop's Pizza, what can I get you?"

Dan either doesn't notice I'm late or knows but doesn't bother to say anything. Everything is back to normal. Except, I can't stop thinking of the beautiful pictures in the *Architectural Digest*.

Later as we clean and close up the shop, I ask Logan, "Hey, did you ever hear of an 'allée'?"

I pronounce it correctly, putting emphasis on the second syllable.

"I don't think so. Why? What is it?"

Logan sloshes more water from the bucket onto the floor by the fryer, and the pong of disinfectant pinches my nose as I wipe down the tables and benches.

"I think it's the correct pronunciation of my name. I typed in *a - l - l - e - e* and it said something about trees and bushes lining a path. They had some pictures and they're amazing."

"Well, that sounds a whole hell of a lot better than an alley! Imagine all the images that would pop up if you had typed *a - l - l -e - y*!"

"Right?! No need to look them up! We get to experience them every day!"

We laugh and chat about all the different uses for alleys: a short-cut, a quick get-away, a parking lot for trash bins, a rat maze, and even a secret hook-up spot.

I blush at this, but he doesn't seem to notice.

On my walk back to the Craigs', I think about all the pictures I had seen that day. The next time I'm at the library, I'll google the closest *allée*. Maybe there's one not too far away and I can go see it. Would they put an *allée* in the city? Maybe Logan will want to go and see it with me.

When I walk into the house, Auntie T is watching the news and doesn't bother to look up. I always ask the same question before walking up the steps, "How was your day?"

Tanaya's been gone almost two weeks now, her answering me usually doesn't happen.

But this time, she looks over and gives a faint smile.

"It was okay, I'm glad I don't have to go back out. My feet are killing me."

Her answering is reassuring, so I walk into the room and sit on the floor next to her.

"Um, I know you're tired, but I was wondering, do you know anything about the pronunciation of my name? That shrink asked me about it the other day and I didn't know what she was talking about."

Auntie T folds her hands and lays them in her lap. Her smile broadens as she remembers something.

"Yes, yes, your name. I almost forgot!"

When I see her expression, I feel warm inside, like she has life inside her still. Maybe she doesn't hate me as much as I think she does.

Auntie T looks into my eyes and whispers, "Of course, you should know."

And then her eyes go dark, her lips tighten.

"Well, I'm sure you're aware, your mom was scared of Tony. The only reason she stayed with him was because she was even more scared of not being able to keep a roof over your head. She wanted to protect you. There are always a few scary people milling about shelters. She didn't want to take you there. And she didn't want Social Services taking you away from her. She didn't care about herself. It was, 'Allee needs this, Allee needs that.'"

Auntie T chuckles.

"She loved you so much, Allee. You were her world."

I don't understand. She uses the pronunciation Dr. Winters was talking about, rhyming my name with ballet.

"Wait, what did you call me?"

"I know, sounds weird, doesn't it? But she always wanted you to be Allee, with the long A sound at the end of your name. She didn't dare call you that in front of Tony. He was quick to mock. When she first called you by name, she told me he … "

She stops and holds my hand.

"Well, never mind him. He has such an angry soul, that man. I'm just telling you that you should call yourself whatever you want, and I will support you."

Her story brings my mom very close. It's a connection that I never knew I had. I was Mom's beautiful Allee.

Auntie T whispers, "And from the look on your face, I think you like the pronunciation your mom wanted."

Chapter 24

Like every other killing near a big city, the story is all over the news but they never show the body. "Young girl" catches my attention, but no one else in the shop seems to be concerned, so I just keep answering the phone and taking orders. Sentences float out of the TV as of no importance, just words the mind grabs: a female body...the bottom of a Mount Penn trail...no identification yet...pink and green backpack.

I freeze at "pink and green backpack" while the voice on the other end of the phone says something about mushrooms and onions.

Dan walks up behind me, takes the phone, and finishes the order. He hangs up and I'm still standing there, staring at the television.

He whispers, "It's time to leave, Allee. I'm taking you home."

I turn away from the television as it cuts to a KitKat commercial and look at him, try to register what he said. As it sinks in, I shake my head.

"No. I have nowhere to go, Dan."

I look back at Logan. "I belong here."

Logan looks over at us as he gives a basket of fries a few shakes and drops it back into the fryer, oil sizzling the hell out of those potatoes. Dan gives me a side hug then goes and turns off the neon 'OPEN' sign by the front door.

"You okay to finish up the last few orders, Logan? Don't bother with the phone if it rings and only unlock the door for people picking up orders. Once the food orders are out, close everything down. I'm taking Allee home."

Logan counts the slips hanging on the line.

"You got it, boss. Nine left. I'll take care of everything here and then close up. Won't bother with the phone. Call my cell if you need anything."

Dan seems to know what to do. I'm tired of trying to figure out what to do, where to go, what to say. Maybe he is right. Maybe it is better to go… home. I climb into the passenger side of the Chevy, numb. Tanaya's backpack. A body.

It's a warm night, but I shiver as he drives out of the alley and turns onto the street.

Dan asks, "How's Tina been, Allee? Anything you think we can do for her? You know, as a community? Some of the shops want to do more."

I don't know what to think of my new role with Auntie T, and I don't know how much to tell Dan. She talked to me about my name, but that's the most she's said to me in the last two weeks.

I decide on, "She doesn't say too much," and quickly add, "She's nice and all, always asking me how I'm doing. But she just walks around the house, like wandering, not sure where to go. She started going back to work. Not every day."

I'm sure she doesn't want me in the house anymore. It's never good to have a liar around. Never know what to expect with a liar. Most of the time, when she walks into the room I'm in, she makes an excuse about something and then leaves. I'm waiting for her to wake up one day and tell me to get out of her house.

But I'm too ashamed to tell Dan about all that so add, "She does eat the food you send home with me. Not much else, but she does eat that."

I remember the conversation like it was yesterday, my promise to Auntie T at the table after Tanaya went out on one of her "studying" nights. I had promised to let her know if Tanaya was getting into any trouble. Lying lumps together with the guilt for not helping Tanaya and the guilt for not helping my mom.

I can't even help myself.

Guilt builds quickly right there in the front seat of Dan's car as I think about all my lies, the news on the television, Mom alone with Tony on the night he killed her, Auntie T ignoring me in the house. I can't breathe, a destructive tidal wave starts outside of me, sweeps up and crashes down into my lungs, suffocating me. My heart beats fast and hard, as if it's fighting to get out of my chest before the wave drowns it.

I grab the armrest, a soft "Oh, god!" escapes my lips.

"Allee, are you okay?" Dan tries to keep one eye on the road and the other on me but gives up and pulls into the abandoned 7-Eleven parking lot.

He turns to me, "Breathe, Allee. Breathe. Look at me. With me. Ready?"

He looks deep into my eyes, trying to lead me out of the dark and scary place. He's holding both my hands. "Slow, deep breath in. Hold it there. Good. Now, slow breath out."

I watch him, listen to him as he teaches me how to do something so basic. He is a life line. I feel the air go in and down, freeing my lungs. My heart slows and the ache subsides with each deep breath. The deep breathing lets oxygen in, diffuses the pain so it can break up and float away. I wonder where the pain is going as I take the deep breaths in and out.

"Breathe," he repeats.

I imagine the pain leaving me with each exhalation. It's filling the car.

I watch Dan and wonder if it will suffocate him. Will he die, too, breathing the toxic air I put out into our space?

I threw the knife away the night I felt Mom so close to me in the shower, when I was trying to drown out the sound of Auntie T's howls. That was my last cut. And I'm determined not to put another pointy object under my mattress. The guilt is crushing, anger bubbling. If there is no relief from a knife, what can I use?

Deep breaths? Maybe. But sounds kind of lame.

What else? There has to be something else.

I look into Dan's eyes, and the answer comes to me — words. Can words ease pain? Is that why Tennessee Williams and all those other authors wrote stories and poems? Can words take the pain and explain it away? Before I lose my nerve, I let the words tumble out.

Between sobs, I fight for air and cry, "Oh, Dan, That's her backpack. The pink and green one on the news. It's Tanaya's! It's all my fault! I didn't help Tanaya, and I let Auntie T down, I lied to her."

The tears flow, and I don't try to control them. They swell up and out. I panic again and gulp for more air.

Dan's words become a mantra.

"Breathe, Allee. In and out, with me. Come on."

As we breathe the same air in a slow rhythm, I stop gulping for air. I'm not drowning. Dan keeps holding my hands, and I don't pull away.

When my body is calmer, he says, "Now, we're not sure the backpack is Tanaya's, so let's hold off on thinking the worst. And what are you saying about letting Tina down? God, girl, you can't keep living this way, keeping everything bottled up! Spill it. What are you thinking?"

His command helps me pull my thoughts together, to try and make sense of the disjointed ideas. I nod and wipe my nose on the sleeve of my sweater and tell him everything: how Tanaya was sneaking out of the house, about the night Auntie T asked if she was missing anything important, if she was working too much to notice that Tanaya was getting into trouble, and how I didn't get help for Tanaya when she was crying the night before she disappeared.

I look down at my hands, they look small in his.

"Auntie T said, 'You'll tell me if anything is going on that I should know about, won't you?' And I lied, Dan. Tanaya asked me to keep it a secret. I told her mom that I would let her know if anything was up. But I didn't."

I look up, expecting anger, but his eyes soften as he looks into mine.

"Oh, Allee, this isn't your fault. No matter what you did or didn't do, this isn't your fault."

My head falls forward, the shame is crushing. His words bounce off like hail on an alley's concrete cinder blocks. Why can't he see? It's all my fault. Tanaya would be here if I hadn't lied.

"Did you tell the cops all you know?"

I keep my head down and whisper, "I told them everything that I think is important. Even about the drugs I found. I replay everything over and over in my mind hoping I'll find information that I forgot. Something that will help." I sit quietly, then add, "They must have told Auntie T everything I told them. That's why she's not talking to me. She knows I lied to her."

I can't believe I'm worrying about my own safety in the midst of Auntie T's grief. I really am a coward. But I ask him anyway, "Do you think I shouldn't be in the house anymore? Like, maybe it's too painful for Auntie T that I'm there and Tanaya's not? And it's all because I lied?"

Dan answers slowly, searching for the right words, "I can't know for sure, but you're probably a comfort to her, Allee. Don't you think?"

I shrug, don't know what to think. I feel more like a burden. Like I'm always in someone's way. I'm just a lie. A living lie walking around in a house I don't deserve.

"Maybe I shouldn't be there, Dan. I don't deserve to be there."

Dan continues, his words picking up momentum as his thoughts clear. "Well, how did you feel when you moved into the house? Tanaya had a mom and you didn't anymore. Was it upsetting to have Tina in the house, interacting with Tanaya? She took care of the both of you, didn't she? Did you wish Tina wasn't there?"

"No." I look up. "I loved having her there. She reminded me of my mom."

Dan nods, "Well then, you have your answer. You may be giving her comfort."

I state the obvious, "Yeah, but she didn't lie to me."

Dan's quiet, scratches his forehead as the reality of that one sentence settles into his awareness.

He doesn't deny this truth but says, "Let's wait a couple of days and then ask her. Right now, we have to be there for Tina. If that is Tanaya they're talking about on the news, we're going to have to support Tina, no matter what."

I have a sinking feeling in my stomach when I think about that.

"I took advantage of Auntie T's trust. There's a chance she won't want me. I can't stay if she doesn't want me."

"No worries about a place to live, Allee. You have people who care about you. You won't end up on the streets."

I'm not so sure, but he starts up the car, and we drive to Auntie T. Words allowed some of the pain to escape, and the air around me diffused it, broke it down, and took it away so I could catch my breath. He drives in silence now. I look out the window, too exhausted to think or feel.

Numb is good.

Two squad cars are parked out front of the row home. Instead of dropping me out front of the house, Dan parallel parks behind them.

"I'm going in with you."

Two officers open the front door and head down the steps toward one of the squad cars. Dread creeps into my gut.

"Do you think they were giving her the news? About the body?"

Dan gets out of the car first, "Let's talk to them before we go in."

I can't wait.

My gut has already told me the body is Tanaya.

I run up the steps to check on Auntie T.

Chapter 25

Auntie T is on the couch, watching the dark TV screen. A female officer sits in the winged back chair in the corner, next to the TV. There are no lights on in the small living room, just a soft glow coming from the kitchen. Not wanting to disturb anyone, I hesitate by the front door. Everything is eerily quiet.

The officer stands. "You're Allee."

The abruptness surprises me and I take a step back. "Yeah, I'm Allee."

"We were talking about you. Weren't we, Ms. Craig?"

The officer looks over at the couch, but Auntie T doesn't look up or respond. My eyes move from one to the other. The officer seems familiar, but I don't know why.

She walks closer to me. "She's tired. I didn't want to leave her alone. She said she'd be fine once you came back from work. Will you stay with her? Do you feel comfortable sitting with her?"

"Of course," I whisper. "I live here."

Saying those words makes shame creep back into my awareness, and I look down at the floor.

The officer hands me a card. "Allee, do you remember me? I'm Officer Smith. I was with you on the night your mom…"

At the mention of my mom, I look from Auntie T, to the officer, and then down at the business card in my hand. I search for some connection, something that will help me make sense of this night. That night. Everything is a blur.

"Are you okay?" she asks. "Do you need to sit down?"

"No. No, I'd rather stand." I'm afraid to ask, but mumble, "Why, why are you …"

That's all I can get out. The images of my mom and Tanaya mix together so quickly, I can't get the words into a complete sentence. Time seems to leave the small room and though I want to keep standing, to be ready for anything, my feet walk me to the wall, and I lean against it. But I don't remember walking to it. What happened in the few seconds from when I was standing in the doorway to when I'm up against the wall? I feel separated from my body.

The officer is explaining something, telling me about Tanaya's backpack and that Auntie T will go and identify her body tomorrow morning.

I interrupt the officer. "I'll go with you, Auntie T."

But Auntie shakes her head, no.

She's so small there, nestled in the corner of the sofa. Her feet are on the jute rug, the same rug I kept staring at when they told me about my mom. But the rug doesn't consume my thoughts this time. All I can think about is Auntie T. The urge to comfort, even though I struggle to find comfort myself, and maybe because I've never found it, fills me with a knowing. I leave the security of the wall. Auntie T doesn't move as I sit next to her. We share the silence. I think words will create a small crack in the dam and send a flood of emotions and more chaos. Then, nothing will be safe. Not even the words.

I'm afraid but move a little closer anyway, so close I put my hand through the crook in Auntie T's arm, around her elbow. It's warm, safe. Auntie T doesn't push me away. I lean in and rest my head on her shoulder. At first, she doesn't respond to my presence. But after a few seconds, Auntie T tilts her head just enough that it touches the top of mine. She lets out a slight sigh. That is all.

Dan comes in and has a whispered conversation with the officer. The door closes behind her and Dan drags the wing-backed chair closer. He places his hand gently on Auntie T's knee.

Tanaya was found. Tanaya is dead.

Chapter 26

TANAYA: IN THE MIND OF THE SEX TRAFFICKED

He said his name is Mike.

I know it isn't. And I don't care. We're characters in a movie. And like a movie, names are made up. It's one of the reasons I liked it when Stretch first called me Yaya and uses the nickname for advertisement.

"Yaya" separates me from Tanaya just as this "Mike" has permission to be his own main character.

Stretch told me I'm a perfect yaya. So I googled it on my phone, to figure out what the hell he was referring to. The Urban Dictionary describes a yaya as amazing in bed because she aims to please her partner, she also loves to cuddle and kiss.

Hmm. 'Bout sums me up.

I also like it when my clients talk about their boring lives, mean wives, and selfish kids. Are their families really all the same? Definitely makes me not want to get married. Their stories are so similar, I feel for them without having to listen anymore.

The blue dolphin pills are my favorite. I usually take them about thirty minutes before a client. Ecstasy blows life into the sensual side of my body so I can give everything to these strangers.

I embrace them all. I fall in love with their sad eyes, their hungry kisses, their groping hands. The feeling of euphoria comes to life in the arms of these paying customers. I rationalize that it is an equal relationship. Symbiosis or symbiotic? Something like that. I wonder about the correct science word or if I'm getting it confused with my homework about symbolism. If only I had a memory like Allee. I chuckle at how bio class is wasted on me. I really don't care. I'm excited now, for the job at hand, and that's the signal I need that I'm ready to take care of "Mike." He should stop talking now. It's showtime.

"I'm sensing you're really sad. Poor thing."

I unbutton his shirt and kneel down to kiss his belly button. Mike lets out a sigh and arches his back as I unbuckle his belt.

"How about you let Yaya take care of all your needs right now, right here? Tell me what you like. I can help you forget all those worries on your mind and give you the love and attention that you deserve."

- - - - -

I'm still high, but getting irritated that Stretch is late, again. It's almost two hours since he dropped me off. And not one message on my phone.

I look out the window and then back at sleeping Mike. I don't want to have to do anything more for him. Or even talk to him. Waiting to leave is always awkward. In the beginning Stretch was in the next room, or waiting for me outside the door. Or, in the room with us.

Occasionally, he'd run to the store or have to go "check on something." I hated that, but it's getting to be all the time now. The longer I have to wait, the more needy the guys become, like I have life answers for them. Or they become so angry they blame me for their messed up lives and get nasty. I need to leave before he wakes up. I shove all my things into the backpack and go outside to call Stretch again.

I don't know where I'm supposed to go next, so I'm pretty much stuck here waiting.

This is the part I need to change about my new life. Maybe I can convince Stretch to get me a car. Gotta get that all figured out before I open my mouth. If I don't present things just right to Stretch, I don't get what I want.

I walk down the cracked concrete steps and call him again, but it still goes straight to voicemail. I slide the phone into the side pocket of my backpack as an old lady shuffles down the middle of the street. She pushes what seems to be her life belongings in a shopping cart. The front right wheel doesn't always reach the ground and spins in the air. There are plastic bags, all different sizes and colors, piled high. And a ragged, old bunny so smushed his nose and eyes bulge through the side of the cart. He seems to be begging to be set free. One tug of the ear swinging through the metal rungs and the rest of him would squeeze out.

I look closer at the woman and know she'll never release that bunny. For whatever reason, she needs that bunny. As she passes, I think about life on the streets. Stretch may be a pain in the ass, but he would never let me live on the streets. The woman parks her cart next to a makeshift tent that sits at the entrance of the alley at the end of the street.

I sit on the curb and pull a piece of paper from my backpack to begin my essay on symbolism. I write and write until Frank's truck rounds the corner. Stretch must be with the new blonde bitch he's been hanging out with.

"Can't be bothered to leave her to pick me up?" I say with a scowl.

Not too sure what to do with the Stretch-and-other-girls situation. He doesn't like it when I tell him he's acting like an ass. He scolds me, slapped me once.

"Stop over-reacting. It's not sexy, and the drama is beneath you."

Whatever. Not worth the slap so I don't talk shit about it anymore.

I shove the essay into my bag and stand as the truck pulls in front of me.

It's not Frank. It's Mouse.

I lean into the open window, and his eyes settle at my cleavage. I'm aware he appreciates the way I look and often catch him staring at me, taking deep breaths whenever I'm close.

As usual, I just ignore it.

"Using the truck to chauffeur around today, huh? Sweet!"

Mouse lifts his eyes from my breasts and smiles. "Come on in. Your chariot awaits!"

I hop up into the front seat. "Love the smell of this new truck! I'm starving! Do you think we can stop at Ceci's for a burger before you drop me off?"

Mouse's smile disappears as he turns the truck off. He dangles his left arm over the steering wheel. "Look, Yaya, I need you right now. How 'bout we make this truck dance? You know…"

He stops talking and lightly touches my arm, brings my hand up to his lips and licks my index finger.

I'm surprised and laugh. "Hold on there. I'm working today and need a break!"

I expect that to be it. That should be the end of it.

But he lunges, pushing me back against the door before I even know what's happening.

"You laughing at me?"

He gets on top of me, his hand up my shirt. I'm pinned under him. My nails dig into his neck and shoulder.

"Get off me!"

But he doesn't stop. He tries to unbutton my pants. I pull the door handle, and it opens, but he grabs me with so much force, I have to let go to protect my head from smacking the dashboard. He leans behind me and yanks the door closed.

"Come on, Tanaya!"

He shouts obscenities, mumbles what he wants to do to me.

I yell at him, "Not even on the tail end of a blue dolphin!"

He grabs my neck and presses so hard my head slams into the door. He leaves go with one hand to lift my legs up onto the driver seat and then kneels on them. I can barely move as he tries to undo my pants again.

I dig my nails deeper into the hand he has on my neck and start jerking my legs all over the place. He lets go of my neck to reach up and steady himself, one hand on the ceiling the other on the headrest. I open the door and push with all my strength against the side of the seat, dragging my legs out from under him. He grabs the top of my pants but as I pull my feet out from under him, he falls backward and hits the driver door. I give one more hard push and fall onto the street screaming,

"Help me! Someone, help!"

As I stand, there's movement near the tent in the alley. A flap is tossed up and a small head peeks out.

I scream again, "Help!" and turn to run up the steps to Mike.

But Mouse jumps out of the truck and stands in front of me. I try to run around him, but he anticipates every turn I make, always blocking my way. I scream his name again and again, trying to reason with him. But he doesn't seem to recognize me.

I yell, "It's me, Tanaya!" I beg, "Mouse, please, don't do this."

Anger distorts his face, and I don't recognize him. His eyes are empty. I am just a means to something he wants. I scream again, try to jolt him back, to remember who I am. His eyes, motionless, fix on me but can't see me. He raises his fist.

"Just shut up! Do you hear me?! Shut up!"

There's a sharp pain on the side of my head. It travels behind my left eye where it explodes. Everything goes black. I'm falling.

Until I'm not.

Chapter 27

Ms. Davis looks all wide-eyed, excited about something. I'm sure I don't want to have anything to do with it, but she plows ahead with the plan anyway.

"I talked to the other counselors and Principal Jones. We're in agreement that we'll have a memorial service, here at the school, at the end of the week."

My first day back since Auntie T identified Tanaya's body three days ago and my guidance counselor is planning a frigging party.

She leans forward. "What do you think?"

What do I think?

Ms. Davis sits motionless, hands clasped on top of her desk.

I think the memorial service at school will be a circus.

I think Tanaya would not have liked the idea.

I think Auntie T won't even walk into the building.

So, I stare at Ms. Davis like she has no clue. It's worse than a normal slouch, my eyes are screaming at her, *What are you, stupid?!*

But I keep my mouth shut, let my eyes do the talking.

She must not know how to read eyeball stares because she sits back in her chair and says, "A memorial service will be good for the school community. Of course, if it's too difficult for you and Auntie T to come to it, we will still have it and keep you in our thoughts and prayers."

Thoughts and Prayers. Gee, thanks.

Next, she'll be asking me to make posters for it or cookies.

Whatever.

Totally oblivious to how wrong this plan is, she continues. "I called Dan. He said he would like to donate pizza and drinks afterward, for the senior class. As a way to bring everyone together."

Maybe I should mention to Ms. Davis about the paper someone threw at my head. And the way no one looks at me anymore. And how I cram a breakfast bar into my mouth as I walk into the school library during fifth period lunch instead of actually eating in the cafeteria. Not one person in this great senior class of hers wants to talk with me, walk with me, hang with me. No one even bothers getting pizza from Pop's anymore. There used to be the occasional student group coming in or phone orders for student parties, but no more.

Seems I've really gotten good at the invisibility thing.

And it sucks.

Ms. Davis looks at me with that concerned look, the one that makes me think she might read my mind and make me cry. I pinch the inside of my wrist and think about Ms. Davis's blouse. She must have packed all her cardigans away until next fall. The blouse is shimmery, with geometric figures intercepting at different angles. It makes me think it's the way personalities would interact if we didn't talk, we'd just move around and through each other. Why am I thinking of this?

Thoughts are so random and randomness seems to keep my emotions in check. I figured that out with Dr. Winters. She pointed out to me one day that I fixate on random thoughts and patterns because it helps me feel safe, in control. By fixating on things, I don't have to think or worry about what's going on right in front of me. Like the jute rug.

Dr. Winters has some good observations. Who would have thought?

Ms. Davis takes a notepad out of her desk.

"We'll have the service this Friday. And then after the pizza, an early dismissal for seniors. Is there anything you'd like to include in the service? A favorite song of hers, or poem? A favorite quote? I'll call Auntie T this afternoon and see if she wants to say something. Hopefully, she'll be comfortable enough to join us."

She looks at me. "We're all worried about you. If it's too much for you to attend, we understand."

The realization that she's just trying to help seeps into my skin. I still think it's a bad idea, but kind of want to do something for Tanaya. Maybe this will help.

I sigh.

"I'm here, aren't I?"

It's what Mom would want, me to keep showing up. Mom is the only reason I still come to school.

I walk out of Ms. Davis's office just as Dorie walks down the hall. She doesn't say anything, in fact she quickly looks around to see if anyone else is in the hall. But then she looks at me, gives a slight nod, and walks away.

- - - - -

Four days later, I walk into the kitchen while Auntie T finishes up a phone conversation with Dan.

"Yeah, thanks, Dan. We'll see you in about ten minutes."

She looks nice, put together. The navy blue dress is patterned with small cream-colored specks. The three-quarter-length sleeves and modest neckline is professional, yet pretty.

Our conversations are still lacking, but I always try.

"You look perfect. Tanaya always loved that dress on you."

Auntie T blinks back tears and nods. "Yeah, she helped me pick it out. That girl always had a knack for style. I talked to her this morning, while I got dressed. Sounds weird, that I talk to her, but I wanted to make sure she knew I was getting dressed up for her." She sighs. "I don't remember to shower some days, Allee. I'm hoping this memorial service will help me get my head a little straighter."

"Yeah, doing something for Tanaya feels right. Like maybe it's okay if we put on a brave face, brush our hair, and smile. For her."

Auntie T walks over to the counter and grabs some tissues.

"People say, 'Let it hurt so it can heal.' Never fully understood that. Now I know."

I look at her and nod. "Like your heart is ripping out of your chest?"

Anguish. There it is, all over Auntie T's face. I can't bear to see it. I walk over to her and slide my hand behind her back, rest my head on her shoulder.

And she doesn't push me away.

"Oh Allee," she says. "I'm so glad you're here."

I let those seven little words wrap around me, heavy like a warm blanket. I hang onto them like the edges of the comforter up on the bed. Once Auntie T knows the extent of all my lies, this feeling will be pulled away from me.

Everything I want to say back to Auntie T is stuck in my throat, so I hug her a little tighter. The heart-ripping-from-my-chest feeling stops with her seven words. It pulses calmly. Something was just set straight inside my head, too. I'm afraid it will leave, get all disturbed again. I want it to stay. Need it to stay.

So I etch those words onto my heart: *Oh Allee, I'm so glad you're here.*

There's a knock on the door, and Dan swings it open.

"Ready? Can I help carry anything out to the car?"

Auntie T sighs.

"No, not bringing anything." And then with a smile, "Just tissues."

We walk out together, and I'm surprised to see Logan in the back seat of Dan's car.

"Hey," I say to him, "I didn't know you were coming."

Logan is dressed in a suit, his black shoes shine like they were just polished.

"I wouldn't miss being here to support you and Auntie T."

I mumble, "Thank you," and slide into the back seat with him. He takes my hand and gives it a squeeze. I wait for him to let go.

But he doesn't.

No one talks as we ride the half mile to school. It's a beautiful day, sun shining. We could have walked. But here, in Dan's car, I have my people. I feel cocooned, safe, no matter what happens at school.

The senior class is assembled in the front half of the auditorium, the other classes are sitting behind them. Up on the stage, there's a large picture of Tanaya surrounded by white, pink, and lavender roses. I gasp when I see her, the life-size picture that seems to look right at me as I take my seat in the front row.

Those roses. I think of the rose tattoo. There's something wrong with all of that. Tanaya hated roses. Peonies are… were… her favorite. Seeing all the roses next to her picture makes me cringe a bit, and I remember her in the bedroom telling me, "Maybe I learned to ignore the thorns."

Ms. Davis walks over to us and gives Auntie T a hug.

"Thank you so much for coming, Ms. Craig. I'm sure this is a very difficult time."

Auntie T gives a weak smile and then asks about the rose flower arrangements on either side of Tanaya's picture.

Ms. Davis turns to them and then back to Auntie T.

"They're so beautiful, aren't they? They were delivered to the school this morning. The note said it was for the services today, and it was signed only with the letter 'S.'"

My breath gets caught in my throat. I want to run up on the stage and get those flowers as far away from Tanaya's picture as I can. My heart is racing, the adrenaline pumping.

But I look at Auntie T, and her sadness stops my crazy. She thinks the flowers are beautiful.

The tattoo, the roses… *S.*

He's making sure his presence is felt by the whole student body. Letting them know that he has control and is very close, aware of everything going on.

When the service begins, all I can think about is running up on the stage and shattering the glass vases. I want to hear them crash to the floor, watch the roses fall, then stomp on the petals.

What is wrong with me?

Principal Jones is quoting Christopher Robin (*eyeroll*), "Friendship is a very comforting thing to have" just as I imagine tying Stretch up and shoving rose thorns into different parts of his body.

Tanaya is close, tugging at me, trying to get me to stop thinking crazy…

My forearms are twitching. My shins are itching. I keep glancing over at Auntie T. She is the only thing keeping me from running up there.

There's movement as the senior class is called to put single white roses in the vase that sits on a table just in front of Auntie T and me. Next to the vase is a beautiful lavender felt box. After placing their roses in the vase, they each drop a note into the box. Ms. Davis is talking at the mic.

"Every student and faculty member, kitchen staff, and maintenance worker wrote a memory of Tanaya so Auntie T and Allee can read how Tanaya impacted all our lives. Let's have silence as they bring up their roses and place their thoughts in the memory box. "

I wonder about all of that. I remember the seniors standing around when she was with Stretch, and he was so angry, when she left Snake Road with him.

And nobody helped her.

Not even me.

They look sincere, sad even, as they walk up to us. Some look right at Auntie T and me. They give us a slight nod, then walk away. I sense Tanaya forgiving them. Auntie T, too.

It's just me holding onto the pain, anger.

And guilt.

I watch them and think about what it would mean to let it all go.

But I can't. I won't.

Chapter 28

At the beginning of each session, Dr. Winters still walks around the desk, hand outstretched as if I'm somebody important. Every visit, and we've had quite a few the past month, starts the same way.

And it's still weird.

She must be bored to death with everybody complaining about their lives that she breaks up the day by taking walks around her own desk.

Lame.

I fake smile and shake her hand.

"So, how have you been this past week? How are you feeling after the memorial service?"

How am I feeling? I think I'm not feeling.

I used to be hyper-aware of everything. But ever since the service at school and the not-running-to-destroy-the-flower-arrangement feeling, the world is dull. I shrug.

"Doing pretty good, I guess. Just trying to help Auntie T. Figuring it out as I go along."

"It must be difficult. For the both of you."

There's something genuine in the way Dr. Winters talks to me, the way her eyes search my face. It breaks down a little bit of the hardness, the protective mound I concrete around myself before I walk into this office. Before the handshake. Before she starts asking questions.

Yeah, I think it's like concrete now, not mud.

I try not to care, not to share, not to break down. I need the hardness to keep Carol Winters away from my deepest fears. The fears I can't even name, shadows of some messed-up shit. So, I don't tell her that lately I wake up crying with no idea why.

She suggested I use a marker to doodle pictures or draw cut marks on my arms. Sounded weird when she first mentioned it, but honestly, at three in the morning, it kind of works.

Well, it wouldn't work if I had kept the knife under my mattress.

But since that's gone, and Tanaya's not in the room with me, I wrap the comforter around me in a big hug, turn on a small flashlight I found in a kitchen drawer, and doodle on my arms. I started with just one black marker, like Dr. Winters suggested, but now I use a rainbow of colors. Intricate designs run up and down my arm. When I focus on the art, the designs, the urge to cut disappears.

Lately though, after I turn off the flashlight and snuggle under the comfortable, I have an irresistible urge to scratch my shins...and do... until they bleed. I think this is another type of self-harm. But, what do I know? They really do itch. As I scratch in the middle of the night, scared to death of the things I can't name, it gives me some relief.

It can't be that bad. It does make me feel...something.

Or, it's some type of contact dermatitis.

I know this shrink would love to figure it all out. But I'm convinced it's a bad idea. If Carol Winters figures it out, Carol Winters still gets to go home and sleep in a beautiful house with a perfect little family. While I return to the bedroom and wait for the Tony nightmares to terrorize me in real-time as my nails shred the skin on my legs.

No thanks.

She interrupts my thoughts with a revisit from last week's session.

"You told me that you hadn't cut, hadn't felt a need to cut. Has anything changed? I want to remind you that there is no shame in self-harm, we just want to find better ways to deal with stress, with feelings."

This is the kind of shit that makes me think that Dr. Winters can see right through me, knows what I'm thinking. Did she just read my mind about scratching the shit out of my legs? It's exhausting, keeping this woman out of my head. I feel like a frigging ninja warrior deflecting her questions.

"Nope, no desire to cut. Threw that knife away and haven't even tried to get a new one." I pull in my upper lip with my bottom teeth and nod. "Yep, that's me, not even thinking of self-harm."

I let out a sigh and then smile at Dr. Winters to convince her all is good.

There is absolutely no reaction on her face.

To convince her, I pull the sweatshirt sleeve up my left arm. I'm right-handed, so the left arm designs are always better executed than those on the right.

"Last week I came across henna art designs on the library computer. I asked the librarian if she could print some of the designs for me. She suggested I check out the book *Henna Art*."

I love that book. Creating those beautiful designs on my forearms makes every crazy, sad, angry, scared feeling drift away. I get lost in those patterns. I choose artwork that will cover over the scars. I'm not brave enough to walk around with my colorful arms showing, but maybe, if I get really good at the designs, I can finally feel the breeze tickle my arms, the warm sun kiss them.

Shorts are out of the question though, until this contact dermatitis thing goes away.

Dr. Winters whispers, "Beautiful, Allee."

She says it in such a way, I know she means it. She looks up at me and smiles, then writes something down.

I still hate that. Don't ask what she wrote, though.

Go ahead and do that writing-down-thing.

I slouch a little bit more.

She looks up again and says, "You know..."

Ugh. "You know," another adult phrase to draw people into a conversation.

"...If we stop cutting without finding healthy ways to deal with emotions, another form of self-harm might develop."

Crap, this woman *can* see right through me.

I don't move, except a slight nod of the head as if to say, "You don't say."

"If that happens," she continues, "I just want you to know it's normal and we can figure out what to do with it if you're not sure. Is there a time of day when you get overwhelmed with emotions? Anxious, scared, or even angry? Or when you're tired? These can be triggers."

I shift in my seat, lower the sleeve back down to my wrist.

"I'm so busy with school and work, I don't really have time to be thinking of my emotions and how to deal with them. I just kind of go through my day, doing my thing." I sit up and nod again. "You know, kind of doing stuff that needs to get done."

"How about sleeping? Are you sleeping well?"

Shit, shit! I take a deep breath and lie, "You know, some nights are better than others, but not too bad. I get a pretty good night's sleep."

It came out so calmly, I almost believe it myself.

Dr. Winters doesn't even bother to write that crap down. She looks at me as if I should say something more.

I feel the hardness chipping away. The blood under my nails freaked me out this morning. The scratches up and down the front of my leg left a bloody mess on the sheets. I blamed it on my period and told Auntie T that was why I was washing my bedding before school. I read on the Shout bottle that it got rid of blood stains. I doused the sheet with the stuff.

Now, I wear long shirt sleeves and long pants. In May.

I look out the window. I'm tired of making up lies, and they're getting hard to keep track of. I told Dr. Winters some stuff, and she seemed to understand. And that marker drawing on my arm was a cool suggestion.

Why can't I tell her everything? Maybe she has other ideas that can help me.

A robin flies up onto the windowsill, for just a second, then flies away. Birds don't have to drop out of bathroom windows or climb down fire escapes. They fly out and up. They don't take sharpened sticks and carve lines into their wings. They just flit around… *free as a bird.*

I feel jealous of that little bird and whisper, "I want to be like that bird."

Dr. Winters follows my gaze, but the bird has already flown away.

I turn and repeat, "I want to be like a bird. But I'm too heavy. I want to be as light as a bird."

Dr. Winters tilts her head. "What's holding you down? I can help you deal with it all. That's why I'm here. No miracles, but there are ways to help you cope, so we can lighten your load. Then, you will feel lighter, better."

I want to believe it, but it sounds too good. What's the saying Mom always told me? *If it sounds too good to be true, then it probably is.*

Hot tears melt more of the hardness, leaving me exposed, vulnerable. I miss my mom. I miss Tanaya. The ninja wants to rest. I look at the empty chair and imagine my mom sitting next to me, leaning over to hold my hand.

Tanaya stands next to her, holding her other hand. I wish I was with them.

But, they're not here. And I'm not there.

I place both my elbows on the arms of the chair and pull forward to the edge of the seat. I close my eyes so I don't have to see Dr. Winters' reaction.

"I can't fall asleep without scratching my shins, until they bleed. And I'm mad at myself for doing it. But it feels good to do it. Sometimes I scratch them in my sleep."

It was honest, and after saying it, the tears stopped. I think Dr. Winters is disappointed, will tell me that she expected me to be further along in my healing. Or some other shit like that.

But she doesn't say anything.

I open my eyes to see what's going on. She has her eyes closed, listening. Remembering? When she finally opens her eyes, we look at each other. I want her to see, to help. I hold her gaze, and she doesn't look away. I think she wants me to see her, too. There's something I said that she understands. She knows what I'm talking about …

"You're soothing yourself Allee, that's all. There's nothing to be ashamed of, or mad at. We'll find healthier ways for you to deal with all the emotions behind a traumatic life. We will. You don't have to figure it out by yourself."

I don't look away. I want this lady to see me. I am not invisible. I've been fighting to keep everyone away for so long. I don't want to hide anymore. I want her to see me, to hear me. I want to undo the concrete and let the hardness ooze away.

Chapter 29

Dr. Winters suggested I stop the after-school-climbing-under-the-comforter activity to see if I sleep through the night better. Somehow, I was able to sleepwalk through school today and managed to keep awake enough through work that I only messed up three orders. I'm so tired, I can't wait to climb under that comforter when I get home, at the acceptable-to-be-under-a-comforter time.

Logan yells from the back line, "Dan tells me your birthday is this Saturday."

I stop counting out the cash drawer.

"I'm not celebrating, so don't get any crazy ideas."

I wrap the bills up and snap the drawer closed.

"Anyway, how does Dan know? And has he mentioned anything more to you about getting the online ordering up on the website? It's like 2005 in here. Christ. It'll make all our lives easier once he gets it up and running."

Logan rolls the mop bucket toward the booths.

"He said by the end of the month, it'll be all set up."

"Thank god!"

"He said your mom filled out a job application for you before you started. That's how he knows it's your birthday."

My heart skips a beat. Or something like that. Whenever anyone mentions my mom there's a rush, or jump, under my heart. Or maybe it's over my heart. Or maybe through it. It's hard to pinpoint where or what it is. The feeling used to overwhelm me, catch me off guard. Scare me. But Dr. Winters told me it's called a grief-burst, and it only happens because of love.

We've been working on identifying that as an emotion I never thought possible, love mixed with sadness. That lady knows stuff. Now I use that unexpected burst to fill the hollowness inside, fill it with Mom. I take a deep breath to keep the rush-rolling around for a few more seconds before it disappears.

Tanaya, too. She bursts into my life from time to time.

Logan continues, with hesitancy, but there's hope in his question.

"So, are you doing anything? Saturday morning, I mean."

My heart skips another beat but for a different reason. Excitement is the feeling I get when Logan speaks to me, or stands close, or looks at me from the fryer. Or holds my hand. Dr. Winters told me that the muddy, concrete-y feeling wrapped around me is really a lot of emotions like guilt, loneliness, pain, sadness trying to protect me. In this case, it's guilt keeping me from feeling like I can enjoy Logan because Mom and Tanaya are dead.

I'm still working on that idea. Even though I have no plans, I lie easily. "Um, you know, I should check with Auntie T. She mentioned something about cake."

Logan laughs. "I don't think you'll be eating cake at nine in the morning. But talk to her and let me know. If you have the time, I'd like to show you something I think you'd be interested in."

He gives a crooked smile which makes me curious.

"Well, if it's just in the morning, I guess that'll be alright."

Logan slides the slosh bucket back into the closet with a bang.

"Great! We'll meet at the Emberton bus loop at nine."

- - - - -

At 9:10 on Saturday morning, Logan follows me onto the bus, and I slide into the seat next to a window that faces storefronts.

"So, now can you tell me where we're going?"

Logan eases in next to me.

"Well, there's no air conditioning where we're going. With long jeans and that sweater, you're gonna sweat something fierce! Why are you always dressed like that?"

I act like his words didn't just stir up a whole lot of anxiety in my gut and give a non-committal shrug.

"I run cold, I guess. Now, stop changing the subject and tell me where we're going."

"It's a surprise and gonna take us about thirty minutes to get there so start talking about something else. I can be a very stubborn, old PIA."

"You're not old!" I punch his arm. "What are you? All of nineteen?"

Logan rubs his arm like I hurt him but then laughs.

"Yeah, but I'm mature, y'know. Mom says I was born an old man."

There's a little hope, close to the hole in my heart, and I imagine my mom there, wanting me to experience different kinds of happy feelings. The feelings are like small gumballs filling up the globe on top of a gumball machine. Dr. Winters thinks it's a good way to visualize enjoyment in my life.

I imagined the first one, purple with the seven words Auntie T told me, "Oh Allee, I'm so glad you're here."

Logan's name is on the second gumball, and it's yellow.

Another, a green one, has a picture of an allée on it. Three gumballs. It's a start.

I like to figure out surprises and ask, "So, half an hour? That means you're taking me out of the city."

"No, and that's the last hint."

He looks past me, out the window, ending the conversation. I know he isn't going to give up any more info, so I watch the other passengers. Their stories seem to emanate from their bodies. I sense mostly pain.

Or, maybe not. But that's what I imagine. The pain I see on their faces could be my own reflection. Dr. Winters called it something like "projection." I don't quite understand that concept either. But everybody looks sad to me. Like they're in pain.

I glance over at Logan to see if he feels it, too. But I don't think so because he looks at me and smiles.

"You good?"

I nod and return the smile, then look back to the people. Like me, they all got up this morning and walked onto this bus. They are all sitting, breathing, waiting to arrive somewhere. Being on the bus with them and Logan lifts my loneliness.

As we transfer onto the next bus, I ask, "Are you abducting me?"

"God, no! You'd make my life a living hell!" But, he winks. "This is actually the way to Clairmont Park. You need to get out of Emberton more. The city is gorgeous. I can't believe you've never been out of the neighborhood."

Whatever. Mom never bothered, so neither did I.

I was hoping today's outing was more and casually smirk, "Oh, is that what we're doing? You're teaching me how to make better use of the bus system?"

"Well, that's not all," but he doesn't give any more details.

For the rest of the trip, I people-watch, breaking away from the things usually looping through my mind. Logan points to a few things around the city, and I sway side to side in my seat, thinking about how fun it is to do something different. There is a rhythm to the ride, and everyone on the bus moves in unison. We're all connected, synchronized, and I love being with them. I put the image of them swaying in their seats onto a fourth gumball, a white one, with me and Logan in the middle of them.

"Okay, this is our stop!" Logan pulls my hand before I even get a good look out the window.

We hop down the steps in the middle of the bus, and I'm glad he lets go once we're off the bottom step because it's so hot, my palms are sweaty. He was right about the sweater and pants, beads of sweat collect around my face, the urge to push my sleeves up intensifies.

Can't let that happen.

We walk, and I refocus my attention on the trees and flowers. When Logan said *city*, this is not what I was expecting. He pauses under a sign that reads HORTICULTURAL CENTER.

"Well, this is it! The start of finding beauty in a sometimes very ugly world. And..." he opens his backpack. "...I packed us a picnic!"

I peek inside and see chips, wrapped Wawa sandwiches, and bottled water.

"We're having a picnic?"

I want to hug him, but instead punch his arm again.

"This is very cool."

Me punching him in the arm doesn't feel very cool, though, so I make a mental note not to do it anymore.

We follow a paved walkway toward the back of the building. It opens to a large space with huge trees, vibrant flowers, and manicured lawns. I stop to take it all in.

"Wow, Logan, this is awesome!"

A long, thin rectangular pool with small fountains catches the reflection of large oaks and the blue sky. White puffy clouds sail through the water, and I laugh at the upside-down world. It's only May, but the sun is brutal.

No Swimming is posted around the ankle-deep pool, but three toddlers are in the water, splashing each other as moms or nannies sit and chat on the low rectangular wall. When the little kids stop running, it seems as if they're standing on the clouds. They put their fingers down to splash, and the clouds ripple away. When they run off to another section of the pool, the clouds rest back on the water.

I ask, "Does that pool have a name?"

"Hmm… not sure if it's named for anything, or anyone. We'll have to pick up a brochure on the way out."

Logan keeps walking, and I run to catch up.

"But y'know," he adds, "that type of low pool is called a reflecting pool. Like the one in Washington, D.C."

To the left, metal horses seem frozen in time as if an ice queen stopped them mid-gallop on the lush grass. A few steps lower than the reflecting pool, a sundial sits in the middle of a small landscaped garden.

"Does it actually work?" I ask and run my fingers across the bronze engravings winding around the circular structure: Roman Numerals are on the outer ring, towards the center ring names of large cities from around the world are separated by the months of the year. The heavy sundial rests on the shoulders of four kneeling women, representing the four seasons. The details are fascinating.

Logan looks closely at the triangle sitting in the middle of the sundial and says, "I'm sure it works. We'll have to figure it out. Has to do with this triangle and its shadow, right? I never learned how to read a sundial in school. You?"

I look at him to make a snarky comment about all the things missing in Emberton's curriculum but stop when I see the trees lined up behind his head. It is as if he's standing at the entrance to a tunnel of trees. I'm speechless and walk past him to get a better look.

Logan walks behind me.

"Okay, so I guess you see why I brought you here… Well, what do you think? This is Cherry Allée."

"God! Are you frigging kidding me right now?"

I walk between the cherry trees lining the grassy path, taking it all in, thirsty for it to fill me. When I reach the end, I turn and look back toward the sundial. Past the sundial, the reflecting pool continues the structured lines of the cherry trees. It's as if the trees are directing me, no, inviting me, to move forward, to see more.

"Here, let's sit on this bench and eat something."

He takes my hand, and this time I don't pull away. He knows what I need. He knows what I would love. He did something totally for me.

This is a new feeling. And I'm not too sure what it's all about.

I look at him and ask, "Why? Why did you do all this for me?"

We sit on a bench under one of the trees, and Logan hands out the hoagies and bottles of water.

"I love the city. I hate all the ugliness, but it's important to remember what's right about it and the good people in it. It may not seem like it sometimes, but there really are more good things, more good people, than not. I just wanted to show you wonderful things on your birthday."

This is something my mom would do. No hidden agenda, nothing asked for in return. He even sits away from me on the bench, his backpack a chaperone separating us.

As we eat, Logan chats about other things he wants to show me around the city, and I allow myself to relax. I'm distracted by the heat of the day and want nothing more than to allow the shade of these trees to cool my body, starting with my arms. I finish my hoagie, then slowly raise the sleeves of my sweater, up to my elbows.

A breeze brushes my forearms, scars are safely hidden under the intricate designs I drew over them last night. Art passed down through the African, Indian, and Middle Eastern generations adorns my arms. I rest them, designs exposed, on my thighs and take a slow, deep breath in. I feel light.

As light as a bird.

Logan announces, "I even packed us Twinkies for dessert! I forgot a candle though."

He turns to hand me the small yellow cake but pauses when he sees my arms.

He doesn't say anything.

With every second of silence, I feel sillier about the designs and reach over to grab one of the Twinkies.

I snap at him, "What, never seen an Indian dotted sun motif?"

He doesn't take his eyes off my arms. "Did you do that?"

Shame creeps into my awareness. Maybe drawing on your self-harm scars is something just me and my shrink are supposed to know about.

I put the Twinkie down and quickly lower my sleeves. The wind is blocked from caressing me, the heat's trapped next to my skin. Tears spring into my eyes, making me hate myself even more, and I hear Tony from far, far away, "Freak."

The lightness is gone as heaviness pours over me. My shins itch.
Logan kneels in front of me.

"Don't hide them. Allee, they're beautiful!"

I want to run. To hide. To disappear. To become invisible.

I want to cut.

I want to scratch.

But I remember what Dr. Winters explained and whisper, "Trigger."
I take a slow, deep breath and repeat, "Trigger."

The panic dissipates.

Logan looks as scared as I feel and asks, "What? Are you okay?
Allee, can you hear me? Are you okay?"

I want Logan to know and slowly push my sleeves back up. He
hasn't moved from kneeling in front of me. He gently touches my forearms, tracing the designs, feeling the scars under them. He slides his
hands under my arms, rests them on my thighs. I look into his eyes,
waiting for the accusations, the disappointment, the judgment.

But there's none of that.

He whispers, "Beautiful."

I look up at Cherry Allée and etch it onto another gumball, a blue
one. On a bench under one of the cherry trees, I sit and Logan kneels
in front of me, my arms cradled in his.

Chapter 30

That following Monday, Auntie T and I are called into the police station. Not so bad, really. I get to miss half of Monday's classes. Hopefully, Auntie T will want a Dunkin coffee after this. I'll grab a biscuit sandwich and not have to bother with my normal library granola-bar lunch.

We're ushered into a small room and introduced to Detective Carter. She doesn't look too old, probably in her thirties. And her blouse is buttoned correctly. She's not too fat or too sloppy or too skinny. She kind of looks…normal.

"Thanks for coming in to talk with me, Ms. Craig," the detective says, then looks at me. "You too, Allee." She points to the chairs and looks down at her notes. "Is that how you pronounce it? Like Ally McBeal?"

Who the hell is Ally McBeal?

I glance over at Auntie T, but she's lowering herself into a chair, eyes fixed on the floor. She's not good at looking at people anymore. Like, maybe she'd rather climb under a comforter and stay in bed for a couple of weeks instead of putting up with questions, stares, and whispers.

I get it.

My seat has a dark stain. I convince myself it's just an old coffee spill and slouch into the chair.

"Actually, my name rhymes with ballet. But a lot of people pronounce it as alley."

"Okay, got it." She writes something on the notepad and then looks at Auntie T. "As the officer said as you came in, my name is Detective Carter. Since Tanaya's body was found in a different jurisdiction, I'm now the lead investigator trying to bring all the evidence together. I'm hoping I can answer some of your questions. And maybe, if I ask some questions, you'll remember something new that we can use to help with the investigation. I have all the evidence and statements given to the police. Do you mind clearing some things up for me?"

Auntie T sits motionless, doesn't answer. The detective turns to me. I'm going to have to do the talking. "Yeah, sure. We were wondering what's been going on this past week. We haven't heard from anyone."

The detective nods. "I've been collecting all the evidence uncovered here and over by Mount Penn, checking into things myself, and talking to people on my own. I apologize no one has gotten in touch with you. I am your point of contact for now on."

I think I should be angrier for her not getting in touch with us sooner. Like the cops earlier, does she think Tanaya just ran away and then slipped and fell off that mountain trail?

She continues, "It says here that you, Ms. Craig, never met the individual called 'Stretch.'" The detective turns to me, "But you, Allee, knew him and didn't like him. Was there a reason? Any specific interactions that you can give more details about?"

"He came into the pizza shop, twice. With two of his friends. His friends didn't talk much. Stretch gave me the creeps. He wanted me to go to parties down by Snake Road. I only went once. He laughed at my job at the pizza shop."

"Did he ever tell you he could give you things? Take care of things? You know, financially?"

I remember the cash he left for me on the counter. "He tipped me fifty dollars for a $30 food order." I lower my eyes and whisper. "I took it."

The detective chuckles. "Well, who wouldn't?"

I'm not too sure and ask, "Right?"

She flips through her papers. "Don't you worry about taking that. Put it to good use."

I nod and she continues. "Anything more, like telling you he would take care of bills or could show you how to make more money?"

"No, nothing like that. It's the way he looked at me that made me feel uncomfortable. I wondered what Tanaya saw in him."

She nods. "Can you tell me a little about his relationship with Tanaya? Did she ever tell you anything, you know, so I can understand what may have been going on between the two of them?"

"She really loved him."

I dig my thumbnail into the cuticles of my other hand. I don't want anyone to think bad things about Tanaya. I want to protect her.

Like I should have done, before she disappeared.

"Well, in the beginning, I think she loved him. But then she seemed jumpy. Like whenever she got a text, she'd tell me she had to go take care of something and then leave quickly. She seemed sad, too. Like she wished things were different. I told her she should break up with him but she said things were complicated."

"Did she ever give a reason why she couldn't break up with him? Why things were complicated?"

"No, but she always had new clothes, shoes, leather jackets, jewelry. Stuff like that. She never came right out and said she owed him anything, but she said Stretch explained to her how much she was worth. Something like that. I told her he didn't own her. Tanaya got quiet after I said that, like it made her think of things. And then she told me I wouldn't understand. It was the last conversation we had."

I can feel Auntie T's eyes on me. I can't look at her.

Detective Carter writes more things down, then asks, "Did the police officers take from the house all the things Stretch bought her? Did you notice if they left anything behind? Or, maybe, if she hid something."

I shake my head. "Auntie T and I had to wait outside on the day the police came to search the house. When they let us back in, they asked us to give them everything Stretch had bought her. That was easy. Everything was hidden in the closet. After they left, the bedroom looked pretty much the same as when I first moved in. All the trash bags stuffed in the closet were gone."

It was like they took Stretch out of our bedroom. Now, the closet only has Tanaya's and my clothes and shoes from before.

But no Tanaya.

I finally look over at Auntie T.

"I haven't found anything else hidden since then."

Auntie T is dead-staring me. My lies are making her hate me.

I hate me, too.

Detective Carter looks at the two of us and lets out a little cough.

"Auntie T, I can come over later today and have a look with you. Will that be okay?"

Auntie T puts her head back down. "Yeah, sure."

It's just a whisper. The first time she speaks. I'm hoping she'll get more responsive to people now that Tanaya's body has been found. The not knowing where Tanaya was made Auntie T lost.

I remember the drugs and feel the need to clear that up again. "Those drugs on her bed a few months after she met Stretch, she wouldn't have done drugs unless he convinced her to use them. Y'know? She wasn't like that until after she met him." I look over at Auntie T. "I just want everyone to know that."

Detective Carter stops writing and looks up at me and then over at Auntie T. "I know this is very difficult for the both of you. I'll do everything I can to find out what happened. Hopefully, by finding out what happened, Tanaya will be able to rest in your hearts. That's my promise, my goal. I can't fix things for you, but I can help her rest within you."

I feel a little hope that maybe Detective Carter *can* help. Doesn't seem like Auntie T even heard her though. She doesn't move.

I've been wondering about Frank and Mouse. "Did you ever find his friends? The two guys he was always with?"

"We've followed up on leads. Frank is the guy most of the kids said was Stretch's right-hand man. He has been helpful but not one hundred percent honest. The other guy is missing." She looks at her notes. "Mouse. I have here they call him Mouse. Can you tell me anything more about them? Are these the guys who came into the pizza shop with Stretch?"

"Yeah, that's them. Stretch got impatient with them, you know, mad if they didn't order their food fast enough. He was either charming or nasty. No in-between. I don't know why people hang around him. They do what he wants, even though he's an ass." I think for a moment. "You know, I feel like Mouse hated him. It wasn't anything that was said. It was more his attitude. Frank didn't act that way, or at least I didn't see it. But Mouse seemed to have a problem with Stretch."

Detective Carter scribbles more notes. Even if it isn't helpful, she's at least taking what I say seriously.

So I add, "Um, it may not be important, but the night before she went missing, we were all down at Snake Road., Mouse put his hand on Tanaya's thigh, and Stretch got really mad. Like, his face was going to explode. Like he wanted to kill Mouse."

Maybe he did, and that's why the cops can't find Mouse. Tony's face would get like that. Anger changed his appearance. Scary as shit.

All this makes me think, *Where's Stretch?*

"So do you know where Stretch is? Have you talked to him?"

The detective takes a big breath in and looks through some paperwork. "Yes. We've pulled him in a few times for questioning." She shakes her head. "Not surprising, he's staying squeaky clean and very cooperative."

Detective Carter leans forward in her seat. "This may be hard to answer, but I want you to be very sure of your response. I'd rather you say, 'I don't know' then make something up just to protect Tanaya. That won't help. I need you to be honest."

I nod, and she asks, "How did Tanaya seem when Mouse put his hand on her thigh? What was her reaction?"

My memory does a slideshow thing, working backwards from when the red Solo cup splashed beer on her boots, the yank on Tanaya's arm, and Stretch's angry face.

Tanaya had spun her head to Mouse, and I could see her profile. Her eyes and mouth were wide in disbelief.

"Surprised. She had a look of surprise on her face and was about to say something to him, but then Stretch pounced on them both."

The detective writes some more things down and then takes two business cards from her pocket. "I want to help, and anything you think of later on, anything you remember seeing or hearing will help with the case. Don't feel bad about calling me, even to ask a question. We look at everything, because sometimes it's a small memory that takes us down a different path, a path that helps us catch the person who did this."

Detective Carter hadn't said anything about my phone call to the police station, about what I saw outside Larry's.

"Did the cops tell you about my phone call? I left a message at the station, about Stretch yelling at Mouse on Fifth Street, outside Larry's Deli, telling him to leave town."

She looks through her notes and shakes her head. "I don't see anything here." She looks up at us, "Frustrating, but not surprising. Since Mount Penn is in a different jurisdiction, outside the city, there's information coming at me from different offices. Tell me what you saw."

I tell her all I can remember about the scene outside the deli, when I was hiding behind the tires: the truck conversation, the slaps, Mouse's cockiness as he walked toward the bus station.

And then I add, "No one said Mouse did it, Mouse didn't admit guilt, in fact, he blamed the other two. I used to think it was Stretch, but the more I think about it, Mouse, Stretch, or Frank could have done it." My heart sinks. "Or, maybe none of them. Maybe it was someone else."

Detective Carter closes the notebook. "That's all good, Allee. I'm glad you didn't approach them. You did the right thing. Mouse is probably far away, but we have our ways of finding people." She hands us the cards. "For now on, you call me, directly. Anything you find out or remember, I want to know about it. All information goes through me now. I'm the one connecting all the dots."

Auntie T places the card in her purse. "Um, where…" she puts her shoulders back and lifts her chin, "Where did she die? On that mountain trail?"

I look at her and reach for her hand. She pulls it away…

… she doesn't want me to touch her.

Detective Carter notices and looks at me with raised eyebrows. then shifts her eyes back to Auntie T.

"It doesn't seem likely, but I can't go into detail. You will have many questions over the next few weeks and I will get you answers to help bring some closure to this nightmare."

Auntie T puts her head down with a slight nod.

"We found her iPhone by the abandoned houses near the boulevard, and that's a pretty good clue. But, because it's an ongoing investigation, that's all I can share with you. We have to keep an open mind, on everything." The detective stands and looks at Auntie T. "Okay?"

"Yeah, sure. Of course." Auntie T stands, too, and looks at me. "I didn't know she had an iPhone."

Her words sound like she wants an explanation from me.

But I got nothing that will make all this pain go away. Tears burn as they collect in the corners of my eyes. I try to remember everything Dr. Winters told me to do instead of hurting my skin. But I can't stop myself. I pinch then pull the thin skin on the inside of my left wrist. I pinch and pull as hard as I can. And the tears stop.

I stand and slide the card into my jeans pocket.

Detective Carter asks, "One more thing, are you aware of any tattoos?"

Auntie T shakes her head. "I saw one on her collarbone when I went to identify her body. It's probably one of those fake tattoos.

Tanaya said she thought tattoos would be a regret she'd have when she got to be an old lady. She said they stretch and fade on old skin. Or worse, get all wrinkly." She sighs. "I guess she didn't have to worry about that. Getting old."

I'm torn between telling the detective what I know about the tattoo and destroying Auntie T's image of her daughter, risk her hating me even more.

Better not to say anything.

Auntie T leaves, and I follow her through the corridors, but just as we're about to step outside, I put my hand on her elbow. She pulls away from me again. I think this shit-feeling about myself is going to stick for a long, long time.

"Auntie T, I forgot to tell Detective Carter something. Can you wait for me here? I'll be super quick."

I run back toward the interrogation room. The detective's standing in the hallway talking to an officer.

"Um, Detective Carter, she did have a tattoo, a permanent one I'm pretty sure. I saw it, but I'm not sure when she got it. She never told me she was getting one, never showed it to me. I saw it when she was sleeping, the night before she disappeared."

If she cares I'm interrupting her conversation, she doesn't show it. The officer walks away, and Detective Carter turns to me.

"Hmm. That's odd, kids post their tats all over social media, but there was nothing on any of her accounts. They usually don't keep them secret. Have you seen anyone else with a similar tat? Is there any conversation going on about them? "

"No, not that I heard. But, you know, I'm not exactly BFFs with anyone. Tanaya never mentioned it. Maybe with Dorie..."

"Just so we're on the same page," the detective interrupts me, "what tattoo did you see?"

"Just one. On her collarbone." I touch my collarbone, remembering. "A small black rose tattoo."

Detective Carter nods. "Okay, Allee, thanks for coming back and letting me know. We'll take it from here and keep you and Auntie T posted on all we find. Do me a favor, keep the tattoo quiet for now. There may be a reason Tanaya didn't talk about it. It's part of the investigation, and the less people know what we know, the faster we can figure things out. Sometimes tattoos are used for illegal operations. I have some people working on it for me."

What?

I mumble. "Sure. I didn't want Auntie T knowing about it. I don't think she would like knowing about some of the things Tanaya was doing."

As I turn to leave, she calls after me, "Allee, take good care of Auntie T. The next few months are going to be rough. But maybe it would be more helpful if you opened up to her. Let her know what you know. Just keep it quiet at school and on the street."

I nod. "Of course."

But I'm not so sure telling Auntie T is the right thing to do. She didn't even bother waiting for me outside the police station. I have to run four blocks to catch up to her.

"You okay?"

She walks even faster and whispers, "I feel so stupid whenever I'm called into talk to these cops. I missed so much in her life. And I don't want to say something that is not what was going on." She stops abruptly and looks at me. "I didn't know she was in trouble. I listen to all you say and wish I had helped. You both needed me. And I didn't know. I was so stupid, thinking all you needed were clean clothes, food, dinner on the table."

She takes a big breath, but not to calm her nerves. The words that come out bite the air between us. "You lied."

I think of every excuse for why I lied: how tired Auntie T always was because of the hours she worked, how tired I was because of the hours I worked, how Tanaya swore me to secrecy, how I was afraid of being thrown out of the house, justifying what Tanaya did, convincing myself it wasn't any of my business.

But it all sounds so lame.

I can't think of anything to say to make it better. I want to say something to make it all go away so that I can feel better. But what about Auntie T's feelings? Telling the truth will hurt me. But telling the truth will help Auntie T.

"I'm sorry. I didn't tell you," I say. "I should've told you, asked for help."

And then, because lying has fucked up my life, I throw the truth out there.

"She did have a permanent tattoo."

Auntie T's eyes widen, "What?! But she didn't want a tattoo." She takes a few angry steps toward me. "What else, Allee? What else should I know that you haven't told me?"

There's a metal bench next to the small community playground. I walk toward it and sit while four or five kids laugh and scream, climbing all over the nooks and crannies of that equipment. Auntie T may not want to sit, but I'm so shaky I don't trust my legs.

The playground activity is a good distraction because I can't bear to look at her. She walks over and stands in front of me, doesn't sit. I look down at a massive dandelion growing through a crack in the pavement.

"He gave her a nickname. She was Yaya."

A whispered sound escapes her mouth. Within that gasp of fragile air, I think Auntie T broke.

I don't even have to explain to her what a yaya is.

She knows.

And then I tell her everything: the cell phone, the different ways she'd sneak out of the house, the Snake Road parties, the piercings, the night she cried in my arms, the way Stretch seemed to be manipulating her, her rose tattoo, the roses next to her picture at the memorial, the "S" signature.

When I'm finished, there's only a brief silence, and then she fires away, question after question. I answer them all as honestly as I can, and as I talk, the story of Tanaya takes shape.

When she's done asking and I'm done answering, she walks away.

And I let her go. The kids slide, swing, climb and laugh.

She'll never forgive me. I'll never forgive me.

Chapter 31

At my next session, Dr. Winters told me to give Auntie T time to "process things." Auntie T not talking to me...I have no words for that feeling. On the fourth day after Auntie T and I met with Detective Carter, I woke up knowing one thing for certain—I need to start my own investigation.

I open the front door as Auntie T walks out of the upstairs bathroom.

I yell up to her, "I'm heading out for a bit. Need anything at Larry's?"

There's a slight pause, and then she answers, "Nope. I have the afternoon shift today. I'll be leaving here around eleven."

I wasn't expecting her to answer, but there she was, answering me. A happy feeling jumps inside me and comes crashing out of my mouth, "Okay. Have a great day. I'll see you later. I'll think of something for dinner and get it together. I'll have it ready so you just have to heat it up when you come home."

I hear myself but can't stop talking. *Ugh!* Not wanting to mess up this perfect moment when Auntie T talked to me, I quickly pull the door closed and hop down the front steps.

I can feel it in my bones, things are going to happen today.

It takes me just ten minutes to walk the five blocks to the boulevard. The houses facing the twelve-lane highway are huge and in different states of decay. Thousands of cars rush past these old homes, day and night, but no one bothers to look at the dying monstrosities. They would have been impressive when they were first built, beautiful even.

But now, they're depressing and dangerous. Even in the light of the morning sun, I'm on edge walking around here. But I need to go back to the beginning. Or, is it the ending? To stand where Tanaya may have breathed her last, to feel the surroundings, see things for myself. My gut will let me know if it's the place where Tanaya's life was snuffed out. I can't just sit around and wait anymore. I need to show Auntie T that ...

I'm sorry.

The words sound too basic. I need to show, not just tell her.

Since her body was found, Detective Carter said there hasn't been any activity in the houses where they found her iPhone, so they called off the police surveillance. They only drive by the area for a nightly check. This morning, I'm free to walk, think, and feel without the cops asking all their questions, crowding my space, or staring at me from patrol cars.

I turn away from the boulevard and walk around the block. These homes face away from all the traffic, so it's more private. This has to be the street. Stretch isn't dumb. He would use this quiet street for his activities.

I lean on a telephone pole and look at the empty houses. Most of them aren't even boarded up. About six of them look ready to collapse. Trees and vines grow out of broken windows and chimneys. It isn't hard to imagine the street at one time filled with kids. Parents calling them into dinner as they shout plans to meet the following day.

I used to watch them on my own street even though I never went out to play with them. It was easier to just be with Mom. Whenever I started friendships, there were questions about my parents and where they worked. Sometimes new friends would want to come and play in my house.

Yeah, that wasn't going to happen.

That's what made it easy with Tanaya. She lived seven blocks away on the other side of Fifth Street—the dividing line between okay and not so okay. I thought she was unaware of my chaotic world with Tony and I liked it that way. I guess we all keep secrets and lies.

She never even asked if she could come over to play. Looking back on it all, it was probably Auntie T who navigated those embarrassing situations for me and Mom. She always had us over to her house. Maybe she told Tanaya why she wasn't allowed over in my part of the neighborhood.

Doesn't matter. I was just glad I didn't have to worry about that in our friendship. Auntie T always welcomed me when I showed up on her doorstep, no questions asked. No questions from Auntie T meant she was plenty aware.

None of that now. Death ended my family and my friendship with Tanaya. All of it collapsed like the last house on this street: a pile of bricks with broken window panes and soiled couch cushions.

Shit. That's too depressing, even for me.

I decide to walk down the block and give each of the standing houses a good look. But not from the pavement. There's an eeriness here. I put a little distance between me and the houses and walk in the middle of the street. Cars don't even bother to drive here. My gut tells me this is it. This is where she died. Somewhere on this street.

Across from the collapsed house at the end of the block, there's a shabby tent nestled at the entrance of the alley. A shopping cart is parked to the side, stuffed with plastic garbage bags. Some are dark, like the ones Tanaya had stuffed in the bedroom closet. Others are clear with trash shoved in them. Some are light green like the bags used at the dollar store.

Why would someone collect trash?

I don't think the person who lives here can be a reliable source for Tanaya's last few minutes of life. But, I walk closer because any news is better than what I have now. There's a pungent urine smell, and I hesitate for just a second, then call, "Hello, is anyone here? Can I ask a few questions?"

Peering into tents is never good. My mind thinks about all the tent shit I've seen on true crime shows: bodies with open sores, syringes all over the ground, human feces, mice scurrying out from sleeping bags, and bugs. Lots of bugs. Street life is not an easy life. For anyone.

I call again, "Hello? I was wondering if I can talk to you."

The flap pops back, and a small toothless woman pokes her head out.

"I'm not hurting anyone. No need to concern yourself with me. Just leave me alone, please."

"Yeah, sorry, but I need to ask a question. I was wondering if you saw a friend of mine around here. A few weeks ago? She would be about my age, a little taller. Darker complexion and longer hair."

She cocks her head and squints. "Maybe. What's in it for me? More coffee, donuts?"

I'm confused until I realize the cops probably talked to her and offered donuts and coffee. Dunkin is at the other end of the alley.

"Yeah, I'll get you coffee and something to eat. What do you like?"

Her toothless grin grows into an open, full smile and she clasps her hands together.

"Big coffee, lots of cream and sugar! And powder cream donuts. Lots of donuts!"

I have a little cash in my pocket, so I take off down the alley.

Whatever it takes, lady. But you better have some information for me.

I only have enough money for two coffees and two donuts so get two powdered-cream for the lady. There's no way I'll be able to stomach anything near that tent. May not even be able to drink the coffee. I order a large for her and a small for me.

When I return, I stand outside the tent looking for something to knock on. Nothing. Hands are full anyway. I roll my eyes and call out as politely as I can:

"Hi. I'm back. Here's your coffee and donuts."

There's a rummaging noise, and the flap lifts.

"Well, come on in," the old woman says. "I made some room for you."

The pungent stench explodes in my nasal passages—the smell of a whole lot of things that have gone wrong in this lady's life. I turn my head away from the tent and gulp down fresh air.

When the acrid smell dissipates, I shake my head.

"Yeah, about that. I'm not comfortable going into your....um, home."

She stares at me, frowning, then cocks her head again and smacks her lips. "Well, what are you going to do, stand out there and talk, holding the coffee and donuts? That's what those cops did. Silly. That's no way to share information." She ducks back into the tent muttering, "You should know better, young lady. Definitely not civil."

"Jesus Christ," I grumble, take another deep breath of fresh air and go in.

The woman giggles, as she scoots on top of a mattress then leans against a backrest pillow. It's rust red and as the woman puts her elbows on the armrests, she folds her hands across her belly. I still don't breathe as I lower myself onto the only chair: a low beach chair. The nylon mesh seat is so tattered my left butt cheek touches the ground. I don't know what to do with my legs. I stick them out in front of me, and my feet push up against the mattress.

I lean forward and hand over the bag of donuts and a coffee. The woman drums her fingertips together, up close to her lips. When she drops her hands to take it, her smile reveals the glimpse of youth, of pure enjoyment, of true appreciation for donuts. I forget where I am, smile and take a deep breath.

Toxic. That's what it feels like. The smell that hits my nostrils strips the lining in my nose. The sting makes my eyes water and my stomach wretch. I press my wrist up against my nose to keep the smell out of my body, out of my head. I search for something to mask the smell. My coffee might help. I flip the lid off and stick my nose over the top. Instantly, the rich earthy aroma pushes the other smells away. I make it appear as if I'm drinking the coffee instead of using the rich smell to hide the stench. My eyes peer over the rim as I watch the woman.

She nestles the coffee between her knees and takes the two cream donuts out of the bag. She holds them in one hand as she smooths the bag on top of her lap. She places one donut at the center of the bag and eats the other one. She makes appreciative noises the whole time she … I can't really say *chews* because she doesn't have teeth … *gums* the donuts. Noises rise from the back of her throat and escape the toothless grin. She licks her fingers when the first donut is finished and giggles in my direction.

I keep my cup in place and smile back.

"My name's Allee, what's yours?"

I use the new pronunciation of my name, letting the long a sound fill the small tent.

"Ooh, la, la! Allee, huh? Like a beautifully tree-lined grove."

She knows what an allée is?

The woman stares at me for a minute, a knowledgeable look in her gaze. It makes me lower the cup for a split second, as if something in the old lady is reaching out, to be recognized, remembered. But the stench invades my nasal passage, and the moment is lost. I raise the cup and peer again from behind it.

"I'm Rickety. I was Posey. Mom is gone, so no more Posey. Only Rickety."

She rocks back and forth, remembering something sad. The grin is gone until she sees the other donut. She clasps her hands together again. The memory disappeared, and she is happy. Powdered sugar covers her chin and chest. I feel like an intruder witnessing the joy of something so simple.

I ask, "Can I call you Posey?"

This startles her, and she glares at me. "Why? I'm Rickety. Call me Rickety."

"Oh, of course, Rickety. I got confused. Thought you were someone else."

I roll my eyes and take a sip of the coffee. To use it as a shield from the smells, I'll have to make sure I don't drink it too fast.

It isn't until the woman rolls up the paper bag, carefully places it in the bucket next to her mattress, and settles back with coffee in hand that I feel comfortable enough to ask questions about Tanaya. I need to be gentle. Treading lightly will be the best way to gain information.

"There's a lot of crime these days. Do you feel safe here, in this alley, in this tent? I bet you hear a lot of things going on."

I keep my tone indifferent, like it's a question that can be asked of anyone. Rickety lets out a disgusting snort. Coffee shoots out of her nose. She wipes it with her sleeve, and I try not to notice. Then she gets serious, lowers her voice, and looks right at me.

"Yeah, cockroaches and rodents. They scurry around, nibble at your toes."

"What? Are you serious?!"

I push up on the armrests to lift my butt off the ground and look around, expecting to see critters crawling all over the place. She snaps her head back and lets out a howl of laughter that fades into a chuckle as she smooths the stained sweatshirt over her boobs. When she's happy with how it's lying, she turns to me, daring me to say something. She stares at me the way Mr. Jenkins looks when he wants us to think, to make connections. I lower myself back onto the nylon half seat.

"You're afraid of the animals and bugs that run around here? I'm sure they're gross. Do they really, uh…" I shudder. "…Bite your toes?"

"Don't be stupid, girl. You smarter than that cop. She wouldn't come in and sit all civil like. Wanted me to stand outside my home to talk."

She hisses and then with a click of her tongue looks at her feet, moving them like windshield wipers for about six swipes, then takes a sip of coffee.

"If you're not civil, why should I talk?" Rickety squints to get a better look at me, "You stupid? Uncivil? No, no, no. You different. Think. Think, girl!"

I search my memory and think about what Rickety said about cockroaches and rodents.

And then it comes to me. The more I think about it, the more it makes sense: Mouse in the pizza shop, Mouse's contempt for Stretch, Mouse's hand on Tanaya, Mouse's rejected look when Tanaya showed surprise at his hand on her thigh, Mouse's anger when Stretch pulled Tanaya away from him. Mouse talking with Stretch and Frank outside of Larry's.

I whisper. "Mouse. It was Mouse."

Rickety lets out a happy squeal. "Yes, yes! You know!" And then she drops her voice, to make a point, "The cops will know when they listen. When they come, civil like, carry conversations and make connections." She smiles at me. "You see, now you know."

But how did she know it was Mouse?

Rickety gets a faraway look until some white powder on the armrest catches her eye. She picks at the larger pieces of sugar and licks them off her fingers.

She mutters, "Mouse, it's me, Tanaya. Mouse, it's me, Tanaya." Once more, in a whisper, "Mouse, it's me, Tanaya."

Tears appear and drop down her face. "Mom, it's me, Posey."

The memory invades the tent and takes her far away.

I lower the cup and with my other hand, reach out and touch her knee. I pull back when, in one swift motion, Rickety's head lifts and turns to me. Her eyes are dark with fear and her voice a whisper, deep and slow from far down inside her, "Rats know where I am. I don't like rats. They shut you up and take you away. Eat you while you sleep. Make you go to sleep and take you away."

Chapter 32

I call Detective Carter as soon as I get home and tell her everything that Rickety told me. She's not impressed with what I did.

"Allee, you can't go rogue on us. It's dangerous. Whoever killed Tanaya, Mouse or someone else, will come for you if they know you're snooping around. Even that old lady, Rickety. She even knows this and stays under the radar."

I snap back at her. "Well, I can't just sit around waiting for you and the do-nothing cops to decide on your next step."

"That's uncalled for. Things take time, and we're working every day on leads."

I let my exasperation release with an eyeroll. But she can't see it so I add, "Whatever."

"Allee, just call me *before* you decide to act on any fresh ideas. You have good insight, and I'll follow up with Rickety because of what you found out today. But let's talk out your ideas together before you try them out all alone. Okay? Can you do that for me?"

Not going to happen, but I manage to tell her, "Fine."

And for whatever reason, Detective Carter believes me and hangs up. Finally, I get to do what I've been dying to do since I left Rickety's tent—take a shower. Once clean, I make chicken salad for Auntie T to eat when she gets back from work.

I attach a note: "I hope you had a good day!"

I add a heart at the bottom of the note and slide it into the fridge. I think she'll like it.

I hope she'll like it.

I head to work with a feeling that maybe I can make a difference. Like, something I do can actually have a positive effect on others. It's a pretty cool feeling, so I label it as ACTION, put it on a tie-dyed gum-ball, and plop it into the imaginary gumball machine inside me.

Between phone orders and all the walk-ins, Logan and Dan listen to my story about Rickety and my follow-up phone call with Detective Carter.

I stop sweeping behind the counter and lean on the broom.

"Detective Carter said they've been trying to find Mouse. After I told her about Rickety, she said she's sending officers down to bring her in for questioning." I shake my head and continue sweeping. "I'm sure Rickety isn't going to like that. She'd be more cooperative if Detective Carter went and sat with her, in the tent. I'll check in on her tomorrow. I feel bad. It's because I said something that they're taking her to the police station."

Dan folds another pizza box and asks, "Why don't you stop back here before you see her? I'll get food together for you to take to her. How about a salad and sandwich?"

I think of how long it took her to gum through the soft cream donuts.

"No, I don't think a sandwich will work. She's more of a soup person."

He nods. "Not quite a soup restaurant here at the pizza shop, but I'll call down to Larry's, see if they want to help out. Call the detective tomorrow to make sure she's back at the tent and then let me know a good time for you to pick up the food."

I've been worried they might not let her go.

"Do you think there's a chance they won't release her? Won't let her go back to the alley with all her stuff?"

"Who knows what will happen once they have her in the police station. But wherever she is, Detective Carter will make sure she's comfortable, safe."

I hope he's right. The detective does seem kind, as long as she doesn't have to go into tents.

"Yeah, hopefully Rickety returns and everyone leaves her alone." I feel weird admitting it but add, "I kind of liked talking to her. She's definitely kooky—and a little spooky. But cool, too, ya' know?"

Logan walks up to the counter and stands next to me. The calm, solidness of him envelopes me without him even touching me. I wonder if he feels it, too.

He says, "They'll probably get info out of her by promising to take her back to her tent. They get info by making promises like, 'We'll take you back soon as you tell us everything you know.' That's the way they work. It's effective. Manipulative as hell, but it works."

Could it be that simple? I'm not sure it'll make Rickety cooperate. I had explained it all to Detective Carter that morning. How, if she went in and sat with Rickety, she would tell everything that happened. But the detective refused. I even explained how to put coffee up to the nose to mask the horrid smell.

"Absolutely not," she said.

I finish sweeping as two younger girls enter and approach the counter. I recognize them from the Snake Road party. They were at the far end of the cleared lot, flirting with Stretch as Tanaya sat with Dorie. They're not part of the regular crowd I see at school, the juniors and seniors. These girls are only about fifteen years old. The blonde, I think she was the girl Stretch was way too much into at the party.

I feel like I should warn them, let them know they're headed for trouble hanging with Stretch and his crowd. But why would they listen to me? I couldn't even help Tanaya.

I grab the notepad and the pen and practice some deep breathing… deep breath in and then slow breath out. From the diaphragm. This is another one of Dr. Winters' suggestions.

"It'll set up a 'pause' Allee, so you can check in with your thoughts and feelings. Deep breathing gives you time to reset, ground yourself when people or situations become too overwhelming."

My last breath out, then I ask, "What can I get for you?"

The blonde backs away from me. "Okay. Listen. Don't be blowing in my face like that. What is your problem? Do you have asthma or some other breathing problem?"

I'm so embarrassed, I put my head down.

I did not actually breathe in her face…Did I?

In order to read the taped menu, she steps closer and leans over the counter, her bracelet dangles. It looks expensive, not like the cheap metal ones from the dollar store. It has a heart lock and a key charm that keep reflecting the light. I want to start a conversation, to see if they know anything about Tanaya's last few days. And if this girl is still hanging with Stretch.

"Cute bracelet. Your mom and dad give it to you?"

The girl brings the hand with the bracelet up to her chest, then fingers the lock and key with her other hand.

"What? This? Oh, no, my parents would never buy me something like this!" And after a short pause. "My boyfriend gave it to me. It's Tiffany."

I can't help myself. "Expensive! You must have been dating for a while. Did he give it to you for a special anniversary or holiday?"

She stares at me, unsure of why I'd want to know, but then sighs and clicks her tongue. "Actually, we just started dating a few weeks ago. He thinks I'm special and wanted me to know that."

She looks down at it and adds, "He said he feels like what we have is what everyone else wishes they had in a relationship." She smiles as if to say, "Don't you wish you were me?"

Which couldn't be further from my mind.

"He must really care for you." I'm afraid to ask, but my insides are telling me to find out, so I add, "What's his name?"

This is too much information for her to share. "Oh, you wouldn't know him. He's older. Didn't go to school around here and doesn't have any younger brothers or sisters."

Part of me is glad she doesn't tell me. What would I do if it is Stretch?

I convince myself there's no reason to believe it is Stretch. And then I realize that because I don't ask the question, I'm probably not that great at detective work.

She looks at the menu. "So what do you think, Nia? Do you want to split a pizza, or get sandwiches? My treat."

"Let's get pizza." Her friend walks over to the beverage case. "Want a soda?"

"Grab me a diet iced tea, thanks." She turns to me. "Plain cheese pizza and two drinks."

I write the order and ask, "What name do you want for the order?"

"Chloe. My name's Chloe."

Didn't Stretch mention a Chloe when he was outside Larry's, talking to Frank and Mouse?

As I write her name, Chloe taps the phone number Stretch wrote at the top of the taped menu with the scribbled *S* under it.

"Or maybe you do know him."

She looks up, blue eyes expecting some kind of explanation.

My stomach flips. "So, it's Stretch, huh?"

I casually rip the order off the small tablet and walk back to the fryers. With shaky hands, I clip it on the line by the ovens.

I whisper to Logan, "She's dating Stretch."

He looks out into the restaurant area and whispers back, "Shit! For real?!"

They slide into the first booth, and I head to the counter area so I can keep them in my peripheral vision, plan out my next move. They're too young, giggling at what each other has to say, heads together, whispering.

Logan comes up behind me.

"Didn't Tanaya say he's like 22-years-old or something?" He shakes his head. "There's no way he should be dating one of those girls."

"If only it was just dating! What should I do?"

"Your call, Allee."

He heads back to the line, shaking his head.

I think of Tanaya. And my mom. Maybe I should say something before it's too late. I bring the disgusting plastic menus up from under the counter to scratch off all the dried-on food, wiping them down while I think.

Will it even help if I say something? I doubt it.

"Order up!" Logan shouts from the back.

I go back to get the pizza and know it's now or never. I slide the pie onto the table, and though I don't know what to say until I actually open my mouth, it comes out clear, with confidence… and probably a little louder than needed.

"I was right, wasn't I? Your boyfriend's name is Stretch."

Chloe scowls. "What's it to you?"

I'm so nervous, everything pours out. I don't recognize my own voice. "He's no good! He's manipulative, and you need to get rid of the bracelet, get rid of him."

I feel my face burning, and Chloe slides away from me in the booth.

Nia barks, "Who the hell do you think you are?"

I glare at her. "His dead girlfriend's best friend!"

Dan comes from his office and walks up behind me. "Allee, Allee, what's going on?"

I point to Chloe. "Stretch is dating her. Giving her presents. She needs to know what he's doing."

Dan puts his hand on my arm, tries to pull me away from the booth. "Come on, Allee. This isn't the way, the place."

But he's wrong. What is the right place, the right time? That's what

I kept waiting for with Tony and my mom. And with Tanaya. For things to just fix themselves. But that never happened. There is no right time for anything. You have to make the time right.

I push him away. "No, Dan! I have to tell them. They have to know!"

I turn to Chloe. "Please, listen to me! No matter what he buys you, says to you, promises you. He'll take your life from you! You'll exist only for what he wants. You'll become his."

Dan tries to stop me again. "Come on, Allee. That's enough."

Logan comes over. "Dan, let her talk. They have to know."

Chloe looks at Logan and Dan. Then back to me. "What are you talking about? Are you jealous or something? You are one crazy bitch!"

I plead with her. "He will take over your life, Chloe. Don't give him your life. He's not worth it."

She fingers the bracelet. "What do you know?"

"I know you are worth much more than what he can promise you. Leave him, Chloe. While you can. Tanaya was his girlfriend. She never got the chance to walk away."

Nia takes a piece of pizza and puts it on Chloe's plate. Without even looking at me, Nia snaps, "Fuck off, skinny pink piggie."

The two of them start laughing, and the familiar shrinking feeling pulls at me. Makes me feel like I'm of no use. That I'm better off invisible.

But at least I told them. And when those words rolled right off my tongue, something happened inside me. At least I said something, and my feelings were set right. I did that, by just opening my mouth. I look at Logan, and he nods.

He gets it.

I turn back to the girls and know one thing. That shrinking feeling? I know how to make it go away. Do something, say something.

"When you need help, Chloe—and you're going to need it—remember what I said. Reach out and ask for it before it's too late."

Nia rolls her eyes, but Chloe looks right at me, sees me. For a split second, something registers on her face. She's not as confident about her relationship with Stretch as she would like people to believe. She senses something's not right.

But then she shrugs.

"Fuck off."

She takes a bite of pizza.

Chapter 33

Nobody's using the computers when I stop at the library on my way to get the soup Dan ordered from Larry's. There has to be another way to deal with the horrid smell in Rickety's tent. The thought of sitting with the stench makes me reluctant to go. But everything else about Rickety makes me want to return. I want to know more about her and how she ended up on the streets.

I type "how to mask horrible smells" in the search engine. Articles that pop up have to do with hospital smells and how nurses can better cope.

"Makes sense," I whisper. I click on the first article. "Hmmm. Let's see."

I don't have a lot of time so I scan the article and scribble suggestions on a piece of scrap paper: vapor rub, essential oils, mint Chapstick, strong mint gum, mints, and coffee grounds.

That explains why the coffee worked the other day.

I close the tabs on the computer and stop in CVS before heading to the deli. The essential oils and coffee grounds are too expensive, but I buy everything else on the list, then hurry to pick up the soup.

Just outside the tent, I put the mint Chapstick below each nostril and pop a mint into my mouth.

"Hello! Posey, I mean Rickety, it's me, Allee! I came for a visit."

Rickety doesn't throw the flap open.

"No, thank you! You told those cops, and they took me away. Go away!"

Guilt washes over me. Those cops probably had to drag her from here. Or, threatened to take her home away. I don't blame her for not wanting to see me. I walk away, but remember the soup and turn back to the tent.

"Look, I'm trying to find my friend's killer." I stand just outside the tent and plead with her. "Please, don't hate me. I didn't know Detective Carter was gonna take you in. I told her to come and talk to you personally. To sit down civil-like here and talk to you so she could hear about everything. But she didn't listen to me."

I sit down outside the tent. "No one ever seems to listen, do they? Please, Rickety, let me in. I brought you food from the deli."

There's a slight rustling, and then the flap is tossed back. She pops her head out and looks at the brown bag on my lap.

"Well, why didn't you say so? Wait here, one minute please."

She ducks back in and comes out struggling with a bucket.

"No worries, just need to freshen up a bit. I didn't expect a visitor. I was mad, you know. You made me mad." She limps, swaying side-to-side as she walks. She dumps the bucket down the sewer and leaves it near the curb, in front of me.

"Can get messy, sticky, you know. You have to care. Take care of yourself. Take pride in yourself."

I think of what was in the bucket and step away from it.

Rickety rubs her hands together.

"Well, come in. Let's see what you have for me today!"

I wonder how long it's been since she washed her hands.

Note to self: hand sanitizer for Rickety next time I'm at the CVS.

For now, I follow her into the tent and try not to think about it. I'm feeling pretty pleased with myself about the Chapstick idea. Not a full barrier, but the candy cane smell definitely tempers the stink.

Rickety plops on the mattress, and I hand her the pint of soup. They packed a salad so I place it on the orange crate next to the mattress. I hadn't noticed an old creased picture on top of the crate because a tattered stuffed blue bunny partially covers it. A woman and young teen are looking into the camera, laughing at whoever took the picture. Their smiles are identical.

I slide the picture out from under the bunny.

"Who's this?"

Rickety doesn't bother to look up or answer. She takes the lid off the carton and squeals.

"Creamy soup! My favorite! Is it chicken? Does it have corn?"

She doesn't wait for an answer but puts the carton to her lips and slurps. She didn't even bother looking for a spoon.

"Wait! I have a spoon for you." I reach into my back pocket and pull out the small bag with the plastic spork, knife, and napkin.

"Oh, you thought of everything. How very civil of you! We like that, you know, people being civil." She smiles at me. "Thank you, dear. Thank you."

She calms and relaxes into the backrest. If she's still mad at me, she doesn't show it. After a few more spoonfuls she asks, "Any crackers? Sometimes crackers are very nice with soup, you know."

I look into the bag and under more napkins, hoping someone thought to throw crackers in with the order. But there are none.

"I'm sorry, they asked me if you'd like a roll, but I said no because I thought it would be hard without..." I'm too embarrassed to say "teeth."

Does the woman realize she doesn't have teeth to chew bread or crackers?

Rickety laughs, flashes her toothless smile at me and points to her mouth, "Because I don't have teeth? You said no bread because I don't have teeth!"

She laughs and laughs until I feel so uncomfortable, I stand to leave. I'm not going to be able to get any information out of her today.

"Oh, did I hurt your feelings? No, no, don't go!"

She keeps laughing but manages to convince me to sit back down. I pop a piece of Double Mint gum in my mouth and take a deep breath. A cool sensation travels up my nasal passages and down my throat.

"Crackers soften in soup. Bread softens in soup. Then I can chomp on it. Next time, add crackers and bread."

She stares at me with that huge open-mouthed smile. I fight to keep my annoyance in check and change the subject by holding up the picture.

"Tell me, who's this?"

"You'll bring crackers next time? Crackers melt in your mouth. You don't need to chew crackers."

I put the picture back on the orange crate and let out a sigh.

"Sure, I'll bring crackers next time. Do you like the soup? There's salad, too."

"Maybe later for the salad. Chomping on salad is hard. But you need to eat veggies, right? Do you care and want me to eat salad?"

She looks sideways at me, an inquisitive look on her face. The laughter is gone. Pensive. Rickety looks pensive.

"Yeah, Rickety. I care. I'd like you to eat the salad, too." I lean forward and put my hand on the woman's leg, but she jerks with a scream, "Don't touch me."

I put both hands up. "Sorry, Rickety. I won't hurt you."

I lean back and slide my hands under my thighs. She looks down at my hands and nods, settles back, and takes a few more slurps. I sit in the quiet, just let her be. I think she forgets I'm here until, without looking at me, she says, "That's me and Mom. In the picture."

"What happened to her? Your mom."

"Don't know. They took her away. She was sometimes nice and sometimes mean. And mostly sad." She thinks for a second. "I think she got feelings mixed up. She didn't know how to be at the right time. Very confusing. Chaos is why they took her away. She was not civil."

I pick up the picture again and think about my own mom. In the picture, Rickety looks about 12 years old, maybe 13. When she was Posey.

I tell her, "My mom is dead."

Rickety shrugs. "Maybe mine, too."

We sit quietly, except for the slurping of soup.

Chapter 34

Ms. Davis looks as she always does when I pop into her office unexpectedly—guarded, but hopeful because at least I keep showing up.

"How are you holding up, Allee?"

I slide into the seat. "Okay, I guess. I decided not to go to prom."

Ms. Davis nods.

"It's just, without Tanaya, I don't want to go." I put my backpack on the floor in front of me. "It doesn't seem right."

Ms. Davis puts her hands in her lap. "That's a sad, but rational decision. At eighteen, you're free to make your own decisions. And you know, Allee, you make really good decisions. Keep trusting your gut to do what is best for you."

Tears start filling my eyes, but instead of pinching my wrist, I look down into my backpack for the letter. That was another Dr. Winters' suggestion.

"Keep your fingers busy with an activity as an alternative to pinching."

Yeah, another good, solid idea that actually works. Sometimes.

I take the letter out of the envelope and put it on her desk. It was Ms. Davis's persistence that even got the university to consider me. I didn't even want to go to college. Kind of still don't want to go, but Ms. Davis cared and knew what to do in case I changed my mind. She made a lot of phone calls for me. Seems like kids in my situation—one parent dead, one parent in jail—can get help for college finances. I just have to keep the grades up and stay out of trouble.

It gets so awkward in the house with Auntie T, maybe having somewhere to go is the right decision.

It takes just a second for Ms. Davis to scan the letter.

"Oh, Allee, congratulations!"

She runs around the desk and gives me a hug. I know it's how my mom would have reacted and don't mind so much. I let Ms. Davis hug me.

Kind of getting used to hugs … as long as people let go after a second or two.

"Pitt isn't so far away! They have great support systems set up there. I'll contact them and help you get situated…"

I interrupt her. "That's okay. I think I can manage. I want to go like all the other kids. You know. Show up and just start something new."

Ms. Davis steps back but holds my hands and smiles.

"That's a great idea, Allee. I'm so proud of you." She walks back to her seat and types on the keyboard. "If it's okay though, I'll write down the contacts for you to reach out for help if you need it. They have services for kids in crisis, and they're available 24/7. You may never have to use it for yourself, but just knowing it's there is a big help. And you might meet some other student who needs help. You'll know how to get it for them."

She keeps talking, and I wish she would stop. The last thing I want is people knowing my shit when I show up in new places.

On the back of the acceptance letter, she puts a Post-It note and writes names and numbers and then hands the letter back to me. Under the UCC Mental Health Crisis Response number, she wrote *and you can always call me* with her own personal number. My eyes fill.

"Thanks, Ms. Davis."

I slide the letter back in its envelope.

"I'm proud of you, Allee. You got this far because you're willing to reach out. Always reach out. It's the people who try to do life by themselves who get into the most trouble."

I think about the people who have been there for me: Ms. Davis, Dan, Logan, Auntie T, even Dr. Winters. My mom used to be there for me. But she never reached out for herself. Mom thought she could handle everything on her own. So lonely.

Ms. Davis whispers, "You okay?"

"Yeah. Sad that my mom didn't know how to reach out. I think she would've walked away from my dad if she hadn't had me."

Ms. Davis sighs, and we sit looking at each other. This is the best part about Ms. Davis, when she's cautious with my thoughts and feelings, letting sentences fill the room and sink in before talking.

And when she starts talking, she usually makes sense.

"I'm not sure about that, Allee. I'm not a mom, but I think she probably viewed you as the most important thing she ever did, ever created." She gives me a weak smile. "You were worth everything to her."

Mom isn't around to ask. But I am starting to feel a little better about not having to know things for sure. Not knowing is okay. Well, that's what I keep working on. It stops the thoughts running around inside my head when I remind myself some things can't be figured out.

"I think I'm going to be alright. You know? I don't know why. For the first time, I think I'm going to be alright."

"Maybe because you believe in yourself. And that's your mom's final gift to you. In the midst of the chaos and the pain, she raised you to believe in yourself. And you get to take that with you, wherever you go."

The end of third period buzzer sounds, and I stand. "Thanks, Ms. Davis."

I'm about to leave when I remember Chloe. "You know, there is some stuff going on with younger kids since Stretch started hanging around. I don't want to get anyone in trouble, but maybe, like you said, they can't help themselves. Maybe someone else will get hurt because I didn't speak up."

"Why don't you tell me what you know, and then I'll handle it from there? Kids have been getting into difficult situations since forever. The situations are different. Kids are the same."

"Maybe." I shrug. "I think Stretch is starting with younger kids. Two girls came into the pizza shop the other night. One said she's dating Stretch."

"Does she go to school here?"

"I've never seen her here. Her name is Chloe."

Ms. Davis writes something down on another Post-It.

I add, "She looks about fifteen."

Ms. Davis does that raising-of-the-eyebrow again.

"Really? Thanks, Allee. I'll check into it. And I'll keep your name out of it." She looks up at me. "Will you do me a favor?"

"Yeah, sure. What?"

"Stretch getting involved with someone much younger may be of interest to Detective Carter. Will you contact her and let her know?"

Seems weird that the detective would care, but I answer, "Okay. Easy call." I swing my backpack onto my shoulder. "I'd better get to class. Thanks again. For everything."

Chapter 35

Dan and Logan hover like drones, whizzing about the pizza shop trying to get all up in my business. I'm suspicious at first, until I realize they must have heard that Emberton's Prom is tonight, and because I'm not there, they're monitoring my mood.

I try to ignore them.

At nine, Dan turns off the OPEN sign, locks the door, and brings out a deck of cards. He tells Logan to make a pizza for us to share.

I roll my eyes, "Is this about the prom? Oh my god, guys, I'm fine! Stop trying to make this night any different than all the other nights. I seriously didn't want to go to prom."

I think about Auntie T, still not talking to me.

"And I didn't just want to sit at home so I came to work."

They look at each other and then back at me. They don't believe me.

"I don't want to be there! The two of you are so annoying, part of me wishes now that I did go! Or at least lied to you that I was there! You're making me feel, I don't know, weird. Can we just be normal?"

Logan nods and heads back to the line, but Dan persists.

"You know, Allee, let us do this for you." He looks back at Logan, then walks closer to me. "You came into our lives, and well, made it a little better. It was your pushing to get food orders online that doubled our sales in just two weeks."

Logan comes to the front. "Yeah, about that, Dan. We're going to have to get more space for all the orders, and maybe another line cook."

He waves Logan away.

"Oh please, you're doing just fine. Quit complaining."

Logan shakes his head but winks at me.

"You don't need the prom," Dan continues. "We get it. But, maybe you can let us do something nice for you because we want to. What's wrong with doing something special for a friend? Logan and I, well, we enjoy your company. We're all here together. Looking out for each other. Our own family."

"Don't you want to go home? Aren't you tired?"

Dan's eyes mist so I look away. How come they can't understand it's uncomfortable for me to have fun? Sometimes I feel like everything will be good, like in Ms. Davis's office last week when I told her I thought everything was going to be okay. But that feeling slipped away when I went home, and Auntie T still wasn't talking.

Maybe good feelings make the bad ones feel worse.

But Mom's smile as she stood on top of the stepstool comes to mind. The two of us laughing on our way to the laundromat. Sitting in the bank together as we opened my account.

And Tanaya. Her smile, the funny way she would snort when she laughed. The bike rides when we were in fifth grade. We used to teach each other tricks on those bikes. Lying flat on the seat, arms and legs extended out. Trying to stand on the seat. Riding with no hands.

These are the memories that are coming into my mind more and more. Each day, I seem to remember another one. The painful memories are still there, but they're starting to lose their sting.

The joyful memories don't seem to be fading. Instead, they seem to be trying to rise up and be remembered.

Maybe I have it wrong. Maybe it's the good times that make the bad times bearable. Besides, Dan is still looking at me. This man will not just walk away.

I turn to Logan. "Well, I am hungry. Half plain, half 'roni?"

He smiles. "You got it, one large pizza coming up, half plain, half 'roni."

Dan walks over to the first booth, wipes it down, and starts dealing cards. "500 rummy? Is that what we're playing?"

I laugh. "Seriously?! That should keep us busy for a while. Get ready to lose, gentlemen!"

- - - - -

It's after ten when the game ends. Logan's the winner and doesn't even gloat.

"Just lucky," he says.

God, whoever gets him for a boyfriend is going to be one lucky girl.

We're cleaning up when the phone rings. I pick it up as I count out the cash drawer, "Pop's Pizza, we're closed, but please call again."

The voice on the other end surprises me, and I stop counting. "Oh, hi, Detective Carter."

Logan and Dan walk over as I slide down the side of the counter and sit on the floor to talk to her.

"We found Mouse," she explains. "He's being detained in a jail in Atlanta, Georgia, until we can bring him back here."

"Really? That's good, right? You got him!"

The detective answers, "Well, we have a long way before trial, but since we have Rickety's statement, at least we can start the process. And most importantly, Allee, he can't hurt anyone else while we build the case against him and get justice for Tanaya."

I nod. "Yeah, of course. Thank god."

My insides feel relieved but nervous, too. What do they call that? Cautiously optimistic. I feel cautiously optimistic.

"Thanks for letting me know. Does Auntie T know?"

"Yes, I just hung up the phone with her."

"Okay. I'll head home soon to be with her. Let me know if I can do anything. Anything to help."

And then I ask about Stretch and Chloe, if she found out anything about them.

She shuffles some papers around and says, "We're following up on leads for a different investigation. But I'm not free to talk to you about that."

That's weird.

Then, she adds, "Look, I have to go, but will fill you in on things when I can."

"Oh, okay. Thanks for everything." I hand the phone to Logan, so he can hang it up as I just sit and get my thoughts together.

"They found Mouse." I pause. I can't believe it myself. "He's in Atlanta."

"Oh, Allee, that's good! They know where he is."

"Yeah. It was because of Rickety that they were able to go after him. They're working on getting him back here."

I remember her saying, "Mouse, it's me, Tanaya." Freaky spooky the way she kept saying it over and over again.

And then I remember what they said on the news when her body was first discovered.

"It was a brutal attack."

The images of Tanaya fighting off Mouse, all by herself, cut deep into my heart.

I wasn't there for Mom. I wasn't there for Tanaya.

The black hole grows.

Frigging gumballs will never fill this dark emptiness.

Logan sighs. "I'm almost finished with the floor. How about I walk you home? Just give me a minute to finish mopping."

Dan nods. "Why don't you two go now? I'll finish up."

I look up at them. "I don't know how I could have gotten through the last five months without you both. Thank you, for everything."

And then, I ugly cry. Streaky, sobby, messy tears complete with snot.

Logan and Dan sit on the floor, one on each side of me. They don't look at me, they just sit there and let me cry.

I imagine what I must look like, sitting between these two guys. In the middle of my cry, I let out a sad little laugh, "Oh my god, are these tears ever gonna stop?"

Chapter 36

MOUSE: IN THE MIND OF A KILLER

Atlanta's finest grabbed me two nights ago as I walked into the warehouse for the night shift. Scared the shit out of me. Seriously, almost shit my pants.

Now, lying here on this thinner-than-a-yoga-mat mattress, my brain relives those last few minutes with Tanaya. Goddamn it. Few weeks on the run and she was finally quiet in my mind. Now, she won't shut up again.

"Get off me, Mouse!" … such a bitch.

She was trying to get out of the car, and I grabbed her. She screamed like I was some kind of monster. I don't get it. I had to be better than the strangers Stretch got for her. I treated her like a person, a princess. Those clowns just wanted to use her.

So did Stretch.

And hadn't she shared her sandwich with me, down on Snake Road?

Fuckin' tease.

I even asked her, tried to talk to her in a nice way.

"Come on, Tanaya, what did that guy have that I don't got? Is it because he pays you?"

I hate that she was making me beg.

She stopped screaming to tell me how much I was hurting her. And that she didn't want to kiss me.

What did she say?

Oh yeah, "… not even on the tail end of a blue dolphin."

Ouch.

Those blue dolphins usually make the girls ready for anything. And everything.

And oh my god, the squirming. That girl could wiggle herself into and out of anything. Before I knew what was happening, she was halfway out of the truck, hanging headfirst onto the street, screaming like she was in a horror movie.

Those screams! I needed to shut her up. By the time I got to her side of the car, she was standing, ready to bolt. I stepped in front of her, and she let out another blood-curdling scream. Then, she was crying, like a baby.

"Mouse, it's me, Tanaya!" over and over again.

"Shut up! Just shut up!" I screamed into her face.

Then, to shut her up, I punched her. She fell against the car and onto the street's cracked asphalt. She made me do it. Why didn't she just do what I asked?

Once she was quiet, I could think. I looked up and down the street to make sure there weren't eyes where they shouldn't be.

Stretch knew how to stay off the radar, keep his business under wraps, that's for sure. No one was looking out windows or walking down the street. Houses were boarded up, businesses abandoned. God, some of the houses were growing their own forests. Even the guy Tanaya was with didn't come to the window. Probably sleeping like a baby after all Tanaya did for him. Stretch said she learned quick. And was the best.

All I wanted was a little taste.

At the end of the street, there was a makeshift tent inside the alley. I had taken a minute to watch and listen. But there was nothing.

Probably strung out on heroin, whoever it was.

Tanaya was sprawled out. When I looked at her, all I could think about was how mad Stretch was going to be. He'd be all over my case for messing with his number one girl. He'd beat the shit out of me, or worse. If Tanaya talked, and I knew she would, I'd lose what little life I carved out for myself.

Looking back, it all seemed so logical. Logic, with a little luck, always wins.

She was already unconscious. She wouldn't feel anything. I dragged her onto the truck bed, climbed on top of her, and strangled her. So easy. She looked like she was sleeping. She opened her eyes for a second, all wide and scary, then went limp. Like she woke from a nightmare and then fell back to sleep.

Frank had a toolbox installed in the back of the truck the week before. It was meant to be. The toolbox key was even on the keychain, and the box was empty. If it had tools, I would've had to lug them all out before putting her in.

What a job that would have been.

I didn't have much time, had to get the truck back, and place the keys near his bed before he realized they were gone. Frank was pretty stoned when I took his keys. Easy to take the truck, hopefully just as easy to put it back.

I placed Tanaya in the box, pulled her knees up so I could close the lid, and then locked it. Before jumping down from the truck bed, I took one more look around.

Nothing. No one. Everything was quiet, a ghost town.

I had chosen north. Nowhere in particular. I'd know what to do once I saw the perfect place. I was so sure of myself, I turned on the radio, and listened to music. Even today, The Angry Waiter's lyrics keep playing in my head, drowning out her screams:

> *Pretty little darlin' with the lacey restraint*
> *Teasing roosters on the street*
> *Counting your chickens*
> *Before eyes even meet*
> *Before eyes even meet...*

Anybody but me, huh, Tanaya? Screw you.

Just turned it off. I had turned Tanaya off. That was all.

I boarded the bus right after Stretch told me to leave the city. It was Tanaya who helped me get away. I had lifted the Altoid tin and the wad of bills from her backpack.

She *had* given me a little something anyway.

The cot's not only flimsy, it creaks when I move. At least I don't have to work in that fuckin' warehouse anymore. Or sleep in a motel room with mouse shit everywhere.

That's pretty funny. Mouse shit. I start laughing and can't stop.

A guard hits the bars with his baton.

"Shut up, Mouse. It's quiet time. Just have to follow the rules for another day. By tomorrow night, you'll be on your way back north." He lets out his own chuckle. "I'm pretty sure you won't be laughing there."

Chapter 37

Since graduating—well, I should be more specific. That's what Dr. Winters keeps telling me; be as specific as possible putting words to thoughts and feelings... Crap like that.

Those last three words are my own, not hers.

Since receiving my diploma—I didn't bother going to the graduation ceremony—I take the bus to my therapy sessions with Dr. Winters. Knowing that I'm heading off to college in a few weeks makes me feel old. Our weekly morning sessions are helpful, but I miss the drop-in visits with Ms. Davis.

I'm not as close to Dr. Winters; she's stand-offish. But she is making me feel more connected to...what? What do I feel more connected to?

I look around the bus at the other passengers.

To them? Do I feel more connected to these people even more now than when I was with Logan on the bus heading to Cherry Allée?

Why do I even care?

We're all just traveling around, doing our best.

I look out the window and see my reflection.

What about myself?

Do I feel more connected to myself?

I rest my head on the window.

Yeah. That's it. Who knew it would be so hard, connecting all the puzzle pieces that felt disjointed inside me when I first went to live with Auntie T? When Mom first died?

There's a new poster hanging at the front of the bus. The graphic is the back of a girl walking down a deserted street. **WHEN YOU CAN'T WALK AWAY** is written in red bold font across the top. I make my way toward it so I can read the smaller print:

Can you recognize the signs of coercion?
Is someone pressuring you to engage in
physical or sexual contact?
If it feels like you are being pressured
to do something you don't want to do,
it's coercion and coercion is a crime.
Know your rights!
You have the right to say no.
You have the right to walk away.
You have the right to turn down a sexual act
because it makes you uncomfortable.

Why was this never talked about at school?
At the bottom of the poster in black letters:

Your sexuality is your gift to self.
No one has the right to take it. Ever.
We are here to help. You are not alone.

And then there's a phone number. I wish I had seen this poster before Tanaya disappeared.

But, she didn't understand what Stretch was doing. She couldn't see the abuse.

She wouldn't have called.

- - - - -

Dr. Winters shakes my hand and then walks back behind her desk to sit. I keep thinking about the poster on the bus and don't wait for her to settle back into her seat.

"We need to help kids. You know, like Tanaya. They fall into relationships and can't climb out. What can we do?"

She sits and folds her arms on the desk. "Sexual exploitation is a huge problem. People think it happens in someone else's neighborhood or in third-world countries. They don't want to think about it happening to the kids in the house down the street or even in their own families." She looks down at paperwork. "Sometimes, it's the parents doing the exploiting."

I stare at her. I don't want to believe that.

But then I think of Tony. Tony manipulating my mom, taking

all her money for his beer and drugs. Beating her up when it wasn't enough, or she was late coming home. Me, having to hide my money from him.

I tell Dr. Winters about the poster. "There was a poster on the bus, about coercion. How come I've never heard about that before? You'd think it would be talked about in school."

Dr. Winters nods. "That would be a good idea."

She reaches into a drawer and pulls out a pamphlet.

"I worked on a committee to put it all down for kids. And their parents. If kids understand what is happening to them, are aware, they might reach out for help."

I scan the pamphlet. It has all the information from the poster and even more places and contacts for help. About 20 shelters are listed.

"We're waiting for the school districts to approve their distribution," she says. "There's so much red tape involved because people don't think it's a problem. Don't want to talk about it."

I wonder if the stores on Fifth Street would put the pamphlets out for people. Probably not. Nobody would want to have a pamphlet about sex stuff in their shop. They didn't even want to hang Tanaya's picture.

But I can try.

"Can I take some? You know, to put in the pizza shop. I can ask other stores, too. They have kids coming and going all the time."

She stands and walks over to a tall file cabinet.

"They're private businesses, they can put whatever they like in their shops. And who better than you to ask them?"

She slides open the cabinet and brings out a handful of pamphlets wrapped with a rubber band. She hands them over.

"Don't be surprised though, if they don't want them in their businesses. This is not a cause people want to be associated with."

I hold them close to my chest and think of Chloe. She won't listen to me but maybe reading something in a pamphlet will make a difference. She could read it without Nia around. Maybe that's better than making a big deal in front of the people who like to hang around Stretch.

Dr. Winters interrupts my thoughts.

"You know, Allee, when you find your voice, you have power. You can make great change, one person at a time."

I don't feel that way. I feel small.

Dr. Winters continues, "They're targeted, you know. The most vulnerable." She sits back down and rolls her chair forward. "That's what others call them. Personally, I think they're very strong, doing the best with what life has dealt them. They are survivors, doing what is needed to stay alive. You learned how to become invisible, and it saved you. You became invisible and waited for your mom. Not that you should have needed to do that. Nobody deserves that. But that's how you survived. Now, you are learning what it means to really live. To have worth by the very fact that you exist."

I think of all the times my mom walked down the alley, whispering for me. When I heard my name, I knew it was safe to come out. She would check me, from head to toe, making sure there wasn't a scratch on me.

She would say, "He didn't hurt you, did he? Are you okay? Let's go get something to eat."

She'd take me back to the house. Tony would be passed out on the couch. Or gone. Mom knew when things were safe, when we could enter the house again.

Dr. Winters lowers her voice. "Some kids have no one to wait for. They run from the abuse in their homes into the arms of someone who promises friendship, a roof over their head, a warm meal. An embrace."

I remember how Tanaya fought to be with Stretch, defended his actions whenever I warned her about him. She found something in him that I couldn't give her. Something she thought was even more important than what her own mom could give.

But why? I don't think this will ever make sense to me. And now that she's gone, I'll never be able to ask her.

I sigh. "It won't really help, will it? They're being offered things out on the streets that they can't get at home. Kids think the new life will be like a fire escape."

"A fire escape? If you mean something that will help them get free from their current situation. Yes, it seems a good choice. Initially, anyway."

This makes me feel heavy inside. "But it isn't. It might even be worse. Helping them is useless. Why would they believe a pamphlet?"

She shakes her head. "No, not useless. Just tough. We get information out there. Set up a lifeline for these kids. It's only when they're ready to make their own decisions that anything we do can help them.

We keep doors open, let them know they have options. Identifying options is the only way someone can change their situation."

Chapter 38

I sit in the front seat of Logan's Ford Focus doubting my next move. Earlier at work, when we started closing the shop, I had told him my plan to pass out the pamphlets at Snake Road. He offered to drive me, and I accepted. Now that we're parked on the side of Snake Road, at the bottom of the path that leads to the gathering spot, I'm not so sure.

I look up the trail and feel the opposite of brave. If I was by myself, I would keep walking down the street, pass this path. But with Logan here, there's pressure to follow through.

I look over at him. "You'll wait for me?"

Logan nods. "Right here, with the window open. Yell if you need me."

The pamphlets are reassuring, and I hold them tighter to my chest. If my words don't come out right, at least it's all written down for people to read. They have everything in them that I can't explain. The clicking of Logan's hazards gives a sense of purpose, like the rhythm of a drum on the way into battle.

"I got this, right?"

He tilts his head and sighs. "Well, I wish you'd let me go with you so it could be, 'We got this.' But, yeah, you got this."

"Thanks, but I need do it myself. I should've gotten help for Tanaya." He nods again but doesn't say anything. "Knowing you're right here, waiting for me, means a lot."

He winks. *God I love that wink.* "Right here. I'm not going anywhere."

I open the door and step onto the narrow path. I can hear voices, just a murmur, and anxiety sickens my gut.

The climb to the top of the hill gets my blood pumping. When I duck into the small opening in the bushes, the vine tickles my neck again, and I ache for Tanaya. I force air in and down. Expand my chest, disperse the ache until it's manageable.

Two girls are sitting on the makeshift bench, one in pigtails, one a redhead. I don't recognize them. They're cracking up about something. Red Head falls off the plywood, and Pigtails falls on top of her. They stifle their laughs. Even drunk, or high on some drug, rules are followed at these gatherings. Too much noise will bring unwanted attention, cops will show up. No one wants to be blamed for that.

I probably should've come earlier, on a night I didn't have to work. Now that it's after 11, they're all shitfaced. I scan the area. There's about fifty kids here at various stages of intoxication. They're never going to listen to me. They'll just laugh.

I'm about to leave, but then I see Stretch sitting on a tree stump on the other side of the clearing. Groups of kids walk by and block my vision from time to time, but there he is. Chloe stands behind him, her hands draped around his shoulders, a loose hug around his neck. Nia and about seven other girls sit just off to the right—like his harem.

I decide to stay. I *have to* stay. If they don't listen to me, at least the pamphlets will be shoved in a pocket or, if tossed on the ground, they'll blow around the clearing. Someone might pick one up and read it. Getting the word out is the first step.

The two girls in front of me stumble around, trying to stand. They hang onto each other and laugh as they fall back onto the ground.

Hilarious.

I walk over to them. "Hey, I'm giving out these pamphlets."

Pigtails takes one. "Awesome! What is it? New band playing?"

She scans the pamphlet and hands it back. "Yeah, no thanks."

I don't take it from her. "Do me a favor and don't litter, stick it in your pocket. You can throw it away when you get home."

She looks at me like I'm nuts, but shoves it into her back pocket. "Whatever."

I walk across the clearing, toward Stretch.

Redhead calls after me. "What are you? A narc?"

A few of the others turn to look at me. I don't care, I have my purpose. I walk toward Stretch, handing out the pamphlets as I go, getting the information out there.

They can read them later.

Or not.

I can't control what they decide to do. Dr. Winters is always urging me to follow through on goals.

Looking like a complete idiot, but following through on my goals…

Stretch hasn't moved but watches me with a grin. Chloe's eyes are wide with a sense of dread while Nia rolls hers, then looks away. I'm about to ruin the good thing she thinks she's got going with this group.

Stretch speaks first. "Allee, right? Tanaya's friend."

I take a deep breath, push the words out with some made-up sense of coolness I didn't know I had. "Yeah. How's it going, Stretch?"

"Good. Everything's good. Dorie and Carissa aren't here. Is that who you're looking for?"

I look around. Come to think of it, I don't see any seniors here, don't even know most of the people starting to circle around.

I raise my voice so they can hear me, "What? Senior class can't be bothered with Snake Road anymore? Was it a wake-up call when Tanaya's body was found? Those who know better can't be bothered hanging here anymore?"

I turn back to Stretch, something registers in his eyes.

His grin disappears as I keep talking, "They loved Tanaya. More than you ever did."

Auntie T and I had read all their notes in the lavender box. We sat together the night after the service and cried. Hours and hours of crying together.

Groups of kids circle tighter around us. Stretch's eyes shift to them, but he doesn't move.

He keeps his voice calm, controlled.

"We're not bothering anyone. Those of us who want to be here are here. Those who don't want to be here aren't. It's a free country."

He stands and faces the crowd, they all nod. He turns back to me, his voice hardened.

"But tell us, Allee, why are you here?"

"Handing out some pamphlets, it being a free country and all. I'm allowed to hand out some reading material."

He shrugs his shoulders.

"Do what you want." And with his creepy grin adds, "Global warming and recycling and all, are you sure pamphlets are good for the Earth? We can all look up information on our phones. Cleaner option and you know it." He sits back down, "So I ask you again, Allee, why are you here?"

Self-doubt clouds my plan. I turn nervously to everyone circled around us. They don't care. I can't make a difference. Stretch is right, it's a free country.

But I remember what Dr. Winters said when I was leaving her office with the pamphlets.

"Start a conversation. That's all we have to do. Get them talking. That's why we can't just swoop in and save them. They need to be aware of what is happening so they can make their own decisions."

The rose tattoo on Tanaya's collarbone. The one flower she hated and he had it stamped on her. And she let him do it. Stretch took options away from her until she could only see him.

Even though my insides are trying to shut me up, my voice is steady, sure of itself.

"Tanaya was your rose. Let's just say I'm the thorn in your side."

He cocks his head. "Well, that's the most interesting thing you've ever said. A little lame. But interesting."

I hand a pamphlet to Chloe. She looks at Stretch, doesn't take it. I hand it to a shorter girl standing next to her. She shakes her head and folds her arms.

No one moves or says anything until Nia jumps up. "What are you on, Allee?!"

Stretch chuckles.

She grabs the pamphlet, rips it, and drops it on the ground. "We don't need you, Allee. Even Tanaya used to talk about how pathetic you are. Leave. You're not wanted here."

Tanaya wouldn't have talked smack about me.

"Don't know what a good friendship looks like, do you, Nia? Tanaya always had my back. Do you even know what that means?"

She pushes me, and three of the other girls move forward, circling me like a pack of she-wolves.

Shit. I didn't think they'd come at me!

Stretch leans forward, stupid-ass grin plastered on his face.

Frank runs from somewhere in the back, looking ready to fight. Stretch puts up a hand, shakes his head, and Frank stands back from the group.

I get it now.

Stretch said it himself outside of Larry's—he doesn't like any-body's shit on him. He won't get his hands dirty. That's why he hasn't been around the last month. Laying low, letting everyone else do his dirty work. Keep us divided, and he has control without ever looking like the bad guy.

I look from Nia to Chloe and then to the bigger group gathered around us. Phones are up, recording. They're waiting for something. I know this pause.

But I'm done cowering. That's no way to live.

I raise my voice, it's shaky, but I continue anyway, "I'm not the enemy. Not asking anything from anyone. Just leaving these pamphlets here and walking away."

Nia's voice is low, a rumble. "Such an asshole, Allee. Take them with you."

I look at Chloe. She lowers her eyes.

Nia looks to Chloe, then back to me, moves forward to block me from Chloe's line of vision.

She gets in my face, "Leave, now, skinny Peppa."

She's wearing a tight halter top, and I see a small black tattoo on her collarbone. She has dark skin, but with the full moon, I can see it's a sunflower. And the stem is curved, matching the stem on Tanaya's rose tattoo. Tanaya would've never gotten a friendship tattoo with an underclassman. Let alone Nia.

Pigtails is just behind her, wearing a camisole. There's something on her collarbone. I walk past Nia to get a better look, it's a small iris tattoo with the same curved stem.

I spin around and look for more tattoos. It's a hot, sticky night, lots of skin exposed. I can make out a handful of kids with tattoos on their left collarbone, all with curved stems...curved like the letter S.

No one moves, they're waiting for me to do or say something. I walk over to Chloe, she takes a step back. She's wearing a corset. There's a white bandage taped on her collarbone.

What's going on?

I look at the tree stump. Stretch is gone, and Frank is nowhere to be seen. Nia grabs my shoulder, forces me to look at her.

"Did you hear me? Leave!"

I stare at her, don't back down. "Afraid of some words, Nia? They're just pamphlets."

She pushes me hard, fast. I fall back, hit my head on the log. She comes down punching and some in the group start chanting, "Fight, fight!" Phones are up.

She's heavy, I can't move. But I get a handful of hair just above her ear and pull with all my strength. Her head snaps to the side, and she stops punching to peel my fingers open, but I hold on, refuse to let go. I stand, her brown, coarse hair tangled around my fist, her nails claw into my fingers.

Chloe runs toward us and grabs Nia's arm, tries to separate us.

"Leave her, Nia, so she can get out of here."

I'm not going to let go of her hair and risk her hands all over me again. She tries to turn and look at Chloe, but her head is immobile.

She stares at me, "Let me shut her up, Chloe! She's a pain in the ass, trying to ruin everything."

"Well, yeah." Chloe keeps her voice down, whispers, "but she's also a fuckin' buzzkill. Let her go. We need her out of here."

No one moves.

Chloe calls out to the crowd, "Stretch already left, he said to keep things quiet. Remember the rules."

Nia's anger deepens on her face, for a different reason. I'm not sure why, but it has something to do with Chloe speaking for Stretch. Nia's angry as hell, but the fight for me has left her.

Why?

She growls, "Fuckin' ass, Allee. I swear. Get your grimy hands out of my hair."

Phones go down after I let go. Stretch isn't even here, yet he still maintains control. They do what he says.

I pick up the scattered pamphlets and walk over to the stump Stretch had been sitting on. "I'll leave these here. Just in case someone wants to read them."

Nia smirks, "Great, we'll be sure to study them. Thanks."

Everyone laughs. I notice a few phones are still up, taking pictures, making a video.

They're waiting for something to happen so I call out, "Did you ever think about Stretch? What he gets out of everything you do for him? He buys you things, but at what price? Tanaya loved him. Gave him everything. And now she's dead."

Chloe steps forward. "You're out of line, Allee. That had nothing to do with him. He was with me that afternoon."

"Don't you care that she's gone? Stretch told her over and over how much he loved her. That he would protect her. She did everything for him. He destroyed her long before she was killed."

They're listening to me, watching. With this last sentence, Chloe looks struck. I said something she already thought about, something she doesn't like.

Nia sees it too and lunges at me. She plows, shoulder first, and I'm in the air before falling on my back again. I don't have time to recover, she starts kicking my side. I turn to protect my ribs, and her boot squares me right in the gut. I struggle to breathe as she continues kicking. I shut my eyes as the tip of her boot lands right at the top of my nose. I move my arms to protect each body part, but she won't stop.

It's growing inside me… the rage that's been wanting to ooze free. It's on fire, igniting from deep down inside until it surfaces like molten lava and explodes through the air.

"STOP KICKING ME!"

I grab the foot that's about to land another kick, and she struggles to keep her balance. I roll towards her, wrap my arm around her other ankle, and pull as hard as I can. She falls. I jump up and sit on her chest, a knee on each of her shoulders. She kicks and squirms, tries to free herself. I put my hands on her neck. Blood from my nose drips onto her cheek. I don't feel any pain, anywhere. The more I squeeze, the redder her face and the stronger I feel. She can't talk, struggles to breathe. She kicks frantically.

And I don't care.

Someone leans over and shoves their phone in my face, the light shines on me. No one is trying to save her.

They're all screaming, "Fight, Fight!"

Stretch left her, and Chloe stands at a safe distance. No one is trying to help Nia.

This realization stops my crazy, and I yell down at her, "Quit squirming and I'll let go."

Her legs go limp, and I roll off her.

"Nice friends."

She's still gasping for air as I stand and turn to the group. They're disappointed I stopped; they fall silent.

But their phones are still recording; so I shout out to them, "Well, I'm outta here. But remember one thing. Stretch is nothing without any of you. He knows it. I know it. And now you all know it. Look who was the first one to leave as soon as we got a little loud, a little out of hand."

Nia coughs and with a raspy voice yells, "You're not worth his energy. In fact, Allee, you're not worth anything. No one cares what you have to say."

"Maybe. But it seems to me that none of you are really worth anything to Stretch. Just saving his own ass. He can easily swap any one of you for someone else." I look at their tattoos. "Rearrange his bouquet whenever he wants. That's all that's important to him. All he cares about. When you're tired of Stretch controlling you, your life is waiting for you. There are people who will help you find it. Good people. Don't be afraid to go looking for them."

They separate as I walk through the crowd.

Off in the distance, I see Logan at the top of the path. With each step, there's a crippling pain in my chest, and it's getting harder to breathe. There's pressure in my nose, and it's causing my left eye to swell shut.

But there's no way I'm going to show I'm hurting. I walk with my head up, straight and proud. This is going to be all over social media.

Probably already is.

Chapter 39

Two days later, I'm doing the best I can to hide the pain in my chest by taking shallow breaths and exerting as little energy as possible. Logan knows and grabs the trash bag out of my hand.

"Come on, you can hold the door for me. But that's it. No heavy lifting for you."

My purple, black, and blue eyes? Can't really hide that. But, you can always hide behind a good lie. Best way to get people to stop asking questions is to make something up and keep it simple: "Tripped getting on the bus and smacked my nose on the step." It worked the very first time I said it. Best way to convince people of the lie is to repeat it, over and over.

It's such a hot July night, the heat keeps spiraling rancid smells instead of letting them lift up and away into the night. The air conditioner broke earlier that day, and there isn't the slightest of breezes welcoming us into the alley.

I've got to do something about the long sleeves and pants. Since Logan knows about the scars on my arm, I slip the sweatshirt over my head and tie it around my waist, "God, I was dying in there!"

He looks at my newest mehndi designs and gives an "I'm-impressed" nod as he tosses the black contractor-grade trash bags into the dumpster.

"Cool. What is that called?"

"Henna."

I ordered some paste cones the week before and tried them out on my left arm a few days ago. The process is intense and involves a lot more concentration than just markers. I had to simplify the mandala pattern, and I can't work the cone with my left hand yet.

I ended up putting the henna on my left arm and sticking with a marker on my right. The henna stays on longer than markers, and I like how the design on my left arm is raised and changed from orange to brown.

"I'm experimenting with designs. This is supposed to be a lotus mandala. But my arm is too thin for the full circle, so I just halved it." I hold my right arm next to the left and laugh. "I tried to match it on my right arm with marker, so it would be the full circle. Well, oval anyway."

My right arm looks so juvenile next to my left arm, even Logan laughs at it. "Everyone has to start somewhere. But, Allee, seriously, I think you got something there. That's very artistic. And cool."

We walk away from the dumpster smells, and I ease myself onto the low concrete wall and ask him, "How come you never talk about your family?"

He leans on the wall. "My family's boring. I have a mom, a dad, two older brothers, and an older sister. They're all out working, living their own lives. I hear from them every once in a while. They come back for holidays. That's all me, Mom and Dad usually see of them. But, I can call them anytime."

"Boring sounds kind of nice."

I pull my knees up onto the wall and give my body's aches and pains a gentle stretch by wrapping my arms around my legs. I look up at the narrow patch of dark sky outlined by tall buildings. Even though I can't see them because of the city lights, there are millions of stars up there, staring down at me. And Logan.

He moves close enough that I'm keenly aware of his arm as it brushes the side of my leg. "No family's perfect, you know. I think you do your best with the people in your life. Gotta be true to yourself. Y'know, listen to your gut."

"You think that's it? Once everybody does that, they'll be happy?"

He chuckles. "Well, it's not easy! C'mon, think about it. We were born ourselves, but everybody tries to make us the way they want. Tellin' us what to believe, how to dress, what we can and can't do, making all our decisions."

"You mean, like we forget how to be ourselves?"

"Yeah. I think people try to find out who they are by listening and looking to everybody else." He shakes his head. "That's not going to work."

"Hmm." He may have a point. Dr. Winters sometimes talks about this stuff, as a way to feel less anxious about what other people are thinking and expecting.

"You think that's what it's all about then? Fulfillment, happiness. Stuff like that?"

"Yeah. It's okay to go to people and ask what they think, but in the end, people would do better to sit and think and listen to themselves."

Tanaya comes to my mind — how lost she seemed in the end, 'gone' before she actually disappeared. She didn't listen to me when I tried to get her to change. Maybe she needed to figure it out herself.

I look at the sky.

"Maybe they can't. Maybe they doubt themselves too much to trust themselves. That's why they trust other people instead. And those people are sometimes no good, selfish, like Stretch."

Logan's silent for a minute but then he grabs my hand and walks in front of me, folds his hands around mine, rests them on my knees.

"Maybe. Maybe they need to surround themselves with people who help them see their goodness. People who'll tell them how wonderful they are."

I smile at him and he leans in for a kiss. My heart's all jumpy. He stops a few inches from my lips.

"No pressure, Allee. You're pretty amazing, and I'm here if you ever want to see if we can be more than friends. I'll hold off and let you take that first step, if it's what you want. I can wait."

I feel the breath of his words on my face. I believe him. All of it, and lean in for the kiss. A tear runs down my cheek and he gently brushes it away.

He whispers, "You okay? We can walk away now, never talk of it again."

I shake my head, "No, that's not it. These freaky tears aren't for you, or us. They just keep leaking. Like I have no control over them. Happy, sad? Doesn't matter. I just cry."

I gently pat my bruised eyes with the sleeve of my sweatshirt. "Can we take it slow? You know? Everything has always been so fast and chaotic in my life. I'd like something to happen, slowly. Watch it unfold instead of crashing into me."

He puts his forehead gently on mine. "Yeah, sure. I'll follow your lead."

Chapter 40

The next day, after school, I stop by Dorie's house. I knock, and she's so pissed off that I'm taking her away from whatever she was doing, she tries to close the door in my face.

I put my hand up to keep her from slamming it closed. "I need your help."

She gives an exaggerated sigh and takes a quick look up and down the street. But then, she opens the front door wider. I'd rather sit out on the porch to talk, but obviously, she doesn't want to be seen with me. I follow her in and hope no one else is in the house. What I have to say makes a lot of people edgy. But, I'm getting pretty good at saying what I have to say. Every time I open my mouth, I care a little less about what people think.

"What do you want, Allee?"

She sits on the couch, doesn't offer me a seat, so I perch on the arm of a plaid oversized chair next to the door.

"You done with Snake Road?"

She smirks, crosses her arms. "What's it to you?"

This may be harder than I thought.

"I stopped by this past Friday night. Lots of new kids, but I didn't see anybody older than 16, except for Stretch and Frank."

Her lips twitch to the side, her eyeballs bore into me. "So? Everyone's getting ready for college. People move on."

"Is that why you stopped going?"

"God, Allee, why do you care? I told you before, people can do what they want. It's not our job to police other people." She leans back. "It's all over social media what you did the other night." She lets out a short humph sound. "Who knew you'd be the one standing up to Nia?"

I feel the heat on my face but ignore it, stare back at her. "I care. I care that Tanaya's dead and that asshole is targeting others."

She shrugs. "It's not up to us to keep people from seeing who they want to see. Or make a few bucks."

Even though no one likes to mention "tricks" or "prostitution," Dorie's too smart not to know what's really going on. "You know it's more than that. Why don't you care what he's doing to them?"

Dorie lowers her eyes, thinks about something she's not ready to say. Instead, she looks up at me and whispers. "It is a free country. Why shouldn't girls, and boys for that matter, be able to get what they want?"

"Oh, come on. Did he ever try to get you involved?" I try to think of something to say, get her to admit he's a trafficker. "Did he ever call you a flower?"

She tilts her head, lowers her eyes.

I shudder, remembering the creepy feeling when he breathed the air around me deep into his chest. "He whispered 'lilies' in my ear. Honestly, that whisper's loud as hell in my brain. Can't seem to shut it up. How 'bout you? Got anything that keeps playing over and over in your head?"

There's a slight pause and then she whispers, "Asters."

I nod. "Dorie, we can help. He's collecting girls, like he's some kind of fucked up vase, or garden. He doesn't see them as anything other than what he can use them for. Clipped from a stem and then given to others for a price."

She bites her nail, doesn't seem sure of something. I don't want to lose her. "Please Dorie. I'm only asking that you talk to the cops. Tell them what you know, you were at Snake Road almost every weekend. You can help."

She stands up. "Nah. Not my thing, Allee. I got other stuff going on."

I don't get off my perch, I'm not done trying. "How did you know not to go with him, to resist what he wanted?"

The edge in her voice slices the air in the small living room. "He has no right calling me anything. Fucking aster? Really? As soon as he whispered it, wanted me in his garden, I was like, gross. And told him to fuck off."

Garden? Is there really a specific garden?

"What do you mean? What garden?"

She plops back onto the couch, "I thought that's what you were talking about…The Garden of Eden. It's his company, gets girls—and boys—to work for him. Even told me he'd help pay for my college tuition if I worked for him. Well, at first he told me I didn't need college and shouldn't go because I could make a lot of money working for him without loan debt." She shrugs. "But I really want to do computer animation, you know, like gaming stuff. When I told him that, he said he would support me."

"But you didn't believe him?"

"God no, he's a sleaze bag. Besides, I have a scholarship. I don't need his help."

The frustration is getting to me. "Come on, Dor, you know the story. Kids go with him because they don't have options. They want things, but have no way to get them 'cept through people like him. They take what's offered. Stretch is just one dangerous option."

"People can always say no. He didn't push it once I said no."

I think of Tanaya and ask, "Why do you think Tanaya did what he wanted? Do you think she really wanted to work for him like that?"

She arches her back, stretches her arms. "God, Allee, why are you so dumb? She liked what he was giving her. It was an option she was willing to take because she wanted what he was giving. And she loved him. She would do anything for him."

For whatever warped reason, Dorie thinks the relationship was fine.

I remind her, "She's dead now."

"Yeah, but he didn't kill her."

My forearms are twitchy, my shins are itchy. I slide my hands between my thighs to keep from picking. "He promised to protect her, didn't he? Wasn't that part of their arrangement?"

She dead stares me.

"I'm just asking you to call Detective Carter. If what Stretch is doing is completely fine, then no harm done. The detective leaves him alone. But Dorie, you and I both know he's plucking those kids right out of their own lives and arranging them how he wants. You had options so could walk away. What happens to kids who don't have options? Or are lonely? Like Tanaya. I think she was really lonely. My friendship wasn't enough for her. Neither was yours."

She looks at me, shrugs a little.

"Auntie T worked more and more hours when I moved into their house. And when I should have alerted Auntie T, I turned a blind eye, because I thought it was the right decision. But it wasn't. There was

Stretch, filling Tanaya with more and more attention. I would give anything to change the decision I made. To have spoken up to Auntie T and show Tanaya what real love looks like, feels like."

I toss Detective Carter's business card onto the glass coffee table, then open the front door.

"They're getting younger and need to know, that's all. A fighting chance. You know something's messed up with what he's doing. In your gut, you know. If you really don't care about the others, do it for Tanaya."

Chapter 41

"If there's nothing else, Dan, I'll head home," I'm at the office door while Logan finishes wiping down the ovens.

Since our kiss last week, I find myself watching him. When he catches my eye, we smile and a warm sensation courses through my body. If Dan sees how goofy we've gotten, he's not saying.

Dan walks from behind his desk, picks up a small wrapped gift.

He calls, "Logan, can you come in here?"

"Yeah, sure, Boss."

There's a silly grin on Logan's face as he walks past me and stands next to Dan.

I ask, "What's goin' on?"

"Well," Dan hesitates, but then quickly hands me the gift. "We want to give you something special for a going-away present. We're proud that you're going to college, and we want to make sure you can still keep in touch with us, your friends."

I give him an awkward side hug and mumble, "Thanks".

I open the small package. It's a Nokia smartphone. The panic comes quickly, smearing dread into my mind, paralyzing me from moving on without Mom. It was supposed to be *our phones*.

But, she's not here, and like Dr. Winters is always reminding me, I am. When the dread, the guilt gets too much, Dr. Winters suggested I tell Mom something, so I whisper, "I miss you, Mom." Sure enough, the bad feelings push away, and an awareness of Mom floods my heart.

Dan interrupts my thoughts, "Logan and I wondered if you'd rather an iPhone..."

I shake my head. "No, this is more than perfect. With this, I can call you both and check in with Auntie T, too. It's what I need. What I want."

I look up and smile. "I love this."

The phone will help me keep good people close.

Logan adds, "If you want, I'll come over and help you set it up tomorrow morning."

I'll probably set it up tonight when I get home, but, I like the thought of him coming over tomorrow, so I nod.

"I'll even walk with you tonight if you can wait about 30 minutes."

I want to wait, to feel his hand in mine on the walk home. But I'm trying to keep from rushing into things, to set up time each day to just think and be. The quiet fifteen-minute walk home gives me time to be by myself after taking care of customers all night. Dr. Winters calls it self-care. I'm starting to think I'm going to miss Dr. Winters when I'm at college.

Didn't see that coming.

And Logan.

Definitely going to miss Logan.

"No, I'm good. I'll see you in the morning, though. That will be nice."

- - - - -

It stormed earlier. The smell of washed concrete fills the night air. I jump over the puddles. Street lights are reflected in the water that settled in sections of broken pavement. Ruining my only good pair of sneakers is a concern. Two weeks ago, they got soaked on the way home from work. Even though they've long dried, I still have to spray them with Febreze to keep them from stinking up the bedroom.

Not Tanaya's and my room.

Just *the bedroom*.

It'll never be *my room*. It was Tanaya's first. I'm the intruder. It's all so sad.

I watched Tanaya change in such a short time. And then snuffed out, gone.

"I miss you, Tanaya." I whisper as I jump up onto the first step of the house.

There are no lights on in any of the windows. Auntie T must be cleaning office buildings tonight.

"Why, hello, Allee. We've been waiting for you."

Two small figures come out of the shadows from behind a box truck that's been parked in front of our house for the past month. In the soft glow of the street light, I recognize Chloe and Nia. Pain sparks on my face, chest, and side. A tinge of green and yellow around each eye is all that's left of the bruises. And the painful memories.

"What d'you want?" I'm not afraid—but definitely curious.

Chloe takes a step closer. "To talk."

"Sure, but the kick boxer is not allowed on my property. She stays by the curb."

"Fuck you, Allee," Nia calls as I turn and sit on the top step. She doesn't come closer, though. She leans on the truck.

I call to her, "Good girl, Nia. Now, we just have to work on your vocabulary."

She stares at me, but doesn't bother to answer.

I won't take them into the house. Not scared, but also not dumb. If anything suspicious happens, if Stretch pulls up in his car, I'll scream, alert the neighbors.

I stopped wearing long sleeve shirts all the time, and in the soft glow of street lights, I see Chloe look at the intricate designs on my arms. She looks up at me, about to ask something. My eyes dare her to start with me, to tell me how stupid they look.

But she doesn't. Instead, she says, "Cool designs."

Then turns to sit on the step just below mine.

She doesn't look back at me. "They took him, you know."`

I have no idea who she's talking about. I can't see her face, but her shoulders are bent forward, her head is down. Nia is still standing on the pavement. I look to her for clarification.

"Stretch, you idiot. They took Stretch, and Chloe hasn't heard anything from him, or about him. What did you do? Tell the cops?" Chloe may be sad, but Nia is ticked off. "We know you had something to do with this. You're so jealous, you can't keep your fuckin' mouth shut, can you?" She's yelling.

I look down the street, to see if anyone is looking out windows. But there's no one. I warn her, "Keep your voice down! And I don't know what you're talking about."

Chloe whispers, "They came to my house the other day, two days ago, and took my phone. The phone Stretch gave me."

Ah, the damn phones. Good. Bastard got himself in trouble. It must have been Dorie, she must've said something. How else would Detective Carter have gotten permission to take the phones?

Chloe looks at me and pleads, "He really cares for me, Allee. And

I need him. What am I going to do without him?"

The desperation in her voice triggers empathy, and I put my hand on her shoulder. Surprisingly, she doesn't shake it off.

"Tanaya always said things like that, too. He's good at making people think he can solve all their problems, to trust him completely."

Chloe nods.

"But," I remember what Dr. Winters said about abusers and try to explain, "he only wants to take care of his own needs, his greed, his need for power and control by making you do what he wants."

Nia's voice cuts through the quiet post-storm night air. "Oh, yeah, goes to show what you know! He loves Chloe. Would do anything for her! You're such a jealous twat!"

She is not good at keeping her voice down on the front steps of a house wedged between 50 other houses. And she is not good at name-calling.

Seriously.

A new guy moved in across the street a few weeks ago with his Fox-body Mustang. Auntie T and I call him *Wheels*. Kind of a mystery, the coming and going of that souped-up car.

He yells out his upstairs window, "Keep it down or I'm calling the cops. This is a quiet, respectable street. Shut up!"

Quiet and respectable until that car comes to life and roars down the street on its way to some grudge race. Whatever. Not worth the effort, so the three of us don't move. Freeze and people tend to leave you alone, forget you're there.

After a couple of minutes, I whisper, "Look, I'll call Detective Carter tomorrow and see if I can find out anything, okay? Will that help?"

Chloe stands to leave. "Yeah. Thanks."

She takes out an older phone, probably the one her mom got her before Stretch infected her life. "What's your number? I'll put it in my phone and call you tomorrow night."

I don't know my new phone number yet. And even if I did, I don't think I want to give it to Chloe. "You know what, call me at Pop's Pizza around 9:30 tomorrow night. We start to clean up then, and Dan won't mind if I fill you in on anything I find out."

"Okay. Thanks, Allee. For trying to help. I'm really worried about him."

I want to tell her she's lucky the cops took him away, but Chloe has the same look that Tanaya had whenever she talked about Stretch.

It's so whacked. Everyone thinks they love him. And that he loves them.

- - - - -

When Chloe calls, Dan tells me to take my time with her. He even lets me use the phone in his office. His desk is so cluttered, I take the receiver off the old phone and pull it over to the couch. Thank god the coil untwists enough that it reaches, and I can sit comfortably.

"Listen, Chloe, he's trouble."

She doesn't agree and starts listing all the wonderful things Stretch does for her.

"He got me an account so I can save money for beauty school, protects me from freaks, buys me whatever I want, loves me…"

I cut her off. "I know. I know how you feel about him. Tanaya used to say the same things, and now she's dead. He may not have killed her, but he's hanging out with guys who are killers. I'm just warning you."

There's quiet on the other end of the phone.

I continue, "Detective Carter said he's 27-years-old, and he's being held on trafficking minors. That's all the information she could tell me."

"Trafficking?! What are they talking about?"

The desperation in her voice tells me the cops aren't going to be able to get a true picture of what's going on from her.

"Listen, Chloe, by law, you can't consent to anything because of your age. Do you understand that? Besides, he's too old for you, and even the law sees there's something wrong with your relationship."

She doesn't make a sound.

"Why do you think he goes for younger girls? Why can't he have a relationship with someone his own age?"

"Because girls his age are old and he loves me!" She screams into the phone, "And I love him!"

This conversation is useless. There isn't anything I can say to convince Chloe, or any other girl that he gets his clutches into, that he's a bad guy. A really bad guy.

"Listen," I soften my voice, "this must be very hard for you. You go to Emberton, don't you?

"Yeah. But I'm thinking of dropping out."

Shit. This is worse than I thought.

"Well, if you ever want to talk to anyone, there's a Ms. Davis in the guidance office, she's legit. She keeps secrets and stuff. I swear. You don't have to worry about her rattin' you out or saying anything about Stretch. She'll help you figure out stuff. Stop in and visit with her if things get too big or too scary to handle on your own."

Chloe sniffles and I ask, "Are you okay?"

"Yeah." But then her tone changes. Upbeat, she asks, "So, did the detective say when he's getting out of jail?"

I let out a sigh. "She can't tell me anything like that. Just that there will be a trial and stuff."

I'm pretty sure Detective Carter would've given Chloe her card when she went to her house to get the iPhone. "Didn't Detective Carter give you a way to get in touch with her?"

"Yeah, but I don't want to talk to her. She's a bitch."

I sigh again. "Trust me, Chloe, she did you a big favor."

She hangs up on me.

Chapter 42

"I'm going to miss you, girl!"

Auntie T walks into the bedroom as I zip up the larger suitcase. The careful packing I had planned for my first semester at Pitt ended up being a shoving match of whatever I thought I needed in whatever suitcase I could find.

"I'm gonna miss you too, Auntie T. Thank you, for everything!"

I slide the suitcase onto the floor, and we both sit on the bed.

"You can call me Tina now if you want. We've been through so much and I don't consider myself your guardian anymore. You being 18 and all, neither does the law—"

"You know what, though?" I interrupt her. "I'm sorry. I don't want to hurt your feelings. And it's nice of you to suggest, to give me a choice." I pause and put my arm around her. "But 'Auntie' connects you to me more. Makes us family."

Then the tears come. Always the tears. Damn the tears. She hands me a tissue and I wipe them away, blow my nose.

"I need to know I have a family."

She nods and puts her hand on my leg.

"Yeah, I get that. Me, too. I didn't want you to stop calling me Auntie T. I thought maybe you wanted to break away from all of this... trauma. And I want you to be able to choose the best way for you to move on. Whatever you want is fine."

"Thanks." I take a deep breath. "I wouldn't have been able to get through any of this without you, without an Auntie T."

She blows her nose, then changes the subject. "How long 'til Logan gets here? It's nice of him to drive you to school. I have some cash to put towards the gas." She hands me thirty dollars, "It's not much, but it'll help."

"It helps a lot, and you know it. He said he'd be here in about half an hour."

I slide the cash into the small front pocket of my jeans. There's another bill in my pocket, shriveled up from a few washes. I take it out. It's the fifty from Stretch, the tip he left on the counter a few months back. Touching it makes me feel sick.

I wrap it in my gross tissue and drop it into the trash can, like it's diseased. Throwing it away stops that sick feeling. I'm freed from the ache, but the air is stuck in my chest. I look up at Auntie T, and she gives me a soft smile.

"Is that the fifty from Stretch? The one you told Detective Carter about?"

"Yeah. I think about how he makes his money, and I don't want to have anything to do with it, y'know? Makes me sick."

She nods. "Knowing what we don't want is an important step in getting what we want."

I force the air in, then let it out. "Yeah. Just have to listen to my gut, right?"

She gives a smile and hands me a thick envelope. I open it. It's filled with cash.

"What's this?"

"I saved all the tip money you gave me over the past few months. The money you gave to help with the bills. It's your money, you should have it."

"But Auntie T, you did so much for me. It was my way to help."

"I know, I know. And believe me, if I needed it, I would have used it. But now, you need it. Use it as an emergency fund while you're at school."

I give her a hug. "Thank you. You've been so good to me, even though I lied …"

She cuts me off, "Forgiveness is something we do for ourselves, Allee. Sometimes, it takes a little while for it to happen." She picks up my hand and gives it a squeeze. "I'm getting there. Okay? In my own time."

"Oh," I stumble on that one syllable as I try to suppress a sob, then quickly add, "Yeah, okay. I, um..." And through my tears I whisper, "Thank you."

She hands me another tissue and then opens her purse and takes out a folded paper. "There is something else we have to take care of before you're off to school."

I should be used to bad news by now, but the dread never ceases to slither into my stomach.

I wipe away the fresh tears and ask, "What's up?"

"As you know, your mom and I were dear friends. And I know all the craziness that went on in that house of yours before your mom, well, left us."

I look away. Auntie T was aware of it all. I knew it.

"Now, never you mind about it. We can't go and undo the mess of our lives. And none of it was your fault."

I look up at her, not so sure, and she puts her hand on my cheek.

"None of it, you hear me, girl? We move on and try and do better by those who have gone on before us. Make them proud."

I meet her gaze, feel comforted, and nod.

"Well, even though you're grown up, I made sure those lawyers and the judge put in a no-contact provision on Tony's sentencing."

I wait for some kind of explanation. She's taking her time, straightens her blouse. After a few of her own deep breaths, she continues, "Your caseworker called. Tony wants to get in touch with you."

Can't say anything, suck my lips in.

"Because of the no-contact provision, it's up to you. He's not able to contact you, and if he does, you need to let them know he's not following his sentence. I will help with that if you want." She shakes her head. "He's a violent man, anything will set him off. Lord knows how he was able to get his hands on a gun."

I don't know either. But I don't waste my time wondering about it anymore. Dr. Winters' words have taken root. I hear them when I need them, "It's okay to tell your mind to stop trying to figure everything out. It's okay not to know."

"The better plan, perhaps, is knowing that because you're 18, when you want, when you're ready, you can reach out to him." She slides her hand around my arm. "Or not. I can't tell you what your mother would've wanted, because I really have no idea. Their relationship was very complicated. You're going to have to follow your own intuition. If that's what you want, you let me know. But I'm not going to tell you anytime he contacts me or the caseworker. Okay?"

"Yeah, thanks. I'm not ready, that's for sure. But knowing if I want to, maybe with your help…"

"No need to say anything more. It's all good, and I'll be here for you."

Auntie T unfolds the paper she's holding. I think it has something to do with Tony and don't want it. I stand and look one more time through the drawers, making sure nothing else needs to come to Pitt with me.

"There's one more thing I want you to have."

I close the bottom drawer. "If it's from Tony, I don't care, don't want—"

"It's not from Tony. It was Tanaya's."

She turns and looks out the window. I sit back down next to her.

"They found an essay in Tanaya's backpack. The backpack at the top of the hill where her body…" She sits silently, gets her thoughts together. "Well, anyway, they need the original for evidence, but Detective Carter made a copy of it for me. I made a copy for you. Tanaya's words are important for anyone who's stuck in a situation and wants to get out. Maybe it will help you someday, or someone you know. I think her words can help people."

She hands me the paper and walks out of the bedroom, shuts the door quietly behind her. I hold the paper in one hand and with the other, slide my fingers over the handwriting. Tanaya is in the room. I read the words aloud. They're just a whisper, but they fill the small bedroom, giving voice to my friend:

Symbolism: Something that reminds you of something else.

Dear Laura,
I just saw a blue bunny squished in an old Acme cart.
He looked out at me with bulging eyes as if to say,
"Help me! I want to get out!"
But he doesn't belong to me. So, I watched an old lady
wheel him down the street to a tattered tent.

Laura, you remind me of him. Or, he reminds me of you.
When I read about you in *The Glass Menagerie*
I thought to myself, "This girl just needs a friend."
If you don't have friends, of course you'll start playing
with imaginary animals and dolls and stuff.

A good friend will tell you to knock it off and
invite you to do something really fun.
A good friend will tell you to wiggle through the metal bars
and free yourself from the cart.
You and the bunny make me think I need to wiggle free.

I'd like to feel good when I'm alone, thinking about stuff.
Instead, I feel all squished-face in a place that's too tight.
You, me, and the little blue bunny,
we need to figure out what's holding us down so we can
squeeze through the metal bars and walk around free.

Discussion Questions

for *Mouth Shut Head Down*

1. Did you have a favorite character in this book? What part of their personality or life situation did you find interesting?

2. Think of Allee, Tanaya, or Chloe and her unhealthy relationship. If she were in your life, would you speak up about the relationship? Write a letter to one of these characters offering advice or a warning.

3. Pick two male characters: Tony, Mr. Jenkins, Logan, Dan, Stretch, Frank, and/or Mouse. Using examples (behaviors and/or words) from the story, how do they develop, support, or contradict different roles in Allee's life?

4. What does coercion mean to you? How did Tony use coercion to control Barb and Allee? How did Stretch use coercion to control Tanaya?

5. Were you surprised how Tanaya died? How did you respond to the idea that someone in Stretch's circle could be a murderer?

6. Why do you think Allee bonded so well with Rickety? How do you think this relationship will continue? Will the relationship be healthy or unhealthy for them?

7. Who do you think was more influential for improving Allee's mental health, Ms. Davis or Dr. Winters? Why?

8. What do you think would have happened to Allee if she didn't have an Auntie T?

9. At the end of the story, Allee is about to go off to college. How will this affect Allee and her future?

10. Do you think *Mouth Shut Head Down* is a good title for this story? Explain. Find instances in the story where the characters show *Mouth Shut Head Down* in action.

About the Author

Geraldine Donaher is an author, speaker, and teacher who uses storytelling to educate and inspire. With a passion for both the written and spoken word, she creates narratives of everyday experiences through fresh perspectives. Geraldine's background in education has shaped her ability to connect with diverse audiences, from young students discovering literature for the first time to seasoned writers seeking to refine their craft.

Through her blog, she shares in-depth author interviews and research insights, offering readers a behind-the-scenes look at the creative process. She also curates The Writer's Flashlight, a unique resource that combines visual and auditory components to help writers spark new ideas and deepen their practice. Dedicated to building community, Geraldine engages with readers through her monthly newsletters where she shares reflections, resources, and updates on her latest projects.

Whether in the classroom, on stage, or on the page, Geraldine Donaher's mission is to inspire curiosity, foster creativity, and celebrate the transformative power of storytelling. Readers can connect with her and explore more of her work at geraldinedonaher.com

Acknowledgments

I researched the sex trafficking of minors in the United States for 6 years before I felt ready to talk and write about it. Because of the sensitive topic, I reached out to professionals with all my questions and relied on 20 years of teaching experience to develop the themes in story form. *Mouth Shut Head Down* is a work of fiction, but I wrote what I learned to be true—to keep minors safe, we need to educate them about coercive abuse.

My deepest appreciation and respect for the professionals who gave of their time: Natalie Proud from covenanthouse.org; Sr. Meaghan Patterson, SSJ, from ahomefordawn.org; Shea Rhodes, Esq., from the Institute to Address Commercial Sexual Exploitation at Villanova University Charles Widger School of Law; and Anne Marie Collins, Vice President/Executive Director from druedingcenter.org.

Some of my questions centered on specific aspects of the story. I am grateful to: Fouad El Chidiac, M.D., for his insights into adolescent mental health; Officer Thomas Rosinski from The Philadelphia Police Department for explaining jurisdictions and detective work; Bridget Murphy, Esq., for answering my questions about courtroom proceedings; Laura Offutt, M.D., for our conversations on adolescent relationships; Gina Jernukian from Soul Survivor Ink, and Sadie Bartch from Clover Tattoo for their insights into the branding of sex-trafficked individuals.

To all the girls I talked to, read about, and ached for. I see and hear as you rebuild, speak up, and stand tall. You are power and resilience.

Beta readers take a story in its early form and say, "Sure, I'll read your book and let you know what I think." You spent those early days with Allee and Tanaya so I could breathe life into the story: Jen Pevner, Alexa Donaher, Caroline Smink, Deirdre Donaher, and Valentina Calipa.

Mouth Shut Head Down exists because people told me not to give up. Thank you for your support Brandywine Valley Writers Group, Haverford Township Free Library Writers Group, Pennwriters, Claudine Wolk, Anne Dubuisson, and my dear family.

For that final push to get it over the finish line: thank you, Jon McGoran for your editorial skills. Angel Ackerman, you took a risk publishing a book with themes that make people uncomfortable. Allee, Tanaya, and all the other characters landed safely in your capable hands at Parisian Phoenix Publishing. Thank you for all you do.

To the readers who spent time with Allee and Tanaya, we all have something to say, we all have a story. I can't wait to read yours.

Just when you think you know all there is to know about
your love for God
your love for a man
and your love for a child…

In a Crisis?

**When every minute counts,
help should be easy to find.**

soul survivor.*ink*

Soul Survivor Ink helps survivors of human trafficking begin new lives by providing access to necessary resources along their difficult journey to healing by removing and covering tattoos and other physical reminders of a painful past.
Contact us at (480) 681-7725 or email us at info@soulsurvivor.ink